SLAVE GENESIS

It was time for another of Mistress Celia's little 'diversions', as she referred to them, and Lulu wondered what new little pageant the older woman might have up her sleeve this time: for she liked variety in certain things, if not in the general appearance of her bedmates.

In the past there had been what she called the 'display stool', which the island workshop had apparently constructed to her own very specific designs, a simple stand atop which sat a short metal crossbar, curved to fit under the sitter's sex and buttocks and with two points to which hard rubber phalluses or vibrators could be attached.

Celia had kept her that way for more than three hours, gleefully taunting her, putting clamps on her nipples, taking them off again, flicking at her flanks and buttocks with the little multi-thonged whip, kissing her shoulders, her neck, her back and counting the number of times the helpless girl had climaxed. It had been a lot but as to how many, it was a numbers thing again. Anyway, by the time the two batteries expired, Lulu was past caring.

SLAVE GENESIS

Jennifer Jane Pope

This book is a work of fiction.
In real life, make sure you practise safe sex.

First published in 2000 by
Nexus
Thames Wharf Studios
Rainville Road
London W6 9HA

The Nexus website can be found at
www.nexus-books.co.uk
Jennifer's website can be found at www.avid-diva.com

Typeset by TW Typesetting, Plymouth, Devon

ISBN 0 352 33503 3

Printed and bound in Great Britain by Clays Ltd, St Ives PLC

Part One

They stood close together in the darkness, though not closely enough that any part of their bodies touched, the low light from beyond the one-way glass wall before them reflecting on to their faces in a series of eerie shadows.

The man was tall, well muscled and fair haired and his skin, had the level of illumination been considerably better, would have boasted an even tan that suggested an outdoor lifestyle. His eyes were a pale grey, slightly hooded lids lending them a somewhat sinister aspect and the bridge of his nose seemed flatter and broader than would be considered handsome.

His manner of dress was unremarkable, other than that the quality of his dark suit and the pale-coloured shirt he wore beneath it were unmistakable, a complete contrast to his companion.

The woman was also tall and the high heels of her long boots brought the top of her elegantly coiffeured dark head level with her companion's. Her figure was magnificent, her full curves and sleek limbs emphasised by the broad, tight leather belt that was drawn about her waist. Her dark-green-painted fingernails were long and tapered and her make-up was as meticulous as it was exaggerated.

The high, arched eyebrows had been carefully drawn, the silver and blue eyeshadow above the heavily mascara'd lashes drawing other eyes irrevocably to the pale-green pupils below. Her mouth, a sculpted carmine bow, was set permanently, it seemed, in a supercilious half-smile, but a discerning onlooker, had there been one, might have noticed one other curious thing about her.

For this beautiful creature, as she stood watching the hapless figure beyond the mirrored glass, did not once blink.

'Don't you sometimes think that all this is just a little archaic?' the man asked, nodding towards the bound girl in the adjoining chamber. 'With our technology, surely we can find a better way?'

The goddess creature did not take her gaze from the prisoner for an instant. 'I sometimes wonder at your grasp of certain elementary principles, Boolik,' she replied quietly, though not for fear of the girl before them overhearing her, for the observation chamber in which they now stood was thoroughly soundproofed. 'Yes, there are drugs, electronic techniques and probably a hundred other possibilities, but to resort to them, without exhausting all the basic methods, would be to admit defeat.

'These creatures may look like us, even talk like us and, in their natural state, a few of them are even beginning to approach a level of awareness that we achieved two millennia since: but they are still, in comparison, little more than wild animals. The difference between us is, say, comparable to the gulf between them and the chimpanzee.

'Genetically, they are within one per cent of each other, but the rest – well, it speaks for itself, doesn't it? As for the training programmes, yes, we could drug them, operate on them again, even change a few minor connections when we effect the original transfers: but we would end up with totally mindless zombies, "things" that are little more than robots.'

'They are close to that now, Salinia, surely?' Boolik pointed out.

The woman shook her head, her first animated movement for several minutes. 'Not at all,' she retorted emphatically. 'Their bodies are almost entirely biological and are grown from the DNA of their own kind, as you well know. True, we still have to rely on a few cybernetic additions in order to overcome one or two little glitches, but, in time, even that problem will be solved.

'You are a lot younger than I, Boolik,' she continued, turning her head slightly in his direction. 'I can remember

2

these J-As at a time when they spent thirty per cent of their lives back in the laboratory – "running repairs", we used to call it. My father assures me that before even that, the earlier attempts seldom lived five or six years and many of them became mindless idiots even in that time, due to synapse failures.'

'I bow to your superior experience and age, Salinia Aj-Laaranuk,' the man said, 'but I still find this compulsive preoccupation with training these bitches by such crude physical methods a little strange. Surely it brings us down to the level of our so-called guests?'

'That's because you have never been directly involved in the programme down here, Boolik,' Salinia purred. 'Perhaps I should ask my father to transfer you to this section for a while? You might find it very educational.'

'I serve to the best of my ability, whatever task I am assigned to,' Boolik replied stiffly. 'However, we all have our different strengths and weaknesses and I am confident that your father understood mine when he appointed me to the Security Office.'

'Father makes few mistakes, if any,' the woman conceded. 'He understands inner natures, ours and human, equally well. That is why the Induction Programme is so successful.' She returned her attention to the prisoner, who had not moved throughout the time they had been observing her – although, had she attempted to, her efforts would have been largely wasted.

Tall and blonde, her figure was as remarkable as Salinia's, though her current garb was even less conventional, consisting as it did of a complicated web of strong leather straps that circled arms, legs, torso and neck, her head then completely covered by a leather mask that hid her features entirely, leaving just two small apertures through which her eyes were barely visible, two even smaller holes beneath her nostrils, and a crown opening through which her hair cascaded down in a long ponytail.

She stood, perched upon curiously arched heels, on tiptoe like a ballerina, backed against a framework of steel tubing, to which she was attached at a multitude of points by means of metal links that snapped on to her body harness, holding her arms wide and level with her shoulders and her legs several inches apart, displaying her hairless mound and the swollen sex-lips beneath it, though not the fine wire that ran from behind her and which, Salinia knew only too well, was connected to the tiny device now inside her vagina.

From the top of her head, a fine chain ran from a ring in the leather, stretching up into the darkness above, forcing her to remain with her chin erect, even if the stiff leather collar about her neck had permitted her to do otherwise.

'It should soon be time for the next stage,' Salinia observed, without apparent emotion. 'Very few of them last longer than this.'

'I'm surprised they last even this long,' Boolik remarked, turning away from the bizarre tableau. 'However, I have work to do and you still have not told me why you summoned me down here.'

'You should have a little more patience, my friend,' the woman said, her smile now widening. 'With a little less impulsiveness, you could go far. You have more potential than you think,' she added, reaching out and touching his arm.

'I have been watching you for several years now,' she said. 'Your mother was and is a good friend and I miss her so much now she spends so much time in the nursery colonies. I promised her I would take care of you as if you were of my own line and I think that you may have talents that are being wasted, with all due respect to my father.

'I have seen the way females look at you, human and J-A alike. If you were not Maayalan Fernik's son ... well, there is no point in my even thinking about that, is there?' Her perfect teeth glinted as she turned. 'However, that does not change the fact that you have a certain quality which would be invaluable in the training programme. Perhaps you would like to put it to the test?'

'Test?' Boolik looked uncertain. 'In what way?'

4

Salinia turned back to the window and stabbed one forefinger towards the still unmoving form beyond. 'With her,' she said simply. 'You may conduct the next test, to establish whether this period of indoctrination has been as successful as it would appear.'

She opened her eyes, blinked against the sudden intrusion of light and then blinked again, trying to work out what was wrong. The room seemed larger than before she had fallen asleep and the colours – that was it! The colours. There weren't any colours. Everything was now in monochrome, like the picture on an old black-and-white portable, except that it wasn't fuzzy the way you'd expect from an ancient television; in fact, apart from the obvious, her vision was even more sharply defined than usual.

'Damned drugs,' she muttered, as she tried to ease herself up on the pillows and turned, automatically, to look down at the IV tube going into her left arm. It wasn't there and, for a moment, Mary McLeod began to experience a feeling of panic, for that line to temporary oblivion had become like a sister during these long weeks of illness.

She sat up, eyes darting about for any sign of the needle, the tubing, the stand, the little electronic self-regulator box, but they were all gone. Gasping, fighting back the urge to throw up or scream out, she clutched at her arm with her other hand. There had to be a reason and . . .

. . . there wasn't actually any pain now.

Why wasn't there any pain? The tumours had been growing and multiplying at an ever-increasing rate; the doctors had told her that so many weeks ago now, it seemed. They had been very gentle, very sympathetic, but also very clear. The two operations had been a waste of time. She was going to die and there was nothing anybody could do about it.

How long, she had asked. A few weeks, maybe; maybe months.

Not long.

5

Not very long at all for a twenty-nine-year-old postgraduate who had just landed the job of a lifetime with one of Europe's biggest multinationals.

The job of a lifetime. How ironic, she had thought, when her lifetime was being cut so cruelly and drastically short. Now it would be the job of somebody else's lifetime and, despite everything, Mary hoped grimly that they had a better crack than she'd been dealt.

So where was the pain?

Why wasn't there any pain?

'I'm dead.' She spoke out loud and the simple act of speaking seemed to relax her. Mary nodded. 'Yup, that's it.' She grinned stupidly. 'I'm dead and this is – well, it's wherever.' She stared down at her arm, at where the IV tube should have been, trying to work out what else it was that was missing: and it was several long seconds before she realised.

There weren't any marks on her skin, not even the slightest blemish – and yet the constant removal and reinsertion of the needle had produced a network of purple bruises and track marks that any Gorbals junkie would have balked at. Gently, she traced over the now flawless skin with her fingers, her eyes unblinking, only the steady thump-thump of her heartbeat breaking the unmoving silence.

At last, Mary looked up again, this time her eyes searching the room for familiar signs, but finding none. Gone was the magnolia-and-oak bedside locker; gone were the two tubular-framed armchairs which no visitor could get comfortable in; gone was the small vanity unit in the corner by the . . .

There *was* no window now. No window, no venetian blinds, no view out over the hills and glens, no faint smell of heather and damp moss. In fact, there was no smell at all. She sniffed hard, as if to disprove it, grabbing at the bed sheet and bringing it up to her nostrils, but there was nothing.

'So, I'm dead, I can only see in black and white and I've got no sense of smell,' she murmured, lowering the sheet again. 'Or I'm dying and this is all a hallucination from the morphine they're pumping into me.'

She yawned, closed her eyes and lay back against the pillows, feeling suddenly very weary.

'Well,' she whispered to the empty room, 'whichever it is, I'm past bloody caring anyway.' She raised her arms, putting her hands behind her head and was suddenly wide awake again.

'Hair!' she squealed, clutching the handfuls of thick, fair locks that now fell forwards over her shoulders. 'I've got bloody hair again!' Her hands flew to her mouth and she began to laugh hysterically, for the gradual loss of her crowning glory from the months of chemotherapy had been one of the hardest things to bear during her long illness. At first, the nurses had consoled Mary with the assurance that it would grow back again once the treatment had been concluded, but as time had passed and it had become painfully obvious that there was only going to be one conclusion to the treatment, it had also been clear that she was going to die bald.

'Oh, yes!' She bunched her fingers into two triumphant fists and punched the air with joy. 'Yes!' she repeated. 'Yes! Yes!'

It was unfortunate, however, that her lack of multicoloured vision prevented Mary McLeod from realising one very important factor. All her life, right from being a freckle-faced tomboy in first school, through to her days as a slightly plumpish, almost attractive university student, she had been a redhead.

And the hair that now grew on top of her head was decidedly blonde.

Her name was Helen Montgomerie and she had been going to die, but that was a long time ago now, or so it seemed to her.

In truth, she really did not know how long had elapsed since the hospital, for they had never told her, dismissing her questions with the reply that it was no longer important to her and that the future was of far more significance than the past.

To Helen, the mere fact that she now had a future again had made any show of ingratitude seem churlish, even if she now seemed to be inhabiting a totally different body from her own. It was even quite easy to accept that apparent miracle for, despite the lack of coloured vision and sense of smell, this new body was, overall, a great improvement on the old, not least in that it was not about to give out on her.

Her face took some getting used to, even though it was considerably more attractive than it had been before, for she had, after all, grown used to seeing the old one in the mirror for thirty-seven years and more. And it was also an odd feeling seeing two more women with identical features to her own, but the freedom from pain and the promise of life overrode all other considerations, especially when they told her of the lifespan she could now reasonably expect.

There was the downside, of course, but that would only come many years into the future and it was easy to push thoughts of senility well to one side. After all, even had the cancer not been ready to claim her original body, she would still have faced the ageing brain process ultimately and now even that had been postponed, at least in some part.

She had spent many hours posing in front of the long dressing room mirrors, giggling at the outlandish costumes they had given her, secretly relishing the admiring glances she knew she would now command in her high boots and tight waist, but then had come the bombshell.

Of course, she knew she should have guessed something like that was coming. Whoever these people were, whatever futuristic techniques their research had developed, this was no ordinary scientific facility. When her mentor, Julia, had explained about the little electronic components that helped keep her new body working, she had laughed.

'Bionic Barbies,' she'd cried. 'What a thought!' She'd turned back to the mirror, smiling her broad, full-lipped smile, perfect white teeth almost dazzling, the perfectly made-up features offering so much promise.

'Look at us,' she'd exclaimed to Julia. 'The Six-Million-Dollar Whores!'

Except, as she very soon discovered, with the exception of the price tag, the joke was about to become reality.

23 June 2002
Inverkeithing, Scotland

For the attention of Doctor Malcolm Fraser

Dear Malcolm,
If you are reading this, you will already know that I am either dead, or have been missing in some way or other for more than twenty-one days and Colin MacIntosh will have passed this on to you, as per my instructions. I trust and hope that this will never be necessary and that one day, my dear brother, I shall be able to explain all this to you in person.

Explain, did I say? I hardly know where to begin, except to say that I wish I had never allowed myself to become involved in all this, but then I have never pretended to be more than human and one of humanity's greatest failings – its Achilles Heel as it were – is greed, although we never admit that it is greed, at least not in the beginning. We justify everything by giving it pretty names and pretending there are other factors involved.

But I digress and this is complex enough without that; not only complex, but also quite unbelievable and I should not blame you if your first reaction, upon reading this, was that your esteemed elder brother had finally taken leave of his senses, that the pressures of his lifestyle had finally taken their toll. Malcolm, I swear to you that I have not, and the enclosed key and instructions will give you access to a safety deposit box in which I have secreted such proofs as I have been able to gather.

And so to the facts, or to those of them I am aware of, for there are pieces of the jigsaw missing, which I am yet striving to acquire.

As you know, my work during the past eleven years has been mainly based at the Charles Stuart Hospice near Braemar, where I have been striving, with others, to gain a few more yards on the never-ending battlefield of terminal cancers. There have been some successes, but mostly only minor ones and the war will remain unwon long after I myself have departed this world, I fear. It is a dispiriting struggle mostly and I have been close to hoisting my own white flag on many occasions.

It is against that background that I ask you to judge my subsequent actions, for initially I was able to grant self-absolution in the belief that I was at least saving some lives that were, otherwise, indisputably lost.

When Professor Jensen approached me with his proposition, although I had serious misgivings at first, ultimately I could see the possibility that here, at last, was a way to ease suffering and extend the life expectancy of maybe thousands of otherwise terminal cases. The money he was offering was only secondary, at least then.

Put quite simply, what he asked of me was this: in certain cases, where the prognosis was death and the patient had entered the very final stages, he and I would jointly certify that death some hours before it actually occurred. It was a simple enough matter and there were two nurses on the staff who were also on his payroll.

Jensen himself is authorised to perform autopsies, although in the cases of inmates of the Charles Stuart these are purely for research reasons, there being no dispute as to the cause of death by the time it occurs. This made the next stage of his scheme quite simple, for the 'corpses' were quickly removed, supposedly to the pathology lab, but in fact, for a few hours, to another facility, just a few miles away.

There the patient's brain is removed and transplanted into another body. Yes, Malcolm, I know that this does sound rather futuristic, but you can believe my every word, for I have since assisted in several of these operations and have witnessed it for myself.

However, there is an even more unbelievable aspect to this process, for the new host body is not a human body at all, but a specially produced – I can only describe it as a 'container'. I should explain further.

Outwardly, this new host has all the qualities and attributes of humanity, yet it is not truly human. I do not

10

know how they do it and I have never been permitted to see this stage of the process, but somehow, whoever is behind Jensen – or maybe it is Jensen himself – has managed to perfect a technique that is part cloning, part genetic modification and part cybernetics.

Basically, when the subject recovers consciousness, she (and they have all been female patients to date) finds herself in a new body that is perfect in every way, responds to her brain's commands, exhibits virtually all normal reflex and motor functions and also, I am assured, ages and degenerates at a rate that gives it a life expectancy of approximately SIX TIMES that of the normal human body.

What condition the brain itself would maintain over such a span I do not know, but Jensen has assured me that even this problem has been surmounted, apparently by some sort of continuous cloning and replacing process. As you know, human brain cells do not reproduce themselves, so if what he tells me is true, this aspect of the entire project, by itself, would represent one of the greatest medical advances ever known to mankind.

Of course, there was no way we could possibly let the rest of the world know what was going on, for our society is conservative in the extreme in such matters and there would have been such an outcry, as you may imagine. Therefore, the fact that all involved were sworn to secrecy was not at all suspicious to me. At least, not at first – not until I had been sucked in so far that it was too late.

However, events since I first became involved in this thing have been such that I am now convinced that there is more to this than simply trying to push forward the frontiers of science without arousing the hostility of the world at large and I am afraid that I may have betrayed my suspicions to the others, however inadvertently. Consequently, I am certain that my life is in real danger, even though it might at first seem inconceivable that people who have dedicated their careers to saving the lives of others might be prepared to resort to taking lives instead.

11

For you see, Malcolm, I am now convinced that this miraculous development – and it is miraculous, whatever else it might be – is not intended to be shared with the rest of the world, not even in the more distant future. Furthermore, the longer I remain involved in it, the more I am certain that there are other agencies at work here, for the clinical procedures involved, the technology required, they are all so far in advance of anything else known on this planet that – well, I just don't know. I simply don't know what to think.

All I do know is that none of the patients (and I have been involved in some thirty cases to date) has ever reappeared in the outside world, or, if they have, not one word has ever leaked to the media, which I find impossible to believe. I am thus led to believe that they are being spirited away to some secret location, possibly for further experimentation: or else, worse still, they are simply being killed off again, though why I cannot imagine.

There is something in Jensen's attitude that troubles me. He seems to regard our patients as little more than laboratory animals and refers to them as 'Jenny-Annes' – not a pun on his own name, but a name derived from 'genetic' and 'android', for that is, in many ways, what these girls have been turned into: genetically modified androids. Perfect female specimens outside, but a veritable Frankenstein creation underneath their flawless skins.

Their old bodies, once their brains have been transplanted, are quickly moved to a funeral parlour and are always cremated afterwards, leaving no evidence of what has happened. I suspect that someone at this parlour is also in Jensen's pocket, but then, as these are almost always closed coffin funerals, there is little risk in any case.

In the safety deposit box, however, you will find several photographs, taken by myself with a miniature camera and at some considerable risk. I am afraid that some of the scenes are quite graphic, but you will also see several 'before and after' pairings, together with biographical details and dates.

12

There is also a brief report concerning one Doctor Keith Lineker, who is in some way involved. You will see that he is connected with a very powerful organisation called Healthglow, *who market various dietary products and own several fitness and health establishments, including an island in the Shetlands called Carigillie Craig, which is where, most likely, these Jenny-Annes end up – if they are still alive, that is.*

I have co-ordinated the results of several discreet enquiries I have commissioned, but although the dossier is quite large, there is little useful substance to it. However, in the event of it coming into your hands, there should be enough, together with this letter, for you to instigate a proper investigation by the authorities. Whatever the truth might be, I urge you to find it and make it public. No matter how bad, it will not be able to cause me any more harm than I have already caused myself.

Please forgive me and try to understand.

Your loving brother,

William

She had finally broken, as they had obviously known she would. Even before the chamber Helen had known that herself and she hadn't even put up much of a struggle when they'd come for her, stripped her and strapped her into that awful harness, drawing the leather bands so terribly tightly and then covering her head in that horrible leather mask, so that her vision was restricted to two tiny pinhole-sized circles and her mouth was filled with that disgusting rubber plug before they zipped it closed.

They had forced her feet into those impossible boots, her insteps arched, her toes cramped, spasms of pain driving up through her calf- and thigh-muscles as she was forced to take her weight, so that the frame to which they immobilised her came almost as a relief, half-hanging as she now was from so many different points.

The little device they had inserted inside her had not been painful, except when the fingers had probed, grasped

13

and drawn out her hidden bud in order to fit whatever it was they fitted to it. She moaned into the gag, but they ignored her, treating her like an animated doll as they completed their allotted tasks.

They had left her alone eventually, alone with her reflection staring back from the glass wall in front of her, the dim lights glinting from her pale flesh and the dark, polished hide that enclosed and held her. All about her was total silence, only the sound of her own heart beating and the hiss of air in and out of her nostrils filling her head until she thought it would burst.

And then it had started. Down there. Inside her. And she began to understand, just as the first waves of unexpected orgasm began to overtake her . . .

Finally, it had stopped and once again there was just the hissing, pounding silence. Perched like a helpless, exotic butterfly, Helen groaned, opening her eyes.

Her entire being seemed to be drained, washed out as though by some spiritual enema. She could feel the thing still inside her, but it was quiet now, a lifeless intruder that had reduced her to a quivering wreck and kept her so for . . .

For how long?

It didn't matter.

The future is more important than the past.

Life. Long life.

A door opened, somewhere to her left, but she could not have turned her head, even had she wanted to. She closed her eyes again and felt the hands reaching up, unclipping the hook from the top of her head. Fingers reached for the zip over her mouth, drawing it back, reaching in and plucking out the disgusting rubber teat on which she had been forced to suck. Opening her eyes, she saw it now for the first time and shuddered as she recognised the spittle-shimmering shape for what it was.

The man stepped back, studying her impassively and she returned his stare, safe behind the anonymity of the mask, aware that it hid all but her pupils from his examination. She felt a sudden feeling of superiority over him, despite

14

the helplessness of her position and his obvious physical advantage.

'Are you just going to stand there looking at me?' she said, her voice sounding muffled to her leather-covered ears. He remained silent, unmoving, and Helen began to experience a feeling of unease once more, for he was an imposing sight.

He was of the people, those men who apparently ran the place, for he had that unmistakably wide gap between his eyes, where the bridge of his nose flattened out, giving his features an almost reptilian slant, though it was in no way repulsive and somehow seemed to add something to his attraction. He was dressed unusually, though, for those of his kind she had seen so far wore either commonplace suits, or white laboratory or hospital-style coveralls, not brief leather shorts and heavy, studded boots.

'Impressive,' he said, speaking at last. 'Very impressive.' His hands went to his belt, fumbling with the buckle and then suddenly the shorts were about his ankles and he was stepping out of them, his penis already thickening and rising.

Helen gasped.

'Yes, that *is* impressive,' she muttered.

He moved closer, the fingers of his right hand closing about his shaft, moving slightly up and down as it continued to grow.

'My God!' she breathed, feeling all her internal muscles tensing.

He laughed, a harsh sound in the empty room. 'It is up to you,' he said, very calmly. 'You may stay as you are, or ...' He did not finish the sentence, allowing the implication to hang in the air between them.

Helen drew in a deep breath and let it out again in a long sigh. 'May I keep the mask on?' she pleaded. 'At least for now?'

He paused, seeming to consider this request, and then nodded slowly. 'Yes,' he said. 'The mouth opening is sufficiently wide.'

Helen gasped again, understanding the significance of this immediately. 'But –' she began and then stopped. Her

15

head drooped as far as the high collar would allow and she let out a little moan. 'OK,' she said, her voice barely a whisper. 'Let me down from here and I'll do whatever you want me to.'

Celia Butler eased herself back against the mountain of soft pillows, stretched her long legs and adjusted the folds of the purple silk robe neatly about her ankles. Her slender feet, arched into golden-strapped, high-heeled sandals, were pale against the black bedsheet. She shook her head, flicking the platinum locks out of her face, and smiled at the girl who stood at the foot of the bed.

She looked about eighteen, Celia thought, but then none of the girls here looked older than their early twenties, so her true age could have been anybody's guess. They had cut her hair short, urchin style – as they did with several of their stable that they knew would appeal to Celia and other female guests of her disposition – and the combination of bobbed nose and tiny rosebud mouth was perfection itself.

Her breasts were firm, but on the small side, the nipples permanently hard, or so it seemed, the narrow waist and boyish hips, the flat buttocks and the slender legs together producing a deliberate waif image. Celia licked her lips, tasting the thick gloss she had just finished applying, her eyes hooded beneath heavy green lids, in the manner of a cat who knows she has got, or is about to get, the cream.

No longer young, Celia was nevertheless still a handsome woman, but as her fifty-second birthday loomed larger on the horizon, she was already resigning herself to the fact that the next visit to her Harley Street specialist would probably have to be her last. Her mother, now in her eightieth year, had joked, cruelly, that if Celia endured many more tucks, she would end up with her navel between her eyes.

Celia sighed, those eyes still not leaving the nymph, her aesthetic nature fully appreciating the narrow gold cuffs about the creature's wrists, matching the slightly broader ones that were locked about her ankles and the wider one still that encircled her long neck. Such a shame, she thought, that such innocent beauty would one day have to vanish beneath the march of time.

'How old are you, child?' she said.

The girl frowned slightly. 'Twenty-four, I think, mistress,' she replied.

Celia barely restrained a harsh laugh. She played out this scene with this particular girl every time she came here and the silly child never seemed to remember it from one visit to the next. 'You *think*, girl?' Celia said. 'Don't you *know*?'

For a second, the girl looked confused, alarmed even, but she quickly recovered and nodded, if just a shade too vigorously. 'Yes, ma'am,' she said, quite firmly now. 'I'm twenty-four. It's just –' She hesitated for the space of two heartbeats, then: 'It's just that I never really pay much attention to the passing of time here, so I get a bit confused now and then. And I've never been very good with numbers.'

'Well, I hope you're not confused as to why you've been sent to me,' Celia grimaced, eyes twinkling. 'What do they call you, by the way?' She already knew the answer, of course, though there *was* another girl here, called Daisy, who could easily have been the twin of this one.

'Laura Jane, ma'am,' the girl said, 'but most people call me Lulu. And yes, I know why I'm here.'

Celia smiled and looked away from her, across to the bedside locker and the collection of accoutrements she had assembled there less than an hour earlier. Maybe she would get them to send Daisy up as well, if things became a little stale later on. For the moment, however, she knew from experience that Lulu was capable of keeping her happy unaided for extended periods.

She patted the bed alongside her.

'Well, little Lulu,' she said softly, 'perhaps you'd better come and sit here beside me and let me put some colour on to those pretty little tits.' She turned, stretched out an arm and picked up the glittering red lipstick cylinder.

Keith Lineker laid the sheaf of paper on the desk and his upper lip curled slightly, as if the sight of the neatly handwritten letter offended him by its mere presence, which in fact it did.

'Where's Fraser now?' he asked quietly. 'This damned thing could have finished us.' He tapped the papers with a finger as he spoke.

Across the desk, the balding figure of Richard Major sat in his usual relaxed posture, hands resting easily in his lap, his grey eyes unblinking. 'He's coming up here with Jensen,' he replied. 'He thinks he's going to get his first look at a brand-new facility. Jensen's told him that there's a position going for him here, if he wants it, and he's coming to see around the place for himself.'

'Here on the island?' Lineker's eyebrows rose sharply and he tapped the corner of the letter. 'According to this, he's already suspicious of the place and thinks Jensen may be having doubts about him, so why would he walk into what could so easily be a trap?'

'Because Jensen has convinced him that we're finally about to go public and will be producing the Jenny-Annes for the bright lights of television, etcetera. He's given him some line about a similar project in America that's about to be revealed, which would deflect some of the outcry this sort of thing would otherwise guarantee.'

'And you're sure he's fallen for it?'

'Jensen is.' Major nodded. 'It would make sense and also settle any doubts in Fraser's mind. We'd take all the flak, then he'd get his new job and new facilities and, once all the crap had blown away, he'd see himself as being part of a team that would undoubtedly be up for a Nobel prize in the near future.'

'How typically human.' Lineker smiled, though his eyes remained cold. He picked up the letter again. 'Have we recovered this safety deposit box yet?'

'Yesterday, late afternoon,' Major confirmed. 'The solicitor picked it up, to avoid any suspicion. I've sent Haarik and Salinia to collect it and bring it back here.'

'What if the solicitor has opened it first?'

'We have to assume that he will,' Major said, his features impassive. 'All lawyers are best regarded as treacherous,

18

regardless of how much you pay them for their so-called loyalty, which is why I have told Salinia to bring the fellow back with them, with the promise of a very large bonus in cash, for services rendered.'

'And then?' Lineker asked, his expression as bland as Major's.

His superior shrugged. 'And then, the good doctor and his lawyer will be found dead in a burning car, the heat having cremated their corpses beyond any chance of an autopsy revealing any slight discrepancies between bodies and brain matter.'

'Ah, I see!' Lineker began to smile. 'A novel departure from our normal subject matter, I think?'

Major was smiling too, now. 'It was Salinia's idea,' he confessed. 'My daughter has always had a rather creative imagination, wouldn't you agree?'

'Certainly her brain has not suffered since being transferred to that body,' Lineker said. 'It seems a shame that –'

'I know.' Major held up a hand to silence him. 'I don't need reminding and neither does she. So far she has held up well, but it can only be a matter of time. Our brain cells outlast their human counterparts quite remarkably, even out of our natural bodies, but we know from the earlier cases that there is a limit after transfer. Better that for her, however, than a lifespan of little more than two decades.'

'Agreed. And she's had nearly a century now, already.'

'Which means,' Major said, voicing what they both knew, 'that she's now on borrowed time.'

'Then maybe her overdraft facility is better than most,' Lineker replied sympathetically.

Laura Jane Meadows had been answering to the name of Lulu for almost as long as she could remember. It had been a pet family name for her, back in those far-off days before she had come to the island, and somehow it had stuck, transcending even the move from one small, sickly body into the new, petite and energetically healthy one she had enjoyed ever since.

19

She was a Type CB-Nine, or was it CD-Nine? Laura Jane had never been very good at remembering a lot of things and that was one problem these people hadn't been able to change. However, she was pretty sure that she had never had a penchant for members of her own sex back in what she privately thought of as the 'old days' – that seemed to have developed since her arrival on Ailsa Ness and she was bright enough to realise that her bisexuality had almost certainly not happened by accident, for there were too many wealthy lesbian guests among the regular visitors.

Not that Lulu particularly minded, although some of the women could be a lot harsher than the men, as she had come to learn over the years; but then pain was only a relative thing and so interwound with the pleasure that it was something she had quickly come to take for granted and hers was an easier life than, for instance, that of the girls in the stable complex, whether the permanent ponies or just those doing their regular stint.

Lulu, along with the other two CB-Nines, and in common with three other similar types, was considered too small for pony-girl duties and her pert breasts did not bounce the way the drivers preferred. In any case, her slight frame, urchin face and hungry tongue were in greater demand elsewhere – Mistress Celia's bedchamber, for example – and her lighter bodyweight also made her useful as a driver in certain pony racing events, which gave her the opportunity to wield a whip, instead of just being on the receiving end of one.

Dreamily, the diminutive Jenny-Anne looked up from between Celia's widespread thighs, her right arm extending, fingers sliding into the opening at the front of the robe, running gently over one heavy breast until they found the firm, swollen nipple. Lulu smiled as Celia let out a low moan of pleasure, dipped her head again and fastened her greedy lips about the now distended clitoris that she had sucked from the sanctuary in which it normally resided.

'Little bitch!' Celia hissed, but there was no anger in her tone. She extended one long leg over Lulu's shoulder, her

20

toes tracing a line down to the flat little buttocks, kneading the cool flesh beneath them as they went. Now it was Lulu's turn to moan, but she did so quietly, anxious not to distract her temporary mistress from her own enjoyment.

'Slower!' Celia gasped, grabbing a handful of Lulu's hair, quite a feat given how little her regular crops left on her head. 'Take it steady, little Lulu. No need to rush. I'm here for the next five days, my sweet little dolly girl.'

The girl was tall, dark-haired and very beautiful and the bizarre nature of her costume did nothing, in Andrew Lachan's eyes, to diminish her appeal – quite the opposite, in fact. She stood there now, quietly waiting in the corner of the room, watching him with unblinking eyes, her face expressionless, the padded bit between her lips a silencing testimony of her obedience and training.

Her name was Jessie and she was a particular favourite with Andrew, a favouritism for which he was, as ever, prepared to pay handsomely: for, in addition to the many obvious delights she offered, her long limbs and firmly muscled buttocks ensured that she was rarely beaten on the track, provided that she was raced singly or not paired with a complete no-hoper. And that latter situation never happened any longer, not since Andrew's vehement complaint two years earlier, for there were fewer more regular visitors to the island than he and fewer still with the sort of wealth Andrew commanded.

The island was his one sanctuary from the hurly-burly of the world in which he normally moved and the cost of his diversionary breaks, though colossal by the standards of ordinary men and even some less than ordinary, was inconsequential to a man who owned and commanded a business empire worth billions. There were also sometimes little favours called for in addition, of course, but nothing that he had ever had to worry about and he knew that, had the need arisen, he would have gladly paid double for his times here.

He finished buckling the studded belt of the skin-tight leather breeches, then reached down and back between his thighs to draw forwards the triangular crotchpiece that would cover his otherwise exposed genitalia, snapping the five studs with practised precision and watching the mute girl's eyes as he did so. He picked up the first boot and smiled towards her.

'Don't worry, Jessie, lass,' he cooed. 'It'll not be hiding away down there for long.' In Edinburgh and in London, as on all his innumerable business trips abroad, Andrew Lachan took care to bury much of his native Highland accent, as did so many of his successful contemporaries, but here, far away from cities and corporations, he slid easily back into the soft burr every time he stepped down from the small helicopter in which he piloted himself on these private trips.

The girl's expression did not change, not even by the merest fluttering of an eyelid, but then, as he knew only too well, none of the girls here ever blinked: a result, Richard Major had once informed him, of the cosmetic surgery techniques employed to enhance their natural beauty to an even greater perfection.

He laced the second boot, wriggling his toes for a snug fit, then straightened up, reaching for the studded collar and the matching wristbands that completed his curious outfit. Almost unconsciously, he breathed in, puffing out his chest, aware that, even at fifty-one, his physique would have been the envy of a good many men half his age and his receding hairline, now that shorn heads were so much in fashion, was no longer a problem.

'You'll be in top form this afternoon, lassie,' he said conversationally, fastening the last buckle and moving over nearer to Jessie. She remained absolutely motionless, a statue of feminine perfection in her equine finery. He reached out, touched the wide girth strap that encircled her like a low-cut corset and checked it for tightness, finding, as ever, that it had been drawn in to its fullest extent.

'Red tack today,' he commented, noting the long boots, with their artfully shaped sole-and-heel combination. Inside the boot, he knew, Jessie would be perched as though wearing a six-inch stiletto and he constantly marvelled at these pony-girls' ability even to walk, let alone run in such footwear. Outwardly, from the ankle down, the effect was that of a horse's hoof and the heavy steel shoes nailed to their underside completed the image.

'But of course, girlie, it all looks much the same shade of grey to you, doesn't it?' Andrew added. That was another peculiar feature of so many of the girls here, their colour-blindness. It had been explained to him that the use of certain drops in the continued treatment of their eyes in order to produce such appealingly large pupils was the cause of this and he had to admit that the finished effect was worth such a small sacrifice. Especially as that sacrifice wasn't being made by himself.

From the front of the girth corset, V-shaped straps descended to either side of her lower abdomen, meeting up at the point of her denuded sex to form a small, slim triangle that passed beneath her crotch, rising again as a single strap between her fabulous buttocks, and buckling to the back of the girth. For the moment, as usual, this gusset device held firmly in place the two rubber dildoes with which she was plugged, front and back, but these impediments would be easily removed at the appropriate time. Meanwhile, she would race with them in place, the tail attached at the rear of the strap billowing in the afternoon breeze, unable to remove them herself, due to the long gloves that sheathed her arms and held her hands clenched into two uselessly balled fists.

Above the girth, more straps formed themselves into an intricate harness, part of which shaped two webbing cones that both supported and elongated her splendid breasts, darkened nipples protruding through tight steel rings set at their tips. Like Andrew, she also wore a collar, but hers was far broader and rising to a slight point beneath her chin, so that she was forced to stand with her head erect and looking forward, her field of vision further restricted by the heavy blinkers to either side of her eyes.

A small, jewelled stud was set in the centre of her forehead, just above the narrow strap that encircled her forehead and, from the cylinder-shaped leather attachment at her crown, her hair cascaded down like a black waterfall. Perfect, Andrew thought, and such a shame that they wouldn't sell her on to him outright, despite his most recent offer of a sum that would have bought a moderate-sized luxury cruiser. Instead, he had had to be satisfied with Major's assurance that, for an additional and not inconsiderable premium, Jessie would, in future, be kept stabled for his exclusive enjoyment.

'You should be well up for it today, Jessie, lass,' he said, giving a gentle tug on the reins that dangled from either corner of her bit. 'What is it now, three weeks since I last managed to get up here? Aye, well, sometimes needs drive, but that means poor little Jessie doesn't get her oats like she's used to, eh?' He patted her rump and then ran a hand down between her shoulder-blades, feeling the smooth, cool flesh beneath his touch.

He reached towards the rack on the wall behind her, taking up the thin crop in his other hand and transferring it back to the right as he moved back around to stand facing her. He held the implement up, but there was still no reaction. He sighed.

'You know I really don't want to be doing this,' he said, his tone apologetic. 'However, traditions are traditions, are they not? And if I take my little pony-girl down to the ring without at least six stripes on her rump, those idiots will be thinking that I've gone soft, will they not? And maybe I'd better be putting my mask on first. Wouldn't do to be forgetting it now, would it?'

He laid the crop aside, moved back to the bed and took up the polished leather mask that would cover the top two-thirds of his face and head, assuring him, once it was in place, of complete anonymity. The other visitors might well share many – if not most – of his tastes, but that did not mean that would place them above using the knowledge of his identity to their advantage at some time in the future.

He tugged the thing into place, adjusting the back lacing that ensured a smooth fit, worked the eye apertures perfectly into position and then took up the crop once more. He tapped it against the side of his leggings, producing a sharp, slapping sound.

'Right then, little Jessie,' he announced. 'You know what to do by this time.'

Head erect, facial muscles frozen, the pony-girl stepped forward, turned slowly side on to Andrew and bent forwards with supple grace, her mitted fingers touching the toes of her hoof boots, buttocks presented high in the air.

'Splendid!' Andrew cried and the braided leather and whalebone hissed through the air for the first of its six strokes. This time the report was far louder and was accompanied by a stifled yelp from behind the bit.

It was time for another of Mistress Celia's little 'diversions', as she referred to them, and Lulu wondered what new little pageant the older woman might have up her sleeve this time: for she liked variety in certain things, if not in the general appearance of her bedmates.

In the past there had been what she called the 'display stool', which the island workshop had apparently constructed to her own very specific designs, a simple stand atop which sat a short metal crossbar, curved to fit under the sitter's sex and buttocks and with two points to which hard rubber phalluses or vibrators could be attached. Several inches from the floor, a second cross-piece jutted out to hold hinged steel manacles, which locked about the ankles, so that even had Lulu's hands not been bound up behind her back, she could not have dismounted the infernal device unaided.

Celia had kept her that way for more than three hours, gleefully taunting her, putting clamps on her nipples, taking them off again, flicking at her flanks and buttocks with the little multi-thonged whip, kissing her shoulders, her neck, her back and counting the number of times the helpless girl had climaxed. It had been a lot but as to how many, it was a numbers thing again. Anyway, by the time the two batteries expired, Lulu was past caring.

Today, Celia announced, she had thought of something completely different, something she herself had never tried before and she had brought with her a very special costume for Lulu to wear – bought in Paris, no less, she informed the curious girl. She instructed the eager Lulu to bring out the smaller suitcase that was standing in the bottom of the large closet and place it on the bed.

Taking her keyring from her bag, Celia unlocked it and threw back the lid and for several seconds Lulu simply stood and stared, not understanding what she was looking at.

'On top is a wig, silly,' Celia said. That much Lulu had already gathered; what she didn't understand was why? If Mistress Celia wanted a girl with frothy blonde curls, she had only to pick up the bedside telephone and one would be sent who didn't need an expensive hairpiece.

'I thought it would be interesting to see what you look like with hair,' Celia said, as if reading her thoughts. She tossed Lulu another key. 'Unlock your collar and cuffs and place them on the shelf over there. You won't need them for now.'

The wig fitted easily over Lulu's own cropped cut and, as Celia used a brush to counteract the compressing effect that the golden curls had suffered during their journey, Lulu shivered and giggled at the unaccustomed feel of hair about her shoulders and back.

'Yes, very sweet,' Celia said eventually, tossing the brush aside. 'Maybe I ought to suggest that they let your own hair start growing out again.' She delved into the case and brought out a pair of pink panties, the legs of which were trimmed with matching ruffles. 'Put these on,' she said, passing them to Lulu, who frowned as she took them, but did as she was told without demur.

As she straightened the soft satin, she realised that it was the sort of garment a proud parent might give to a pampered five-year-old, as part of that very special party outfit and, when Celia shook out the dress, her suspicions were confirmed.

'This makes me look like a little child,' she muttered, as Celia carefully fastened the buttons at the back. And indeed, with the ruffled neckline and puffed sleeves, the short skirt with its sewn-in layers of stiffened net petticoats making it flare out about her narrow hips, it was quite true.

'But you are a little girl, Lulu,' Celia smiled, flicking a finger at a stray blonde curl. 'Just a scrap of a child with no tits and hardly any bum. Why, if your face wasn't so pretty, you'd be more like a boy, wouldn't you?' She returned to the case and took out the lacy pink knee-socks and Lulu perched herself on the corner of the bed and dutifully drew them up her legs.

'And now these,' Celia said, holding the shoes out like twin trophies. 'I'll put them on for you. They might be difficult for those little fingers.' Lulu struggled not to laugh, for the pink patent slippers, with their dainty ankle straps and tiny buckles were, she thought, the most hideous things she had ever seen, let alone been expected to wear, but she was too well trained to argue. Neither did she protest when Celia drew the lacy gloves over her hands, adjusting the frills about her wrists with far more fuss than was necessary.

'Now stand up and go to the closet mirror,' Celia instructed. 'I want you to see how pretty you look in my presents.'

Rustling with every movement now, Lulu rose to her feet and crossed the bedroom floor, swinging the closet door open so that she could see her reflection in the full-length glass on its inside. This time she did let out a laugh, but one glimpse of Celia's rapidly darkening face behind her brought her up short.

'It's very pretty, ma'am,' Lulu murmured. It wasn't a lie, she told herself, for the outfit *was* very pretty, exactly as its designer had intended it to be – very pretty for a small girl child. And that, Lulu realised, as she stood staring at herself, was exactly what she now looked like. Perhaps, she told herself, the mistress was getting broody, although she was surely a bit old for that sort of thing now.

Celia was closing the case now, carrying it back to the closet herself and Lulu stood aside, watching her, unsure of what she should do or say. Taking the course that was invariably the best in these situations, Lulu decided to remain motionless and silent.

She did not have long to wait.

'I think, Lulu,' Celia said, walking back to the bed and stretching out across its width, 'that it is high time you learned about men.'

A bit late for that, Lulu thought to herself, but she demurely lowered her head and went along with the game.

'You see, my little angel,' Celia continued, picking idly at the bedcovers, 'a girl needs to know that she isn't really missing anything, otherwise she might begin to get silly ideas into her head. Do you understand what I'm saying?'

'Yes, ma'am,' Lulu whispered, keeping her eyes lowered.

'Good.' Celia picked up the bedside phone, keyed the single button and listened. Her call was answered almost immediately. 'We are ready, now,' she said simply and replaced the receiver on to its cradle.

'Nets all stowed, Tommy?' In the small wheelhouse, Duncan Robertson stood wedged between the wheel and the locker behind him, feet braced against the increasingly alarming pitch of the deck beneath them.

In the gloom, Tommy MacIntyre nodded. 'Aye, everything's in and battened down,' he said, peering through the spray-soaked screen to where the bow of the little trawler, *Flora*, was disappearing into the heaving sea with growing regularity. Not that Tommy was particularly worried.

At twenty-four, he was scarcely more than a third of Duncan's age, but had already seen more than eight years aboard the elderly vessel. Indeed, he wasn't even the youngest man aboard any more, not since John MacAndrew's son Billy had joined the crew.

'Looks like it's building into a right little bugger,' he remarked, reaching inside his waterproof for the tin in which he kept his cigarettes and lighter. 'Reckon we'll get in ahead of it!'

The wizened skipper shook his head, wisps of white hair dancing about it like an animated halo. 'Not a chance, laddie.' He grimaced. 'And it's my own fault, too. I should have known the wind would back like that, never mind the

28

bloody BBC forecasters.' He nodded towards the small radio set above his head as he spoke. Below it, the small green screen flickered and blinked, but they both knew that radar was next to useless in these sort of seas.

'Aye, well,' Tommy said, finally extracting a cigarette, 'if you didn't guess it, no other bugger will have.' The lighter flicked into spluttering flame and he inhaled deeply. 'Guess we'll have to run with it, then?'

Duncan nodded. 'Aye, straight into the teeth, lad, and this'll get worse before it gets better, so I'd be obliged if you'd pop below and see if either John or that little scamp Billy can get a brew going while they can still keep the stove alight.'

'Do you fancy a drop of something in it?' Tommy suggested, turning towards the door.

Duncan pulled a wry face and cleared his throat noisily. 'Does a woman have a fanny between her legs?' He snorted and then swore quietly as a particularly large wave sent a jarring tremor the length of his craft.

Tommy paused, grinning, his teeth white in the reflected instrument lights. 'I'll take that as a "yes" then, shall I?' he said, as the first tremor was followed by a second and, for just a moment, the smile disappeared from his face.

There were two of them and Lulu guessed that both men had to be guests, although their masks made it impossible to identify them, even if they were visitors she might have encountered before.

The taller male, who was heavily built and dark, wore elasticated leggings, with a wide belt about his waist and studded cuffs about his wrists. A slim collar sat loosely about his thick neck and Lulu was reminded of pictures of old-fashioned circus acrobats, though the heavy, laced-up boots and the sinister highwayman-style mask rather detracted from that image.

In one hand he carried a short, coiled whip, in the other the leather looped handle of a chain leash, the other end of which was clipped to his companion's collar, an altogether thicker and tighter device than his own. This second man was much slimmer, his body effeminate almost, though the naked organ that hung limply between his bare thighs, a thin strap about its base and another passing behind his heavy testicles, would not have looked out of place on a much more muscular frame and certainly seemed to compare favourably with the bulge beneath the first man's leggings.

His mask was an all-enveloping hood that extended from the wide collar and, as Lulu studied him closer, she saw that the eye apertures had been zipped closed, leaving him blind and completely dependent upon his 'master'. Not only that, but the smooth lines of the thick rubber were distended where they covered the mouth and Lulu guessed that the zipper there had only been closed after the insertion of a sizeable gag.

On to his feet had been locked a pair of women's high-heeled boots and his arms, which were cuffed loosely behind his back, were sheathed in opera-length latex gloves, their black surfaces rippling against the lights and throwing his pale flesh into even starker relief.

'Good morning, Master Eric,' Celia greeted the bigger man. 'And who is this worm you have brought today?'

'Good morning, madam,' Eric replied, in a surprisingly well-modulated voice. 'I trust I find you well.' His mouth twitched into a half-smile and he jerked on the leash, causing the smaller male to stumble forwards a couple of paces.

'This worthless piece of excrement is called Loin,' he continued, tugging the leash again to emphasise his words. 'He doesn't deserve the name he was given originally, so I have taken that from him.' He flicked idly with the coiled whip, striking the bound man's penis lightly, which made him start back. 'The only useful thing about him is this.' Eric laughed. 'So Loin is what I now call him.'

And I wonder how many thousands of pounds or dollars Loin has paid to be mistreated and humiliated in this way, Lulu mused to herself, but quickly dismissed that train of thought. There were too many numbers involved, anyway.

'Well, Loin,' Celia purred, standing up and crossing the stretch of carpet between herself and the two newcomers, 'we'll have to see if you've been well named, won't we?' She reached down, taking his organ carefully in the fingers of her right hand and Lulu was close enough to see the tremor of anticipation this induced in the hooded man and saw that the limp shaft had immediately started to respond to her mistress's cool touch.

'Perhaps,' Celia continued, 'we should let Loin see what a delicacy is in store for him eventually.' With her free hand, she reached up and drew back the zipper over his right eye and Lulu caught a brief glimpse of one blinking eyelid as the light flooded in. Using Loin's steadily thickening shaft as a tiller, Celia turned him about, so that he was peering straight at Lulu.

'Isn't she a sweet little thing, Loin?' Celia said and suddenly pressed her long right thumbnail into his swelling flesh.

A muffled grunt escaped from behind the gag and mask and Loin's shoulders hunched forwards in pain. Celia did not release the pressure for several seconds, but continued talking in her silky tones.

'But pain is pleasure, Loin, surely?' she taunted. 'And my sweet Lulu needs so much pleasure. She may look so sweet and innocent, but she really is a wicked child, so you must both be punished, mustn't you?'

More grunts and gasps followed, but Loin dutifully bobbed his head in agreement and acquiescence. At last, Celia released him, the vivid red mark testimony to the strength of her grip, yet miraculously, it seemed, Loin's penis had continued to grow all the while and it now stood nearly fully erect. Lulu swallowed hard, anticipating the moment when it would ultimately force its way into her.

But first, she had another duty to perform.

At a nod from Celia, she skipped forwards, dropped to her knees and raised her mouth to him, her lips parting for her tongue to trace his length from the tight strap above his scrotal sac, right to the very tip and the burgeoning, reddish-purple knob. The blood continued to force its way in past the restrictive harness, veins beginning to stand out through the translucent flesh. Again Lulu's kitten tongue

31

moved down and up and this time she parted her lips wider at the zenith, drawing him into her mouth, though only for an instant.

Celia laughed, took hold of Lulu's shoulder and drew her back on to her haunches.

'Filthy little bitch,' she said, though not unkindly. She patted Lulu on the top of her blonde curls. 'Born to suck cock, as well as cunt, I see. Well, I think we have proof that this wretch is well named, all right.' She stepped away, motioning with a jerk of her thumb for Lulu to rise and do the same.

'Lay him over the foot of the bed,' she ordered, addressing Eric, 'and whip him soundly. And if you mark the bedding, you dirty little bastard,' she hissed to Loin, 'I'll have that thing pierced and ringed and locked back to a dildo in your arse.'

Loin needed no urging from Eric and, seconds later, he was face down over the end of the bed, his knees on the floor, his masked face buried in the soft covers.

'Wait!' Celia cried, as Eric let out the whip and brought his arm back for the first stroke. The big man paused and let the lash fall back loosely on to the carpet. Celia stepped forwards, grasping the six-inch length of chain that ran between Loin's wrists. 'No,' she said, 'this will never do.' Her hand moved up, lingering on the heavy steel ring that was set into the back of the kneeling man's collar. After a few seconds, she seemed to reach a decision.

From another case in the bottom of the closet, she drew a pair of heavy leather mittens and handed them to Lulu, turning back to Eric and nodding down at the hapless Loin.

'Remove the cuffs,' she said. 'Lulu will secure him more suitably. You know what to do, little girl, don't you?'

Lulu nodded. Loin was about to be made even less comfortable than he already was and, as Celia returned again from the case, holding a broad belt and a set of broad leather cuffs, Lulu set about working the mittens on to his unresisting hands, zipping them closed and rendering his fingers useless, locking the wrist straps into place to prevent any chance of removal.

Each mitt tapered to a point, where a ring no less sturdy than that in Loin's collar was attached and from which dangled an equally strong-looking snap link. Deftly, Lulu folded each arm in turn, forcing it high up between the shoulder-blades, until she could attach the links to the collar ring. It was a very painful form of restraint, as Lulu knew only too well herself.

Celia, however, was not through yet. Bending down herself, she locked one of the cuffs about each of Loin's ankles, paying out the chains, which Lulu saw were not connected to each other, but to another pair of separate snaps. The belt went about his waist, drawn cruelly tight and buckled off so that another large ring sat exactly in the small of his back. With a grunt, Celia stood up.

'I think you should complete the task,' she said to Lulu, a smirk on her face; and a few moments later, Loin's legs had been drawn up double and cuff chains attached to the belt, so that most of his weight, other than that proportion that was being supported by the bed, was bearing down on his knees.

'Check that he's still hard,' Celia said casually, 'and then fit this.' She held up the hard rubber phallus, with the narrow base that would prevent its being easily ejected by the sphincter muscles. 'I'll leave it up to you as to whether you want to lubricate it first.'

So, she wasn't dead after all, Mary realised eventually, but something was very wrong, nonetheless: except it seemed churlish to describe being pain- and drug-free for the first time in months as wrong, she was forced to admit to herself.

However, as she sat on the edge of the bed, bare legs dangling just clear of the spotless tiled floor, there could also be no arguing with the fact that . . .

. . . well, at any rate . . .

'I mean, this is crazy!' she said, her voice sounding echoey in the empty little chamber. She looked down at herself and stood up again, raising the hem of the simple white hospital gown to reveal her legs to their fullest extent.

... it's not possible ...

'These are *not* my legs!'

... I *am* on drugs ...

'And these aren't my bloody boobs, either!'

... or crazy ...

'Jeez, it can't be! Oi!' She crossed over to the door again: a plain, wood-grained panel, windowless and with a simple handle. She had already tried it, only to find that it was locked, but she rattled it again and pounded on the timber with her other hand.

'Hey! Out there! Somebody answer me!' She stopped, turning to look for something that she might use to make even more noise, but there was nothing. The hospital-style bed was fixed to the floor and contained just a rubber-covered mattress and the single sheet that had been over her when she first regained consciousness and, that apart, there was nothing.

She swung round, renewing her assault on the door, this time pounding with both fists, but still nobody came. Eventually, her hands beginning to ache, she stopped, returned to the bed and slumped down on the edge again.

'*Much more sensible.*'

'What?' The voice had seemed to come out of thin air and the metallic tones made Mary jump as if an electric prod had been applied to her spine. She leaped up, looking about furiously, but there was no sign of any speaker, nor of any means by which the unseen voice could be observing her.

'*Sit down, Mary. Please.*'

Confused, Mary found herself obeying, trying to work out if it was a male or a female giving the orders. It was hard to tell.

'Who are you?' Her voice sounded tremulous to her ears. She tried again. 'More to the point, *where* are you? And what's happened to me?'

'*All in good time. For the moment, it should be more than enough for you to know that you aren't going to die. Doesn't that please you?*'

'Well, yes, of course it does.' Mary drew a deep breath, closed her eyes for a second and fought to marshal her confused thoughts. 'But – well, I don't want to seem ungrateful or anything, but ... well, shit, this is all a bit much.'

'*Your new body, you mean?*'

'Of course I mean my new body.' She sighed. 'Look, I'm sorry if this isn't quite the reaction you were expecting, but this is kind of scary for me, you know?

'Last thing I remember was being in that side ward, tubes sticking in me everywhere, smashed out of my brains on morphine and whatever. I was pretty skinny by then, though I used to be ... well, slightly chubby, shall we say – before I got ill, that is – and I was about five feet two, give or take.

'Now, unless this room has been scaled down one heck of a lot, I must be around five eight, I've got legs that I only used to dream of having and a bust that's, well, it's a bust, isn't it? Even before I lost all that weight I was pretty flat-chested, but now –'

'*You have a thirty-eight-inch, C-cup bosom and yes, you now measure five feet eight and one half inches in height, weigh one hundred and forty-four pounds and your other so-called vital statistics are a twenty-two-inch waist and thirty-seven-inch hips. Quite standard procedure.*'

'Yeah?' Mary couldn't help looking up when she spoke, for the voice was definitely coming from somewhere above her. She let out a little snort and then lay back across the bed, adopting what she hoped would seem a nonchalant pose.

'Listen,' she said, surprised at how calm she now actually sounded, 'there are about a million and one questions which are buzzing round this poor bewildered head of mine, but one in particular springs to mind. Why?'

'*Why "what" in particular? Why are you alive? Why are you here? Why do you have a different body?*'

'Ah, so it *is* a different body? Come to that, why doesn't that really shock me? Have you got me on some kind of brain-damping drug?'

'*A very mild sedative, just to guard against shock.*'

'Probably just as well.' Mary sat up again, pursing her lips. 'OK,' she said, at last, 'let's start with "why am I here?" and "where the fuck is 'here' in the first place?" shall we? Then let's go on to things like why I've got a new body, one which appears to have been snaffled off some glamour model and how in heaven's fucking name you put me in here, or have you just grafted on a few bits?'

She lifted the loose sleeve of her gown and examined her shoulder closely, squinting slightly to try to bring it into focus better.

'Mind you,' she quipped, letting the sleeve fall again, 'if these bits have been grafted on, my compliments to the chief mechanic. I can't see the welds. Oh, yes – and that's another thing. Why can't I see colours any more?'

'So many questions, but that is only to be expected. All our subjects react in much the same way, though you appear to be handling the transition much better than most.'

Mary shrugged. 'Well, I'm sort of beginning to understand how the condemned man must feel when the governor arrives with his reprieve about five minutes before he's due to drop. Maybe, once the novelty wears off, I may feel a bit different.'

'Maybe you will, but I understand you have a particularly strong character and bore your earlier sufferings with great fortitude, so we have great hopes of you, Mary.

'As for your questions, they will all be answered in due course. Very shortly, you will meet Kelly, who will be your mentor and tutor. She will explain those things you need to know and will be responsible for your future training.'

'Training? What training?' Mary barely stopped herself from laughing out loud. 'I've had all the training I want, thank you very much. Fourteen years at school and another four at university and a double first to prove it.'

'I'm afraid your academic training and qualifications, impressive though they are, will be of no use to you here. Your future training will be of an entirely different nature, but then, as I have already said, Kelly will explain everything.'

'You reckon?' Mary retorted. 'Well, maybe she can start with this one.' She raised the hem of her shift and peered down between the tops of her thighs. 'Maybe she can

36

explain why I don't appear to have any pubic hair – that'll be her starter for ten and then we can work up to the harder questions for bonus points!'

Eric used the whip expertly, cutting a criss-crossed pattern of stripes across Loin's buttocks, thighs and lower back, raising vivid welts, yet never breaking the skin. The painfully bound figure hardly reacted to each pistol-shot blow, simply jerking slightly under the impacts, the little thongs that hung from the base of the embedded dildo twitching between his thighs, and barely a sound coming from behind the mask. All the while, Lulu was made to kneel beside him, her arm and hand inserted between his body and the mattress, fingers gently massaging his burgeoning erection, though not with sufficient urgency for there to be any imminent danger of an orgasm.

She was also instructed to count the lashes as they fell and she had reached twenty-four before Celia called a halt to the punishment and demanded to know whether Loin was still erect. Lulu confirmed that he was and then, at Celia's further instruction, leaned forwards to unhook the ankle chains from the waist belt.

Now it was Lulu's turn to bend over the end of the bed, but she was not required to kneel, simply bending at the waist and extending her arms so that her splayed hands rested on the footboard and steadied her stance as she hovered over the crouched figure beneath her.

'Remove his gag,' Celia said.

Lulu extended one hand about the rubber-shrouded face, found the zipper and drew it across, her fingers returning to search for the plug within. Slowly, she withdrew it and heard Loin gasp as he sucked in a lungful of air.

'Put it in your own mouth,' Celia ordered.

Lulu raised it to her lips and saw that it was shaped like a stubby penis, the black surface slippery and glistening with Loin's spittle.

Slowly, she opened her mouth, pressing the slimy object between her teeth and down on to her tongue, gripping it to prevent it slipping out again. If Celia did not use a strap to keep it in place, Lulu knew that she did not dare release her grip on it, for if it fell out before it was time, her mistress would be very angry with her.

'Turn around, Loin,' Celia said.

Between Lulu's widespread legs, the bound slave struggled to comply, but without the use of his arms it was a clumsy and awkward process. Eventually, though, he succeeded, kneeling so that his face looked up directly into Lulu's pink, satin-covered crotch, his head almost enveloped in the rustling layers of petticoats, which had dipped at the front when Lulu had bent over, while at the back they had risen, exposing her scantily protected bottom completely.

'Begin,' Celia said to Eric. 'And take your time.'

The lash whistled through its brief arc and the first line of white fire exploded across Lulu's unpadded bottom. She bit hard down on to the gag, but still a yelp of anguish squeaked past the wet rubber and her hips shot forwards, thrusting her already damp crotch against Loin's captive lips. As the first icy agony gave way to the heat of rising desire, she felt his lips and tongue beyond the serrated roughness of the unzipped mask, the moist warmth of his mouth pressing hard against the thin satin that separated one wet orifice from another.

By the third stroke, Lulu was no longer bothering to lift herself clear of the trapped face beneath her. Instead, she began grinding her sex hard against it, the combined heat spreading out through her entire body, the crotch of her frilly panties sodden now. Dimly, she heard Celia's slow count, but by now the pain was secondary to the rising tide of lust and the numbers whirled in a meaningless cloud before her glazed eyes.

'Stop!'

Eric let the lash fall and stepped back.

Lulu groaned past the fat penis in her mouth, saliva dripping from her chin as she sucked frantically on the rubber.

Celia stepped forward, scissors in her hand. 'Up, you little slut baby,' she hissed and a moment later the satin panties fell away in her hand. Roughly, she thrust Lulu downwards again and this time the long tongue rose to meet Lulu's descent, probing between her lower lips, its rough surface rasping across the tip of her throbbing bud.

Lulu let out a long shriek and air hissed down her nostrils. 'Continue,' Celia commanded and the lewd dance commenced again. If Lulu had earlier considered Loin's plight, trapped beneath her, arms crushed against the foot of the bed by their combined weight, her full attention was now focused on herself and in particular on that part of her which had now become the centre of her entire being.

She screeched and gurgled, eyes bulging as her body spasmed violently, love-juices pouring into the willing receptacle beneath her, taut buttock muscles clenching and unclenching as she surrendered to the inevitable defeat. She was hardly aware when the whipping finally ceased, only briefly conscious that the lips and tongue ceased their homage as their owner was pulled up and thrown back across the end of the bed by the powerful Eric, but she needed no telling nor urging, vaulting up and straddling her helpless lover, seizing his massive erection and impaling herself upon it in one movement.

She felt the stubby gag being pulled from her mouth, and willingly sucked in its replacement, scarcely feeling the retaining strap that was buckled about her head, but seeing the bobbing extension that now reared so obscenely from beneath her nose. With a snort of triumph, she lowered her head, thrusting the phallus into the mouth that had so recently worshipped her, filling it and driving deep into Loin's throat.

And, when the hard hands seized her buttocks, prising them wide, the hardened knob pressing against her one orifice that remained unfilled, Lulu gleefully thrust back, relaxing her sphincter muscles to accommodate the pulsing organ . . .

Tommy MacIntyre slowly forced his eyes open, coughed several times and was violently sick, bile and sea-water spewing from between his bruised and battered lips. His stomach muscles kept contracting long after there was nothing left to vomit and for several minutes he lay there, not quite sure where he was, nor how he had got there, just knowing that he was alive, though not convinced that death might not have been the kinder option.

At last, his gut reflexes relented. Eyes still closed, he spat several times, trying to clear his mouth of the foul taste and finally, head throbbing, began to haul himself up into a sitting position.

Overhead the sky was a clear blue, gulls circling beneath a warm morning sun, a far cry from the conditions of the night before and the storm that had finally bested the gallant little *Flora*. His memory of the events in those final moments before the huge wave had flipped her into mid-air were still hazy, but, as he sat now amid the rocks on this boulder-strewn beach, his clothes already steaming in the early warmth, he knew that Duncan's faithful craft was by now on the bottom of the seabed and Duncan and the others, in all probability, were there with her.

Why Tommy had been spared, what had saved him, he had no idea: but he was grateful to the lifejacket and to Duncan for reminding him he had forgotten to strap himself into it initially. He turned and looked out to sea, the water now as flat as a millpond, so typical of the cantankerous nature of the seas in these parts.

He tried to stand, but his knees were still too weak and he leaned back against the nearest large stone, fumbling for his inside pocket, amazed when his fingers closed over the tin that was always there, amazed even more that its watertight qualities had held throughout the time he had been in the sea.

He drew deeply on the cigarette, exhaling a long plume of smoke that hovered in the still air above his head, and studied the vista, trying to get some idea of his bearings. The beach was in a tight cove, long headlands stretching out to either side, doubtless what had offered enough of a barrier to the storm seas to prevent the waves dashing his brains out on the rocks when he had floated ashore during the night.

Tommy closed his eyes, his mind picturing charts, his memory searching for some sort of match.

'Ailsa Ness,' he said aloud, eventually. 'Either Ailsa Ness, or perhaps Jockie's Knee. Got to be one of those two. Oh, shit!'

He knew both the small islands well enough, though he had never landed on either, but the *Flora* had passed both at some distance on many a trip and they were clearly marked on all the large-scale charts, despite their diminutive sizes. And that was the problem, for they were so small that nobody lived on them, which was going to make life very awkward for Tommy MacIntyre for the foreseeable future.

Detective Constable Tim 'Geordie' Walker replaced the telephone handset and looked across the double desk that separated him from his latest 'skipper'. Detective Sergeant Alex Gregory had been stationed in the Highlands and Islands for almost all her eight-year career and Geordie wondered if the pretty brunette would have lasted half that time if she had had to serve her time back in his native Newcastle.

Not that he personally had anything against women officers, not even when they were his superiors in rank: but it took a particularly tough breed of female to survive where he came from and Alex Gregory, though apparently bright and efficient, somehow just did not convey the impression that she might have the sort of steely core required in order to qualify. Her legs, on the other hand . . .

Geordie hid a grin and reached out for his cigarettes and lighter.

'Filthy habit,' Alex retorted, feigning her usual disgust. 'Stunts your growth, too.' She smiled and Geordie, who stood six feet four in his socks, returned the gesture.

'That was the Coast Guard, by the way,' he said, lighting up and sitting back in his chair. 'Got a trawler missing. The *Flora*, apparently.'

'That's Duncan Robertson's boat,' Alex said, her eyes narrowing. 'He probably just stood off and waited for the storm to blow out. It certainly was a nasty one last night.'

41

'Maybe,' Geordie conceded, 'but there's nothing from his radio and the wind dropped a good five or six hours ago now. His daughter reported him overdue about an hour back, so they've got the cutter on the lookout and apparently the Navy boys have got a couple of choppers up on exercise, so they've diverted to take a look.

'Why the hell they're telling us all this and why they've also come through to CID and not to the front desk, I can't imagine.'

'Then you haven't yet heard about Morag,' Alex said, shuffling a sheaf of papers into a neat pile.

Geordie raised an eyebrow. 'You're right, I haven't,' he said. 'Tell me more.'

'Morag is one of the switchboard girls at Central,' Alex explained. 'As you know, all official calls are routed through the one main number and then rerouted to the appropriate station from there. In Morag's book, one department is much the same as any other, so long as she puts the call through to the right station. Front desk was probably engaged, so she just flicked our switch.'

'Bloody funny way to run a railroad, if you ask me,' Geordie grunted. 'Hasn't anybody tried having a word with the lass?'

'Not in the last twenty years, as far as I know,' Alex said. 'Firstly, she talks at a hundred miles an hour; secondly, she's got an accent so thick even we natives have trouble understanding her; and thirdly, she's got a very nasty temper and you're likely to find yourself answering calls for half the division if you get on her bad side.'

'Hasn't anyone thought of sacking her?'

'Sack Morag?' Alex exclaimed, eyes widening. 'You can't be serious, as the man said.'

'Why not?'

'Well, because she's Morag, she's probably ten years past retirement age and has worked that switchboard since it was steam-driven, certain locals are convinced she's a witch, and, well, sacking Morag would be akin to shooting a Teletubby in cold blood!'

* * *

The woman stood framed in the doorway, a quite stunningly bizarre sight, her blonde hair piled high above a perfect oval face and, beneath this, a stunning figure that had been dressed in a fashion guaranteed to display its proportions to their best, if somewhat unusual, advantage.

From neck to toe, she appeared to be clad in some sort of elasticated, pale-coloured body-stocking – 'appeared' to be only because her legs, from near the tops of her thighs down were shod in highly polished, stiletto-heeled boots, matching the tightly buckled wasp-waisted body belt that reminded Mary of pictures of old-fashioned corsets she had seen in magazines.

Scrambling to her feet, Mary stood and confronted her. 'Let me guess,' she said. 'You must be Kelly.'

The newcomer inclined her head slightly, her mouth curving into a delightful smile that did not reach her unblinking blue eyes. 'And you are Mary,' she said, 'our newest Jenny-Anne.'

'Jenny-Anne?'

'I'll explain a little later. It's just a little joke of the Doctor's.'

'Doctor Fraser?' Mary asked. 'Is he here?'

Kelly shook her head. 'No, Doctor Lineker,' she said. 'You won't have met him yet. He's in charge of the project and it's thanks to him you have your new body.'

'I see,' Mary said. 'And I suppose it was his idea that I shouldn't be told in advance about all this? Some people might find the shock a bit too much, surely? I mean, I'm just a bit dazed myself, for that matter.'

'And quite understandably so,' Kelly agreed. 'But in practice most of our girls are so grateful that they are not going to die that they adjust very quickly indeed, as I did myself.'

'You?'

The other girl nodded. 'Yes, me too. About twenty years ago now.'

'Twenty – what?' Mary's mouth fell open and she stood staring at the other woman for several seconds, searching for the right words. 'You can't have,' she said, at last,

43

shaking her head. 'I mean, you don't look even as old as I do.'

'As old as you *did*,' Kelly corrected her, 'but then, of course, you won't have seen yourself yet. Come along with me. The dressing rooms are only just at the end of the corridor.'

The island was definitely Ailsa Ness. Tommy was no longer in any doubt as to that, as he stood high up on the one large hill that dominated the tiny patch of land: for across the water, looking deceptively closer than the five and a half miles he knew it to be, stood Carigillie Craig, with its unmistakable pair of stunted hilltops that had earned the place its predictable nickname among the equally predictable local fishermen. Beyond Carigillie, he could see the darkish purple humps that were East and West Kellicksay and, further across, on the edge of the horizon, the distant outlines of the Outer Skerries.

Scanning from left to right, Tommy squinted against the sun, shading his eyes with his hands as he searched for any signs of shipping, but as far as he could see, the sparkling water was as devoid of life and movement as a dead, beached whale. However, he reasoned, it was still fairly early in the day and any trawlers who had beaten the storm back to their home ports would likely not be putting out again until well into the afternoon.

He scanned towards the north west again, for in that direction lay the much larger islands of Yell, Fetlar and Unst, which between them made up the bulk of the northern third of the Shetlands and it was from this direction he was most likely to spot the first shipping. In that direction, too, lay home, on Yell itself, where by now, he knew, his sister Lois would be worrying herself silly over him.

As would Duncan's two daughters. And John MacAndrew's wife, Maggie, poor Billy's mother and now, although she wouldn't yet know it for sure, almost certainly a widow. Pushing such thoughts from his mind, Tommy sighed, turned and resumed his climb, eyes now looking for any pieces of dried bracken, his hand reflexively patting his pocket to make sure that his cigarette tin and the all-important lighter it contained were still there.

'This is crazy!' Mary exclaimed, finally finding her voice again. 'Why? I mean, how?' She was standing before a mirror that occupied most of one wall in the dressing room Kelly had led her to, her 'mentor' by her side. The glass reflected back two females who, apart from the manner of their dress, were as alike as two peas in a pod.

Not only did Mary now look six or seven years younger, not to mention, as she had to admit, a great deal more attractive, she could have been Kelly's twin.

Or her clone, an unbidden voice whispered.

The smile had not left Kelly's face and now she motioned towards the two swivel chairs that stood waiting by the long dressing table unit opposite the mirror wall.

Obediently, Mary followed her to them and they sat down.

'It's really very simple,' Kelly began, crossing her booted ankles. 'Of course, it isn't simple at all, but we don't have to worry ourselves about the scientific ins and outs, just the bare outlines.

'You see,' she continued, her voice steady and annoyingly quiet, 'these new bodies of ours are created by a process that involves genetic modification and some sort of cybernetic technology. I don't understand the details myself, but then I don't have to. I was just grateful that I wasn't going to die at the age of fifty, which was unfairly young, I thought: though not as young as in your own case, I understand.'

Mary was doing some rapid mental arithmetic. She stared at Kelly in disbelief. 'Fifty?' she echoed. 'Plus you said twenty, earlier. That makes you seventy!'

'Sixty-nine, actually,' Kelly replied quite calmly.

Mary looked at her and then down at herself. 'So these bodies don't age: is that what you're telling me?'

'Not outwardly,' Kelly agreed. 'And even on the inside they are far more robust and long-lasting than a normal

45

human body. I am told that we can expect to live up to six times as long as we would have done in the normal course of events and that we will probably only age in appearance by about ten years or so.'

'So why do we die in the end anyway?' Mary demanded. There were a thousand other questions she knew ought to be more urgent, but her head was still in turmoil from these revelations.

'Our brains eventually wither and die,' Kelly explained. 'The rest of the body remains quite functional and will be passed on to another subject in time, but, as you may know, human brain cells are the only ones that do not reproduce themselves and die off at a steady rate during the normal lifespan.

'Doctor Lineker has been able to stall this process considerably, by using a cloning and replacing technique he has perfected over many years, but it is only a delaying process and has certain disadvantages.'

'Such as?'

'Such as the replacement cells not being quite as efficient as the originals. From the age of about a hundred or so onwards, we can expect to experience such symptoms as memory loss, disorientation, slight hearing loss – only what an aged human would normally expect a few years earlier than that, even.'

'Except that an old man or woman with those problems would expect to be dead within a few years of their onset, at the very least. I think that's an awful fate, having to live for maybe two hundred years, having gone ga-ga up top.' Mary tapped her head for emphasis, but the prospect did not seem to worry Kelly.

'If we go "ga-ga", as you put it,' she said, 'then we probably won't even be aware of it, will we? Besides, we do get a very long active life in exchange first.'

'Is it a good trade-off, though?' Mary persisted. 'The thought of it terrifies me and I'm telling you now, when the time comes and while I've still got the intelligence to know about it, I'll find the nearest bus and throw myself under it.'

Kelly smiled even wider and shook her head slowly. 'Apart from the distinct lack of buses here,' she said, 'you would not be allowed to terminate the life of your body. These things are very expensive to create, even in their more basic form.'

'Basic form?' Mary said. 'They don't seem *that* basic to me. Or is this the deluxe version we're in?'

'Not in your case,' Kelly replied. 'As you have already noticed, you can see only in black and white, which is all the basic requirement you need. And you have no sense of smell, which is surplus to your current status anyway. Both refinements require complicated modifications, which means time and money – lots of both.

'However, you may graduate to earn these later, depending upon your performance: and there are other little bonuses as well, though you do not need to know the details at this stage.'

'Maybe not,' Mary retorted, 'but there are a few things I *do* still need to know.' Her brain was slowly beginning to reorder itself now and her initial feelings of shock, disbelief and euphoria were now beginning to concede ground to an uneasy suspicion.

'For a start,' she said, 'how come I've been given a body like this one? This face makes me look like some sort of bimbo – yeah, sorry, I realise we look the same, but it's true, nonetheless – and this figure is, well, look at you, for a start! That's hardly girl-next-door look, is it?

'Also, I take it there are more of us Jenny whatsits than just we two,' she ploughed on. 'Do we *all* look identical? 'Cause that's going to make for severe paranoia, or something close to schizophrenia, I reckon.'

'Actually, there are several different basic models of body and face,' Kelly said. 'We are both Body Type C, Facial Type B, Hair Type Fourteen, or CB-Fourteens for short. In theory, there could be more than a thousand combinations, but in practice there are about fifty, with up to four Jenny-Annes sharing any one given combination.'

'So that must mean there are nearly two hundred of us!' Mary exclaimed, eyes widening still further. 'Are we all here, in one place?'

'Not all of us, no. Here, there are about a hundred of us. The others have been moved out to different locations, but there are new arrivals almost weekly now. The Jenny-Anne programme is expanding at an ever-growing rate, I am told.'

'And *you* still haven't told *me* where this silly tag comes from.' Mary snorted. 'Why are we called bloody Jenny-Annes?'

'Doctor Lineker has a rather odd sense of humour, I guess you'd say,' Kelly replied, uncrossing her ankles and starting to stand up. She tapped her chest, between her impressive breasts. 'As I said earlier, these bodies are the result of some very advanced genetic modifications and Gen, or Jenny, is an abbreviation of that, but also, inside here, certain of our biological functions are now controlled by cybernetic methods, which would make us, if you know your science fiction, part android.

'Thus we have Genetic Androids – Jenny-Annes,' she concluded. 'It's quite sweet, really, once you get used to it.'

'Seems I've got a lot of other things to get used to first,' Mary said grimly. 'And there's this place, for a start? Where are we? I'm willing to bet this isn't the Charles Stuart and no one could keep a hundred of us a secret back in Glasgow. Are we even still in Scotland?'

'The Shetlands, actually,' Kelly said, opening a drawer and pulling out something that looked soft and pale. 'This particular island is privately owned by Doctor Lineker's people and is one of the most easterly. You won't ever have heard of it, I'm sure, and the name is scarcely important: but if it makes you any happier to know, it's called Ailsa Ness.'

'Now there's a report that a helicopter's down last night.' Geordie Walker's tone indicated his annoyance at the constant interruptions. 'What the fucking hell do they expect us to do about it?'

Alex Gregory made a tutting noise and pushed aside the file in front of her. 'Language, Constable Walker,' she said, in mock reproof. 'For that, it's your turn to go and get the

48

coffees. After which, you make a careful entry in the daily log, including details of names and ages and all the other crap of those believed to be on board. Was it a Navy machine?'

Geordie shook his head. 'No, some private buggy, they said. Does taxi runs out to one of the smaller islands. I understand there are quite a few of those things whirling about up there, most days.'

'Yes, quite a few,' Alex agreed. 'That's why we have to keep a comprehensive log of even the most trivial incidents. You know our brief up here. We might pretend to be just ordinary plods, but three CID officers on an island this size . . .'

She did not finish the sentence, nor did she need to, for Geordie Walker, although only arrived on Yell less than a week, knew only too well why they were here. It was his three years in Newcastle's undercover drug squad that had been as responsible for his transfer, as much as his final run-in with the Bozzy Harper organisation that had required that he make a quick exit from his native city and find somewhere nice and remote to lie low until the remainder of the outfit, including the half-insane head of it himself, had finally been tracked down, rounded up and put safely out of harm's way until they were too old to represent a threat to his continued health any longer. Bozzy's brain may have been half-eaten away by his own stock-in-trade, but the man still had a long memory and was all the more dangerous because of his state of mind.

The prospect of spending a couple of years on this remote outpost had not been especially appealing to Geordie, for the work was mostly routine and most of such drug busts as it did result in were generally carried out by the coastguards or the Royal Navy and usually well out to sea, but at least that remoteness assured him of a daily routine that did not include looking under his car for unwelcome modifications of the pyrotechnic variety every time he parked it up for even a few minutes, nor sleeping with a loaded .38 under his pillow. Especially as Geordie had an almost pathological hatred of firearms.

'But surely a regular taxi run between islands isn't worth our attention?' he said, pushing his chair back. The mention of coffee had reminded him that he hadn't had any breakfast that morning and it would be a chance, while the kettle was boiling, to nip out to the little bakery along the street.

'Probably not,' Alex agreed. 'But get the names, all the same. I like to know who's moving about our patch – and over it.'

'Well, whoever this little crowd were,' Geordie retorted, standing up and ducking past the dangling lampshade on his way to the door, 'they'll not be moving about our manor any more: at least, not under their own steam. According to Central, the chopper hit a headland and exploded on impact. There were no survivors.'

'Do I *have* to wear this damned stuff?' Mary McLeod stood unsteadily before the mirror, finding it difficult to maintain her balance in the unaccustomed high heels and walking, she knew, was going to be something of a nightmare. Not only that, but Kelly had insisted on pulling the corset belt so tight that breathing was a challenge now and she was very conscious of the way it thrust her new breasts into prominence, the stretchy, clinging fabric of the body-stocking doing little to counter that effect.

'This makes me look like a right tart!' she sniffed. 'Yeah, OK, no offence meant, doppelgänger mine, but it bloody well does. There's absolutely nothing left to the imagination in this, is there? What's the purpose, I'd like to know? And what happens if I just take it all off again?'

'That would be very stupid of you,' Kelly said, her voice suddenly hard. 'The consequences would be most unpleasant and besides, you might find it harder to remove the belt and boots than you expect. The buckles at the rear of the belt are automatically locking and you will see that the laces at the tops of each boot pass through a sort of ferrule, which also acts as a locking device.

'The straps are tough enough anyway, although there is a fine mesh of thin steel woven between the two layers of

50

leather and there is a very thin, but very strong steel strand running through the centre of each bootlace. It would require some very professional cutters to get through either, unless you happen to have the key – which you don't,' she added.

'Ye gods and little penguins!' The pet oath slipped out under Tommy MacIntyre's breath as he lay low in the heather, staring at the scene below his vantage point. He had seen the figures from the top of the hill, but had not bothered trying to hail them as the wind, such as there was of it, was against him and the distance too great.

Now he was glad that he'd made that decision and that the gradient had been far too steep to make the first part of the descent on that same side of the hill. Instead, he had been forced to backtrack and then begin a circuitous route around the southern slope, his approach here masked effectively by the thick outcrops of gorse bushes, so that Tommy had been able to see the true nature of what was going on below just before the participants would have been able to see him.

Dropping low, he had crawled slowly forwards, until he had finally reached the edge of a drop that had to be at least thirty feet, to where the ground levelled out into what should have been wild meadowland at the very least, but which was, in fact, an obviously well-tended stretch of grass, in the midst of which stood an oval track, its dull pink surface divided into four wide lanes by means of three white painted lines.

Had he happened upon the place when it was deserted, Tommy MacIntyre would have scratched his head and racked his brains to try to figure out why someone should want to put a running track – for it could have been nothing else, even without what he was watching now – in the middle of a supposedly deserted island that wouldn't have been large enough to support even a medium-sized flock of sheep.

Now, however, there was no need to wonder – at least not over the reason, even though that reason was plenty cause enough in itself for wonder of a different nature.

Hardly breathing, Tommy lay motionless, hardly able to believe the evidence of his own eyes.

There were four carts on the track in all and another two standing off to one side, though the term cart hardly did the little vehicles any justice. Buggy might be a better word, he thought, or perhaps even chariot, for they were clearly designed as racing vehicles, light in construction, with one huge, spoked wheel each side and a small raised saddle seat to accommodate the driver.

Each driver controlled and drove a team of two, who were hitched with a central shaft between them and guided by means of long reins that ran back over their shoulders and it was the sight of these teams that had set Tommy's pulse racing, for these 'ponies', for want of a better name, were human.

And female.

And, as near as damn it, naked!

Mary McLeod stood clutching the handrail that ran along the front of the gallery, staring down at the scene in the long hall below, her mouth wide open in disbelief, her unblinking eyes as round as saucers. Behind her, Kelly stood in silence, arms folded across her chest, watching her closely.

At last, Mary managed to tear her gaze away from the tableau and turned back to face her supposed mentor and tutor. 'That's – that's barbaric!' she blurted out. 'And there's no way you can tell me those girls down there are happy with that sort of treatment.'

In the hall, four human pony-girls were being harnessed in pairs to two racing buggies, their handlers and drivers manoeuvring them with practised ease, hitching reins and chains, clipping on bells and brasses, while the four creatures, rendered dumb by their bitted harnesses and helpless by the cruel gloves that held their arms to their sides, stood like statues atop the awesome hooves in which their legs appeared to terminate.

'You can't treat women like animals,' Mary continued to protest.

Kelly inclined her head slightly. 'We are all animals of one kind or another,' she replied. 'And yes, those girls are quite content with their treatment. They have been trained over a long period of time, as we all are – as you will be, shortly. Every one of us must be trained in many different skills.

'Of course, most of us will only race occasionally, but there are some who take to it better than others, some who are better suited – temperamentally, that is – and they are selected for the permanent stables. They lead quite a privileged life, I can tell you. They are pampered and spoiled beyond anything the rest of us can ever hope for.'

'Like pedigree bitches, or thoroughbred mares, you mean?'

'I suppose there is a degree of comparison,' Kelly conceded. 'For myself, I'd prefer to think of them in the manner of a favourite in the sultan's harem. The very best are actually reserved for only one master, although the grooms will exercise them daily in between, of course.'

'Oh, of course!' Mary sneered. 'Couldn't have them getting lazy and fat, could we? Well, if you think I'm going to stand there and let some pervert strap me into a harness and then parade about like a potential Derby winner, you can think again.

'I've seen enough. More than enough,' she added, casting a last look behind her. The first buggy began to move off, accompanied by a jangling symphony of bouncing silver and brass ware. 'I want out of here,' Mary growled.

'I demand to speak to the head honcho and right now would be a good time,' she continued, planting her feet firmly astride and praying the heels wouldn't betray her. 'OK, I know I owe you people my life, but there *are* limits and *that* –' she jerked her thumb in the general direction of the arena below '– *that* goes well beyond them.

'I'll happily repay whatever debt I owe. I've got a few thousand pounds in my savings account and some shares my grandfather left me, plus I'll either work here in some way, or else I'll go back to my job in Glasgow and we can agree a monthly sum.'

53

'I don't think you understand,' Kelly said quietly. 'You cannot go back to Glasgow. Your old job will have been given to someone else now, in any case, but even had it not, they can't risk letting you back into the outside world. Not now and probably not ever. You see, as far as the rest of the world is concerned, you're dead now.

'Your old body was cremated some while ago; your savings will have gone to your next of kin, along with your shares and anything else you owned. The only thing left out there of the old Mary McLeod will be a few photos and cherished memories – and both of those fade a lot quicker than you might think.

'Your past is your past now and the only matter of any importance is the future, which for you – for me, for all of us – lies here. And yes, we will repay what we owe, though how do you put a value on life, Mary?

'And why do you think we have been made the way we are now? These people – our so-called saviours – they aren't some benevolent charity, nor are they state-sponsored. They may not actually be perfecting their science for money itself, but they certainly need cash and loads of it. That's where we come in.

'Those men down there – the drivers and even, possibly, some of the handlers – they're not everyday common Joes. There won't be a single one of them who isn't worth at least a couple of million pounds – usually a lot more – and they pay a king's ransom every time they come here to the island.

'Yes, they may all be warped, kinky, call it what you want, but not *all* of them are so bad. Some of them can be quite kind and, once you get used to it, this isn't such a bad place to be. We are well looked-after, we don't get sick, we eat well and no real harm can ever come to us.

'Even those whips don't have the effect you'd expect. Look, I'll show you.' Kelly reached behind her, to where a small rack was bolted to the wall, to which was clipped a variety of whips, straps and crops. She selected a particularly vicious-looking crop, flexed it between her hands and then, without warning, brought it around in a scything arc.

The leather landed across the top of Mary's left thigh with a high-pitched crack and she jumped back in alarm, but, to her surprise and disbelief, the only sensation was as if someone had slapped her with an open palm. It stung, but not that badly.

'You see?' Kelly exclaimed triumphantly. 'When they gave us these bodies, they arranged it so that our responses to pain were dulled by about eighty per cent. So, when you see those pony-girls being whipped into action, they aren't really feeling much of it at all. And the whip marks fade quickly, too, I promise you.'

'Somehow, I don't think that makes me feel a lot better about things,' Mary said, shaking her head. 'The whole idea is – well, it's demeaning, isn't it?'

'Any more demeaning than someone having to spend fifty years on their hands and knees scrubbing lavatory floors?' Kelly asked. 'That's what my grandmother did and then she died at the age of sixty-five, looking eighty and feeling a hundred and ten.'

'That would have been a long time ago,' Mary pointed out. 'Given that you're nearly seventy yourself, that is.'

'Maybe so, but there are still women suffering all over the world, who would gladly change places with any one of us. Come with me. There's someone I want you to meet.'

Mary hesitated, but finally moved to follow her.

'OK,' she agreed, 'but then I want to meet the boss man. I'm sorry, but you won't convince me otherwise.'

Kelly halted, turning back with a look of genuine consternation in her unblinking eyes. 'I hope I can,' she said earnestly. 'I truly hope I can. Because the mechanism that they use to dull our pain responses can easily be reversed.' She paused and shook her head. 'And intensified,' she added darkly.

Keith Lineker closed the heavy oak-panelled door quietly behind him and walked slowly and noiselessly across the thick-pile carpet towards the two armchairs by the huge, empty fireplace. The one other occupant of the room, Richard Major, looked up at his approach, but barely seemed to be seeing him there. Eventually, however, Major raised a hand and indicated for Lineker to take the other chair.

'I'm really sorry, Rekoli,' Lineker said, breaking the silence as he sat. 'I wish there was something I could say or do, but ...' He made a gesture with his hands to indicate the futility and Rekoli Maajuk, or Richard Major as the outside world knew him, nodded tersely.

'They should have waited till after the storm, Ikothi,' he said, his voice hollow. 'Salinia always was so damned impatient and impatience is supposed to be a trait reserved for damned humans.'

'She would have been anxious to get Fraser here, in case he changed his mind,' Keith Lineker – Ikothi Leenuk – said quietly. 'She knew the importance of her mission.'

'And so they took off with a storm blowing up and killed themselves, plus five very valuable guests as a result.'

'I suppose there's no chance –?'

'None at all,' Major cut him short. 'She was definitely on board and the helicopter exploded when it hit the ground. All nine of them would have been killed instantly, even Salinia. It wouldn't have mattered, not even if we had been there when it happened; a further transfer would have been impossible.'

'Then at least it was quick,' Lineker said, avoiding Major's eyes. 'We can be thankful for that.'

'And maybe for something else,' Major said. 'Maybe the explosion will have destroyed the evidence of your handiwork.'

'And maybe not,' Lineker said. 'Modern forensic techniques – at least what passes as modern out there – don't miss very much.'

'Assuming there is an autopsy, of course.'

'There will be,' Lineker assured him. 'The aviation authorities will want to make sure that the helicopter wasn't full of drunken idiots and the Customs people will want to check for other things. This area is rife with drug-smugglers, as you know.'

'Then we must act quickly, before they have time to get too inquisitive. We must bring Salinia's body back here. Where have they taken the bodies: do we know that yet?'

'A small private facility, just outside of Burravoe, over on Yell,' Lineker said. 'It's some sort of research establishment, but the head doctor there is also licensed by the coroner's office to perform post-mortems. They don't think it justifies full-timers up here.

'Ordinarily, of course, it wouldn't, but nine bodies will occupy this fellow for a little while. If we are lucky, Salinia may be near the end, which will give us more time. At least Haarik was second-generation, so there will be nothing from his corpse to arouse any suspicions. I have already sent Boolik and Rezarda, on the assumption that Salinia was indeed among the casualties. I thought it best not to waste any time waiting for confirmation.'

'And they will bring my daughter back here?'

'Not yet, I'm afraid,' Lineker replied carefully. 'Eight bodies where there should be nine would arouse suspicions anyway. That is why I have sent Rezarda. She will remove only what needs to be removed. Afterwards, the absence of certain elements will be blamed upon the damage caused by the explosion.'

'And what if they arrive at Burravoe too late?'

'I have taken care of that. The good Doctor Lomax is attached to the main coroner's office in Lerwick. He will ensure that he is in a position to intercept any untoward reports from Burravoe. I have instructed him to telephone the fellow at Burravoe and tell him that he has been appointed to oversee the case.'

'And might that not arouse even more suspicion?'

'Nothing we cannot deal with. If our people get there in time, there will be no calls and Lomax will simply telephone the fellow again this evening and inform him that the case has been transferred to whoever is really supposed to be responsible for it. If not, then the call to Lomax will be this unfortunate pathologist's last.'

The main stable areas were at one end of the vast underground complex, reached by means of a long, high-ceilinged corridor, which eventually opened up into a broader central concourse, with rows of wooden half-doors along either side.

At the far end, the area opened up wider still, to allow for storing the myriad assorted carts and buggies, as well as dozens of wheeled stands that held hundreds of items of tack, harnesses, bridles, boots, whips, crops and ornate, feathered head-dresses. Away to the right of this area were two further large corridors, which, Kelly explained, led to the outside and to the large indoor hall they had been looking down into earlier.

'There are outside races most days,' she explained, 'but today it's mostly the occasional ponies involved, so the majority of the regular girls are in their stalls, or else up in their respective masters' quarters. It's not all racing for them, you know,' she added, with a sudden grin.

She turned towards the left-hand row of doors, passing several, upon which Mary saw there were small brass plaques, although the writing on them was too ornate and too small to decipher without getting closer and she did not want to betray any overt curiosity. Eventually, Kelly came to a halt in front of the eighth door, reached up for the latch and swung the top section open.

'This is Jessie,' she said, looking over her shoulder to make sure Mary was still behind her. 'It's quite all right for us to go in and see her, but of course she isn't allowed out, not without her master or a groom and certainly not without full harness. It's part of the ritual down here, you see,' she added, as if that was sufficient explanation.

Stomach fluttering, Mary followed her guide into the dim interior of the stall and was forced to turn away as the powerful overhead lamps blinked on, bathing the area in a brilliant white glow. In the far corner, she was vaguely aware of a figure rising to her feet, but it was several seconds before her eyes adjusted to the glare and several more while she stood and stared at this apparition.

There was little difference between her outfit and the ones Mary had seen on the pony-girls in the arena, she guessed, but now, close up, the intricate harness, and the way in which it seemed to make its wearer appear even more vulnerable than if she had been completely naked, was quite breathtaking.

Jessie, her mouth held firm by the fat bit between her full lips, returned Mary's gaze unflinchingly and there was even the hint of a smile at the corners of her mouth. Kelly, meantime, had stepped back, but now she moved forwards again, reaching out a hand towards Jessie's bridle.

'Your master has left the island again,' she said, speaking to the unmoving pony-girl, 'so I guess it's safe to take this thing off for a while. Here, hold still and let me do it. The girls here are kept permanently tacked up whenever their respective masters are in residence,' she explained, for Mary's benefit.

'All this,' she continued, nodding around to indicate the spartan stall and the straw bed upon which Jessie still stood, 'is for the benefit of the visitors. Ah, that's got it,' she said, pulling the bit from Jessie's mouth, although Mary noted that neither girl made any attempt at removing the rest of the bridle from about Jessie's head.

'Now,' Kelly went on, tossing the bit into the straw, 'this probably looks a bit rough and ready to you. It's meant to. But the straw is synthetic and doesn't prickle like the real thing, the water trough over there is only used to keep the mouth wet and, over in that corner, that tack rack actually conceals the door to an inner room, which is where Jessie sleeps whenever her master is away, which is probably eighty per cent of the year.'

'But she still gets to sleep on this straw stuff, on a hard floor, for the other twenty per cent,' Mary grunted.

'Only for a few hours at a time,' Jessie said, her sudden interruption almost causing Mary to start backwards. For some unknown reason, she almost hadn't been expecting the exotic creature to have the power of speech, so strong was the illusion created here.

'And not everything is as it seems,' Jessie continued, her voice rich and warm. She used one of her incredibly shaped hooves to drag a section of the straw to one side, revealing something black beneath it. 'A rubber mattress,' she explained. 'It's filled with thousands of little air pockets and is very comfortable. The mattress on my regular bed is made from the same stuff.

'My real quarters are a little different to this,' she continued. 'Perhaps you'd like to see?' She turned and led the way across to the rack Kelly had earlier indicated. 'I'm afraid one of you will have to operate the catch,' she apologised, holding up her gloved fists. 'I can manage it with these on, but it's a bit of a struggle.'

The inner room was as different from the stable stall as was possible to imagine. The floor was thickly carpeted, the bed was wide and covered with a silky spread and there was a marbled vanity and dressing unit against one wall. In the centre of another, a sliding panel had been drawn back, revealing a television screen and to the side of that was a small shelf unit, filled with books.

'There is a bath and shower unit behind that cupboard door,' Jessie explained. 'It is shared with the next stall, but neither of us can enter it if the other is already using it. Pony-girls are not allowed to fraternise with other pony-girls – not the full-time among us, anyway.'

Mary stood in the centre of the chamber, looking about her, wondering what it was that was missing. There was no window, of course, just a grille covering a ventilator high on one wall, but there was something more. Suddenly, she had it.

'There's nowhere for you to keep your clothes and stuff,' she said. 'Or is there storage under the bed itself?'

By way of reply, both Jessie and Kelly began to laugh.

Mary looked from one to the other in bewilderment. 'What's so funny?' she demanded. 'It was a simple enough question, wasn't it?'

'You explain,' Kelly said and Jessie nodded, the loose rings to either side of her mouth bobbing.

'These are all the clothes I need,' Jessie said, indicating the leather that criss-crossed her body. 'This room is for me to retreat to, but I am never allowed out as anything but what I have chosen to become.'

'But what about those things?' Mary protested, pointing at the long hoof boots. 'Surely you don't keep them on round the clock?'

'They are removed for me to bathe and fresh ones put on afterwards,' Jessie replied. 'One of the grooms sees to it. If you look closely, you will see that they are locked, similarly to your own boots. I do not have a key. Nor can I remove any of my harness, even when these gloves are taken off.

'A pony-girl may not alter her outward appearance in any way, other than to repair make-up damage, but even that is rare. Has Kelly explained to you that our make-up is semi-permanent?'

'It is?' This came as news to Mary, who had quite docilely allowed her mentor to transform her features earlier. 'How permanent is semi-permanent?' she demanded, rounding on her lookalike.

'Thirty or forty days,' Kelly replied, 'though there is a reagent that can be used if a master wishes to make any major alterations to a girl's image.'

'I've landed in a madhouse,' Mary said, tottering across to the edge of the bed and sinking down on to it. It was, as Jessie had promised, very comfortable, but the thought of having to sleep in it, complete with all that harness and those long boots, did not bear thinking about.

'It's all a question of getting used to it,' Kelly explained soothingly. 'Jessie will tell you – she has a good life here.'

'I do,' Jessie intoned. 'I am treated well, fed and exercised; I have plenty of recreation time and every three months or so I am allowed to leave here and return to the main island for a five-day break, during which time I can dress as I choose. However, I have also chosen to forgo those breaks for more than a year now.

'My master is given to making sudden visits unannounced and I should not like him to arrive and find me not waiting for him. He would be so disappointed.'

'This master of yours,' Mary said, biting her lip, 'does he take you to his bed often?' Jessie nodded. 'And do you sleep in it, or does he just make use of you and then have you sleep on a little straw mattress in the corner?'

'I sleep in the bed with him,' Jessie confirmed. 'And yes, in harness, usually bitted,' she added, anticipating the next question. 'Unless he needs my mouth for other purposes,' she finished, her lips twitching.

61

'Bloody hell!' Mary breathed. She looked again at Jessie's useless hands. 'Don't you ever get to take those off, either?'

Jessie looked down at herself, apparently having forgotten about the mitt gloves. 'When I am in here for any length of time, yes,' she said.

'So why don't you take them off now?'

'Because I am due for an exercise run quite soon now and it would be a waste of time and effort. Besides, I have no use for my hands just now.'

Mary leaned back across the bed, spreading her arms wide behind her to support her weight and looked up at the other two women.

'Don't either of you ever wish you could go back to the outside world?' she asked.

They looked at each other and shrugged in unison.

'What for?' Kelly said.

'There is nothing left for me to go back to,' Jessie replied. 'Everyone I ever knew will be long dead by now. I was forty-six when I was brought here and that was more than fifty years ago.'

'But that – that would have been during the Second World War!' Mary protested. 'Science hadn't got anywhere near that far advanced back then, surely? No one had the sort of technology to clone bodies like this?'

'I can assure you that these people did,' Jessie said. 'I was born in nineteen hundred and six and I can remember the Great War. My father and two uncles were killed in the trenches.'

'You're not kidding, are you?' Mary stood up again, pacing back and forth in the confined area, mind racing. 'You really are nearly a hundred years old,' she said. 'Yet you look about twenty-five. Not only that, you don't seem to care that they keep you here like a pampered show pony and hand you over to some guy who treats you like he owns you.

'I reckon the shock has got to you,' she went on, stopping and turning back to confront Jessie. 'Either that, or this brain deterioration stuff has already set in, in your case.'

62

'You're still so very new here,' Kelly said, before Jessie could reply. 'In a little while, you will start to readjust, as we all have. Yes, I can understand how you can stand there and accuse Jessie of being some sort of simpleton, but you should never knock what you haven't tried.'

'Oh, yeah? Well, I ain't gonna try this, that I can tell you.'

'Listen,' Kelly urged her. 'I'm trying to tell you. They'll *make* you, don't you understand? Why do you think each new girl is put with one of us older hands? It's because we once felt as you do now and tried to resist and suffered for it as a result.

'Of course, very few newcomers ever listen, but some do and that saves them a lot of unnecessary trauma. And these people don't even have to hurt you in order to bring you to heel, though they certainly could if they chose to.'

'So, what do they do? Tickle us into submission? Make us die laughing?'

'You're nearer the truth than you think,' Kelly replied tartly. 'But it's no laughing matter, I promise you. The thought of being hung up, helpless and brought to one orgasm after another for hours on end might – just – sound appealing, especially to some people. In reality, it is a worse form of torture than being whipped.

'You want to beg to be released while it's happening, then beg for it to start up again when they pause it. Except you can't beg, because your mouth is stuffed full with a fat rubber cock and all you can do is dribble and squeak behind a horrible mask.

'In the end, you'll do anything – and I do mean *anything* – rather than go through it again. That's why I tell you, it'll be easier in the long run if you just go along with it. Once you get used to it, well, it's OK.'

'Bit like being hit over the head with a hammer,' Mary rejoined. 'Nice when it stops, eh?'

'Listen,' Kelly said. 'I've got an idea. When is your next exercise session, Jessie?'

'Quite soon,' Jessie said. 'I never bother about exact times and I never know them anyway, but if my master is gone away, I must have been asleep for several hours, so one of the grooms will come to take me out shortly now.'

'Then what say I have a word with the grooms,' Kelly suggested, 'and have them trot you out as a pair? Jessie is the best there is to learn from,' she told Mary.

Mary looked at her, aghast. 'You gotta be joking, lady!' she spat. 'I'm not going anywhere looking like that!'

'It'll happen anyway, sooner or later,' Kelly said, sighing. 'Usually, of course, pony-girl training doesn't come till much later, not until a girl has been properly broken and trained in other aspects, but if you are prepared to show willing, it will count very much in your favour.

'No one's suggesting that you'd want to join Jessie here as a permanent, but we all do stints down here anyway, so why not give it a try? I'll be on hand and I give you my word that it'll only be for an hour or two, three at the most.

'C'mon, what harm can it do? You won't be showing the grooms anything they haven't seen before and they'll see it soon enough, anyway.'

Mary shook her head and turned to study Jessie once more. Eventually, she appeared to come to a decision. 'I must be getting as mad as the rest of you,' she said levelly. 'Three hours, you say?'

'At the most.'

'Swear on your mother's grave?'

'She was cremated. I saw her will.'

'Swear on your own then,' Mary retorted. 'Because I'll bloody kill you if you're lying to me!'

'Please sit down, Amaarini,' Richard Major said. He was still sitting in the high-backed armchair, which he had not left now for several hours. The woman, Amaarini Savanujik, better known to the island's visitors as Amanda Savage, lowered herself into the seat recently vacated by Keith Lineker, crossed her long legs and waited.

'Thank you for coming so promptly,' Major said, at last. 'And please, may we take your commiserations as read? I know how much you thought of my daughter and, as Ikothi Leenuk and myself have already agreed, no amount of words can bring her back to us.'

'Of course, Rekoli Maajuk,' Amaarini agreed, inclining her head slightly forward. 'I do understand.'

'And you will also understand that our programme must continue,' Major said. 'Salinia would not have had it otherwise, as we both know.' He paused and took a deep breath.

'It will obviously take a long time for all of us to get over this tragic loss,' he continued, 'and we shall all grieve, no doubt, in our different ways. But meanwhile, decisions must still be taken and someone must be there to take them.

'Therefore, Amaarini, I am inviting you to take over from my daughter as head of the Jenny-Anne training programme. You have worked with her now for a good many years and I know she both liked and trusted you, respecting your judgement as I have been able to respect hers.'

'I would be honoured,' the woman replied sombrely. 'I just hope I can prove worthy of both your daughter's trust and your own.'

'I am sure you will, Amaarini,' Major said. 'And now, to business. You have several new arrivals, I understand? How are they progressing?'

The two grooms were both male and looked as though they were in their early thirties, but by now Mary was not prepared to take anything for granted where physical appearances were concerned. If they were to be believed, Kelly was nearly seventy and the languid Jessie about thirty years older, yet neither of them looked a day over twenty-five, so who was to say that these men weren't at least a hundred and fifty?

The two men, however, did not have the same aura of physical perfection that seemed to be the main attribute of the Jenny-Annes. While they were in no way unpleasant on the eye, their facial characteristics were slightly unusual, in that they both had rather flat bridges to their noses and their eyes seemed slightly further apart than might be expected, yet both were well built, the sleeveless leather vests and shorts showing off their physiques to their best advantage.

They were called Hugh and Michael and were obviously used to working as a team, for they wasted no time and little effort in preparing Mary for her first training session.

She was taken to a nearby empty stall and quickly stripped of boots, corset belt and body-stocking, the pair working so quickly and efficiently that Mary had little time in which to be embarrassed. Not that either of them seemed remotely interested in her naked body, except as a focus for their professional expertise.

Before she had recovered her wits properly and had the opportunity to analyse exactly what it was she had agreed to, they were cinching her waist into one of the tight girth corsets and as Hugh, the slightly darker groom, made the final adjustments to the straps on that, Michael was already throwing more harness straps over her shoulders and feeding her breasts into the conical webbing that would produce the same distended contours as Jessie boasted.

The collar was then swiftly fastened about her neck and she was led over to lean back against the wall while her hoof boots were drawn up her legs and painstakingly laced tightly into position, one groom working on each limb. To Mary's surprise, although they elevated her feet to the same extent as the boots which Kelly had put on her, they seemed somehow far more comfortable and the broad hoof extensions made balancing a good deal less traumatic.

'These must cost a fortune to make,' she remarked, staring down at her new footwear.

Michael raised a finger to his lips. 'No talking,' he warned. 'Pony-girls do not speak, not unless instructed to by a master or a groom. Now, stand up straight and take a few steps forwards. Yes,' he said, when she complied, 'not bad at all. A very good fit.'

Even in her heels, the two grooms were half a head taller than Mary and had little difficulty in fitting her bridle, scooping up her hair into a high ponytail and passing it through the tubular projection at the crown, tugging the various straps into position, adjusting buckles, until finally they were ready to bit her.

For a brief second, Mary almost balked, but the warning gleams in two pairs of eyes were enough to convince her otherwise. Dutifully, she opened her mouth, parting lips and teeth to admit the padded bar, surprised to discover that there was also a slightly curved projection on the inner edge that pressed down on her tongue, rendering speech even more improbable than had her mouth been filled with just the simple rod.

Standing there, as they now drew the long gloves up her arms, guiding her fingers to form fists inside the tight mitten ends and then lacing the leather sleeves so that they clung to every contour, Mary felt a curious thrill run through her body, for whether this had been inevitable or not before, now there was certainly no way back and, as they clipped the snap links that kept her already useless arms tightly against the sides of her girth, she understood what it meant to be totally helpless.

She was unable to resist, or even to protest; it had taken them less than twenty minutes to transform her into a copy of Jessie, but there was yet more to come, for in her stall, Jessie had been missing one vital part of her costume and neither she nor Kelly had thought to warn Mary of this.

The V-shaped crotch strap, as it was buckled to the front of her girth, gave Mary no cause for alarm. From its design, she guessed its purpose and position and at least it meant that her sex would be covered. But then, as she was expecting it to be drawn back and up between her legs, they produced the two dildoes.

She tried to squeal her protests through the gagging bit, but even if her words had been coherent, she knew that the grooms would not have been dissuaded. Thoroughly oiled in preparation, the two shafts found no obstruction to their passage and slipped easily into her, even the rear phallus – which was a surprise to Mary, almost as much as the feeling that it produced as it was eased fully home.

67

As the gusset was finally buckled into place, preventing any hope of her expelling the two invaders, Mary felt a series of new tremors spreading throughout her, working up and around, yet leaving her in no doubt as to their source. The grooms stepped back and away from her, exchanged satisfied smiles and then smiled at her in turn.

'A natural, I think,' Hugh said. 'Look at the colour in her cheeks.'

'Almost perfect,' Michael agreed. 'She'll be even sweeter when that hair grows out a bit.'

'Walk forwards again, pony-girl,' Hugh instructed.

With the two phalluses making her feel as if she might burst at any moment, Mary hesitated, but it was plain that she would have to walk soon enough anyway. Not just walk, in fact, but run as well; impossible as it seemed, these people actually expected her to run like this.

Biting into the bit, she took a hesitant pace.

Instantly, the rubber beasts seemed to come alive inside her and she gasped, air forcing itself down her nostrils, as a small squeak escaped past the bit.

'C'mon, forwards,' Hugh repeated, reaching out for the ring at one side of her bit and dragging her towards him. Unable to resist his superior strength, there was nothing else for Mary but to follow him and suddenly she understood how a certain type of personality might find a certain type of appeal in living like this.

'Slow her, Hugh,' Michael warned. 'Better give her a blocker shot first. Look at her face, man. She's going to come on the spot if you keep this up.'

And, as Mary tried to shut her ears to his words, she knew that he was not far wrong . . .

The sight of the flamboyant pony-girls racing around the track below had been so mesmerising that Tommy had not heard the guards approaching. He hadn't even given a thought to the possibility that he might be in any danger, but now, as they dragged him down the foot of the hillside, his hands cuffed behind his back and his legs still weak from whatever charge that curious rifle had fired at him, he cursed himself for his stupidity.

His two captors were male, a little older than himself, with fairish hair cut close to their skulls; they wore simple dark-blue coveralls, on the breast pocket of which was a small gold logo that meant nothing to Tommy. It wasn't much of a uniform, but then, he realised, these two goons didn't need big hats to emphasise their authority. They were strong, very strong and half-dragged, half-carried him between them as if he had been no more than a child.

He had expected to be taken right down to where the races were still continuing, but instead they turned away into some trees. Tommy's stomach somersaulted with fear.

'Hey!' he croaked, finding his voice at last. 'Get off me, you great pair of lummoxes. You can't just grab innocent people and treat them like this.'

Neither man appeared to hear him and they certainly made no attempt at a reply.

He tried again. 'Listen, fellas,' he whined, 'I'm not meaning you any harm and I wasn't really trying to spy on you. My boat went down in the storm last night and I was washed up here. All I want is to get home to a hot bath and a decent meal. It's none of my business what games you lot want to play. This is private property, I guess, and you're miles from anywhere, so it's no one else's business either, right?'

They came to what appeared to be an impenetrable stretch of thicket, but one of his captors reached into his pocket, drew out what at first sight Tommy took to be a mobile phone and jabbed at the keypad with his thumb. Immediately, there was a low hissing sound and an entire section of the undergrowth started to slide away to either side.

Tommy looked from one to the other of the men, really panicking now.

Mary's first outing as a pony-girl was an experience she knew she would never forget, not even if, as she had been led to believe she now would, she *did* live for another two hundred years. She would never have got through it without whatever it was that they had injected into her body via the small compression gun.

The sedative, as she assumed it had to be, began to take effect immediately, so that now, when Mary walked forwards, her head no longer felt as though it was about to explode, though the heat between her thighs did not seem to abate quite so noticeably. Apparently aware of this, the two grooms led her gently at first, allowing her time to grow accustomed to the sensations that the two dildoes were producing when she walked and it was several minutes before they decided that she was ready for the next stage.

Out in the wider area of the stable section, Jessie was already waiting, harnessed to the left-hand side of the shaft of a plain black buggy. A third groom stood nearby, holding a long, flexible carriage whip and Mary guessed, quite correctly, that he was to be their driver. As she stood for Hugh to fasten her own traces – two heavy links from the shaft to her girth strap and then a long driving rein clipped to each side of her bit – she suddenly realised the full import of what was actually happening to her.

These men, people she had not even met less than an hour ago, had handled her as clinically and neutrally as if she *had* been a young filly in a riding stables, stripping her of what little decency her original costume had provided and putting her into a harness and bridle that rendered her totally at the mercy of anyone who happened along.

Not only that, but she was perched on high hooves and expected, in tandem with a docile creature who claimed to be nearly a hundred and who did not seem to find any of this either alarming, nor even unusual, to pull a cart on which one of the men would sit and, presumably, use that whip to encourage them if their efforts did not match his expectations.

She wanted to shout out to them, call for Kelly, tell them that she'd changed her mind, but it was too late. The bit, with its gagging extension, prevented her from uttering any intelligible sounds at all and her one attempt produced an embarrassingly horse-like series of squeals and whinnies, which seemed to cause a certain amount of amusement among the trio of men.

'Steady there, girl,' Hugh said soothingly, patting her right buttock gently. 'You all go through the same feelings first time out, I know. It'll pass soon enough, I promise. Mac's a good driver – the best, in fact, which is why he gets to exercise the likes of Jessie here. She's valuable property, is Jess, and we don't let just anyone near her, I can tell you.' He turned to the driver and nodded. 'All yours, then, Mac,' he said. 'Get them back in about two hours, if you would. You can always take Jessie out again solo, if you think she needs the extra exercise.'

Mary nearly balked again when she realised that Mac was taking them up into the open air, for the thought of being seen publicly in this humiliating role was almost too awful to dwell on; but she quickly realised that Jessie was powerful enough to drag her along with her, if necessary, and two sharp flicks of Mac's whip across her shoulder-blades also warned her that he was anticipating some show of rebellion and was ready to deal with it quite summarily.

At the top of the long, sloping tunnel, two heavy doors slid silently open at their approach and they emerged from between what appeared to be two large clusters of bushes, straight on to an area of open grassland, through the centre of which ran an arrow-straight pathway of stone chippings, wide enough to admit the buggy and the two girls who ran shoulder-to-shoulder before it.

The wide blinkers meant that Mary could not see much of her fellow pony-girl, just flashing glimpses of her hoof boots as they trotted along, but she could hear her steady breathing above the clatter that their steel shoes made on the stones and the creaking and clinking of buggy and harnesses. For her own part, Mary was sure she would die of asphyxiation, for the tight girth corset made breathing hard work even at a standstill and this was fast becoming torturous.

Behind them, she heard Mac calling out instructions. 'Whoa, there, Jessie, girl, don't pull so. Steady now, or you'll wear this poor filly out before we've started. That's better, girl: just a nice slow trot until she gets used to it and we see what she's capable of.'

Gasping, panting, her legs feeling like lead, Mary barely had time to think, but it did occur to her oxygen-starved brain that if this was a nice slow trot, Jessie and her fellow pony-girls must be as fit as Olympic athletes, if not fitter: and, had she been able to, she would have thrown her arms round Mac and kissed him with relief when he finally reined them to a halt. She felt the movement of the shaft as he alighted and heard his boots crunching as he walked up and around in front of her.

'You move well, girlie,' he said approvingly and reached out a hand to wipe away the traces of spittle that were trickling from either corner of her mouth. 'Your new body is a lot faster, fitter and stronger than the one you had, but it still needs exercising, proper diet and regular work to bring it to its peak and keep it there.

'It'll maybe not take as long as you'd be thinking, either, little Mary, but it will be hard work for the first few days. Jessie here can cover a hundred metres, pulling cart and driver, in twenty seconds from a standing start and the next hundred in fourteen. Take her out of harness and give her a pair of running spikes and she'd run the distance quicker than the current world record – the man's record, that is!

'Aye,' he said, noting the look of disbelief in her face, 'that's the measure and the value of what you've been given here, girlie. You've plenty to be grateful for and you've hardly started learning yet.' His right hand came up and cupped her left breast, the thumb moving around to press and knead the nipple.

A violent shiver shot through Mary's spine and he grinned at her. 'You'll doubtless already know that your body doesn't feel pain very easily,' he said. 'But it experiences pleasure like you'd never believe and, once it gets used to that, it'll crave ever more and you'll not need the blockers.

'Of course, not all Jenny-Annes are quite the same. You're supposed to be near enough identical, but it doesn't work out like that in practice. Some are far more sensitive and receptive than others and I reckon you're one of those.

'I tell you, Mary lass, if I was doing what I'm doing to you now and you hadn't had that shot back in your stall, you'd be going crazy.' He stroked the back of his hand across her other nipple to prove his point and Mary, despite her determination not to let it show, shuddered again and let out a plaintive little mewling moan. To her relief, he did not repeat the contact.

'Just to let you know,' he said, winking. 'I don't know when you'll come to the stables proper, but I'll be looking forward to seeing you when you do. Jessie here is off limits, as are the other exclusives, but you won't fall into that category for a good while yet.'

He grinned. 'On the other hand,' he added, patting her shoulder, 'you're good stock, girl, so you never know your luck. And now,' he said, starting to move back towards the buggy, 'it's time for another little trot. Let's get those lungs working.' He paused, grasping the top of the wheel rim in readiness for mounting. 'Just try to let the top part of your chest do the breathing. Take it shallow and steady, but faster than usual. Listen to Jess and try to take your timing from her.'

As the buggy creaked beneath his weight and she felt the shaft settling between them, Mary found herself stupidly wondering why it was that Mac's Scottish accent seemed to come and go with such annoying regularity. And also speculating on just what he was keeping hidden beneath those leather breeches.

Trying to banish the latter thought with a shake of her head, she braced herself for the kiss of the whip that would signal for them to move off again.

Part Two

'You've been very quiet all morning, skip.' Geordie Walker set a mug of coffee on the desk in front of Alex Gregory and took a noisy slurp from his own, smacking his lips against the heat of the murky fluid.

Alex looked up in annoyance. 'Geordie, will you please stop calling me "skip"?' she said. 'I keep telling you and you keep doing it. This isn't Newcastle, nor the Met and neither is it a television police drama. The only Sweeney up here is old Gerry MacSweeney at the Victoria Arms.

'Actually,' she corrected herself, 'that's not quite true. There are probably a dozen Sweeneys and MacSweeneys somewhere in these islands and yes, before you say it, half of them probably are interbred. But then what sort of police force is it that gives a Geordie DC a nickname like Geordie when they're all bloody Geordies anyway?'

'The sort that's brought up on brown ale and worships at a licensed house every Sunday.' Geordie grinned. 'Actually, I got the nickname when I was working in the Met anyway and it sort of stuck and there were only two of us shared it when I went back to Tyneside anyway. If it worries you, you can call me Tim.'

'I've got more important things to worry about.' Alex grinned. 'Which is why, as you say, I've been a bit quiet.' She tapped the loose pile of paperwork in front of her. 'It may be nothing, but I've been ... well, just call it a feeling.'

'Feminine intuition?'

74

She glared at him. 'Don't you dare!' she warned. 'Call it a copper's intuition, if you like, but here we don't tolerate sexism, not even when it's meant as a joke.'

Geordie held up his free hand in surrender. 'OK,' he said, 'point taken. So would you like to try it on *this* copper's intuition? Two heads and all that?'

She nodded. 'Can't hurt,' she said. 'Mind you, as I said, it may be nothing, but I gave up believing in coincidences automatically a very long time ago.'

'So what gives?'

Alex lifted her mug, sipped tentatively at the contents, realised the odious brew was still far too hot and set it down again. 'Remember the car crash three days ago?' she said.

Geordie furrowed his brow. 'Doctor bloke?' he said.

Alex nodded. 'Name of Frederick George Deacon,' she said, referring to her handwritten notes which sat atop the pile. 'Originally from Wales, he came up here to head up some sort of research project over near Burravoe. Effects of certain GM-derived medicines or some such.

'Car came off the road in the early hours, went over a fifty-foot drop, exploded on impact. Not much left of either vehicle or driver.'

'Any other vehicle involved?'

'Doesn't seem to have been. Sergeant Mackay handled the case. It's uniform's territory.'

'Seems reasonable enough,' Geordie said. 'So what's your interest in it?'

'Idle curiosity – at first,' Alex said. 'I just happened to be scanning through the daily bulletin yesterday and another name cropped up: someone I know vaguely. He was a friend of my father's, way back: a chap called Hughie Lomax, lives down in Lerwick now.'

'What about him?'

'Well, it seems that he managed to fall off a ladder while trying to adjust his satellite television dish and broke his neck as a result. Died instantly, according to the medics who were called to the scene.'

'Old boy, was he?' Geordie prompted.

Again, Alex nodded. 'Elderly, at any rate,' she said. 'Late sixties. It's here somewhere,' she added, flicking the pile of papers with her thumb. 'He also had an arthritic hip, according to the neighbour who found him, so he had no business being up a ladder in the first place.'

'Maybe not,' Geordie agreed, 'but some people are just too bloody stubborn to know when they're beaten. Or were there other suspicious circumstances?'

'No, none,' Alex admitted. 'Just a coincidence, as I said. You see, Hughie Lomax is also a doctor – *was* a doctor, I suppose I should say. Nothing that special, just a GP who also did a bit of consultancy stuff for one of the local hospitals down there. He also had connections with the Lerwick coroner's office,' she added. 'With his experience and seniority, they often called him in to give second opinions and stuff like that.'

'And?' Geordie shrugged. 'I still don't see anything but a very tenuous connection. Two quacks die within the same twenty-four-hour period – so what?'

'So,' Alex said carefully, 'I also heard something quite interesting about George Deacon. It appears that he's been up in these parts for a good many years and that, among other things, he also once spent a couple of years working as a pathologist in Swansea. Very respected man, by all accounts.

'Which was why the coroner's office occasionally called him in to perform post-mortems for them, to save sending doctors here, there and everywhere. As you can imagine, we don't get a lot of people dying around here and most that do die from old age.'

'There aren't that many people up here, full stop,' Geordie concurred. 'So is that your point? Two doctors, both connected to the coroner, both now dead? You'd need more than that, ski– I mean, sarge.'

'Alex will do,' she said, and tried the coffee again. 'Ugh!' she made a face and put it down once more. 'This stuff is revolting. Now, where were we? Ah yes, two doctors, both retained by the coroner for occasional autopsy duty, both suddenly dead, apparently *not* in suspicious circumstances.

'And then we have this.' She drew another sheet of paper from the small pile and waved it between them. 'Remember the helicopter that came down in the storm the other night? Well, they recovered nine bodies and took them over to Deacon's place. Apparently they have a large refrigerated store, so he got the job of checking them over, what was left of them.'

'And? Anything suspicious there?'

'Not so far. The coroner had to send someone up after the crash, but apparently there wasn't a lot to see or do. The chopper hit *terra firma* with a bit of a bang, so it was more a case of playing jigsaw puzzles and seeing how many bits were missing from the box. Quite a few, apparently, but then that's hardly to be wondered at, given the circumstances.'

'So nothing obvious there?' Geordie said. He moved around to his own side of the double desk and sat down, reaching for his cigarettes and lighter.

Alex replaced the report sheet into the pile and sat back in her seat. 'Nothing obvious,' she agreed. 'Nine deaths from a helicopter crash that happened in a bloody great storm, one man dead from a car smash and another who fell from a ladder. It was just that ladder that was bothering me.'

'Because the guy should have had more sense than to go up it?' Geordie asked. 'Excuse my "isms", or whatever, but the man was a Jock and you Jocks are even tighter than we Geordies. I'm surprised he even splashed out on satellite TV in the first place. It's full of old rubbish anyway!'

'Except for things like news, current affairs programmes and documentaries, and Hughie Lomax, like a lot of people up here, lived in an area where it was impossible to receive terrestrial television unless you erected a two-hundred-foot aerial mast. Satellite was an easy alternative – the *only* alternative, rather.

'Now, if his television reception was so important to him that he'd risk climbing a ladder to realign a bloody great dish, it might be reasonable to assume that he'd have some

77

sort of cover on his household insurance. In fact, I know for a fact that Sky Television offer their own insurance to people up here as part of the package.

'So, given that the big storm probably blew his dish around offline, it would have been covered by insurance. Even if the cause wasn't the storm, Hughie Lomax wouldn't miss the chance to claim that it was. As you say, he was a Jock and we're . . . well, we prefer to call it canny.'

'I take it you've checked that he was insured?' Geordie said.

Another nod. 'Yes, and he wasn't,' Alex replied.

Geordie shrugged. 'There you are then,' he said. 'He *was* just trying to save himself a bit of money.'

Alex fixed him with a curious smile, her eyes gleaming.

In a small, windowless room, several miles and many islands distant, Tommy MacIntyre struggled back to consciousness, trying to piece back together the scrambled fragments of what had happened after the two guards had led him down into that underground passageway.

There had been another man, very tall, though vaguely similar, facially, to the two who had captured him, but the details were very hazy and his head hurt when he tried to focus on them, as did his eyes when he first tried to open them.

Tommy groaned and tried again, but something was still wrong, for everything seemed to be grey and blurred and his chest felt strangely heavy. He tried to relax on the soft mattress, his fingers clenching and unclenching, counting slowly until he reached fifty.

This time the room at least swam into sharper focus, but still everything was a dull monochrome. He raised a hand to his head, wondering if one of them had hit him. Maybe he was suffering from some sort of concussion, he thought groggily. And then he looked along the line of the thin sheet that was covering his prone body and his eyes jerked wide open.

With a small cry – had that noise come from *him*? – he struggled into a sitting position, thrusting the sheet from him in sheer disbelief, until, when it reached the tops of his legs, he kicked it away to slide to the floor in a crumpled heap.

He parted his legs and for several seconds sat looking numbly at what the sheet had been hiding, every muscle in his body frozen into helpless inactivity, except those that controlled his stomach, which was now heaving frantically.

And then he fainted.

'And that's where you're wrong, Mr English Policeman,' Alex cried triumphantly. 'Hughie Lomax was insured once, but not for the past eleven months – mainly because his eyesight was starting to go and television put too much of a strain on it. He gave up watching the box and relied on good old steam radio instead when his last TV licence ran out a year ago.

'And, like the good, upright citizen he was, he also had his satellite receiver taken out, though he kept the TV set, as it was in one of those big cabinet things and was a piece of furniture as well. As long as it couldn't receive signals, he wasn't breaking the law by not buying a new TV licence: though why he was bothered, I don't know. The last TV detector van that came up to the islands ended up with a series of flat tyres and a carrot stuck up its exhaust.

'But that's just by the by,' Alex continued. 'The important thing is that Hughie Lomax's satellite dish wasn't insured against damage, *because he no longer had any use for it!* Even if it had shifted position in the wind, he'd have had no way of telling it anyway, would he?'

'So he wouldn't have any need to be climbing a ladder to fix it,' Geordie finished for her.

They looked at each other in silence for a few seconds. Alex was the first to speak. 'Which means,' she said, speaking very quietly, 'that we have at least one suspicious death after all.'

'Which may be connected to the car crash,' Geordie continued.

'The driver of which was also connected, though after the fact, with the nine victims of a helicopter crash,' Alex concluded.

'You think we could have eleven murders? Seems a bit
... well, this isn't exactly Chicago, is it?'

'Maybe not, but there's one other thing. Hughie's
telephone is routed through one of our wonderful little
local exchange repeaters – works a bit like a mobile phone
– and, as such, it's easy to check on its usage.'

'Which you've now done?'

'Which I've now done,' Alex confirmed grimly. She drew
out another of the papers. 'At seven-twenty-six on the
evening before the car crash, Hughie Lomax received a
telephone conversation lasting just over four minutes. It
came from a number registered to the Marlin Research and
Development Trust, Burravoe.'

'Let me guess,' Geordie said. 'The Marlin Trust was run
by George Frederick Deacon?'

'Frederick George, actually,' Alex corrected him.

'Interesting,' Geordie said, 'but maybe not that
suspicious. If Deacon was working for the coroner and
Lomax was also involved at the Lerwick end, maybe it was
just him reporting in.'

'Except that Lomax wasn't involved in the chopper
crash case. Since his eyesight started to give him trouble,
he'd been cutting back on all his duties and the coroner
hadn't used him in a long while.'

'Maybe Deacon knew him personally and was just
asking for a bit of advice?'

'Maybe. I thought of that. But then, just after Deacon's
call to him – twenty seconds after, in fact – Lomax made
a call himself, to a rather posh mobile service that relies
upon satellites to get signals to very remote places. In this
case – and it took me a lot of string-pulling to get the
information – the phone in question is registered to a
company called Healthglow who operate some sort of
health farm operation on an island near here, called
Carigillie Craig.'

'And the helicopter that crashed also operated out of
Carigillie Craig,' Geordie said. 'I remember. I logged all
the details, like you told me to. Yeah, Healthglow, that was
it. Most of the victims were apparently guests on their way

80

there, plus there was the pilot and the daughter of Healthglow's big white chief.'

'And those guests also included another *two* doctors,' Alex added. 'I checked your log entry this morning.'

'These islands don't seem to be very healthy for the medical profession, do they?' Geordie quipped. 'Any connection between these two and the other two?'

'Not yet, as such, apart from Healthglow is connected somehow at both ends,' Alex said. She took another mouthful of coffee and swallowed it, this time without comment. 'But I'm sure there is one,' she went on, wiping her mouth with the back of her hand, 'and we're going to find it!'

It had taken four of them to restrain and dress him, for Tommy had fought and struggled all the way, despite two shots of sedative fired into his arms. Not until the third dose hissed into his buttocks, his now very curvaceous buttocks, did he finally begin to succumb and they were able to complete their task with a lot less fuss.

'You bastards!' he hissed, when they showed him his new self in the mirror, hating the soft feminine echo of his new voice. 'You bloody bastards!'

None of them replied and, as the ultra-sexy bimbo-like figure stared back at him, Tommy wanted to cry, but the tears would not come, any more than his new eyes could blink, or even see colours. Perched on the high-heeled boots between the two male guards, he fell silent, wishing now that he had gone to the bottom of the North Sea with the rest of the ill-fated *Flora*'s crew.

For Mary McLeod, three days had passed in a blur, three days in which the memory of her few hours as a pony-girl was never far from the forefront of her mind: for, despite the blocking effect of the sedative injection, she had finally climaxed violently and not just once.

Afterwards, Kelly had removed her harness and bridle and helped her to shower in the little room behind the stall in which she had originally been tacked up and then led her back into the main area of the subterranean complex, to where they were to share a small, cell-like bedroom for the immediate future.

Mary was painfully aware that Kelly had known how she would react to her treatment, but her mentor diplomatically avoided the subject and concentrated, instead, on teaching her a host of rules and regulations. At the same time, Mary was able to glean a little more information, not only about her own circumstances, but about the people who were behind this strange place, although even Kelly's information on this point was sketchy.

'I suspect that they're very different from us,' she said. 'You can see that the men have slightly strange features and some of the younger women, too. The older women end up in bodies similar to our own. Apparently – and I couldn't swear to this – their natural bodies wear out too quickly, usually by their middle to late twenties, and if they get pregnant before that, the act of childbirth usually kills them, either there and then, or very shortly afterwards, even if they're still only in their late teens.'

She imparted information very succinctly, in the manner of a lecturer and it came as no surprise to Mary when she learned that, in her former life, Kelly had been a schoolteacher in Bristol. Not only that, but Kelly was not her original name.

'We're free to choose different names, if we wish,' she explained. 'They have to be approved by the masters, of course, and they try not to have too many of us with the same name, to avoid confusion. I chose my name because it was very trendy in the outside world at the time.'

'What were you called originally?' Mary asked, intrigued.

Kelly wrinkled her nose. 'Mavis,' she said simply. 'Which was all very well in the nineteen thirties, but . . .'

Mary nodded sympathetically.

She learned that Kelly had formulated a theory as to the origins of their masters. The former schoolteacher had discovered that the colony had once been based in the South American jungles, but when intensive logging had pushed civilisation further and further into the previously inaccessible interior, they had been forced to look for a new home. A small group of them had already established a base here in the Shetlands during the early nineteenth century, acquiring the titles of several of the surrounding islands over a period of time, using different names and companies, so a large proportion of the Amazon community had crossed the Atlantic to rejoin their former companions.

Other groups had gone to the remote Pacific islands and yet another was now based somewhere in southern Africa, and individual members were dotted around the entire globe.

'I think there are more actual groups, as well,' Kelly told her, 'but it doesn't pay to get too nosy.'

'What about these guests we're supposed to be here for?' Mary asked. 'Don't they ask questions themselves?'

'Maybe,' Kelly said. 'Then again, maybe not. Most of them are here for one thing only and then gone again and I doubt it would worry them where their service providers come from.'

'What about us, then?' Mary persisted. 'Don't these guys think it's a bit funny when you tell 'em you're pushing seventy?'

'No,' Kelly snapped back. 'Because I never tell them. It's strictly against the rules and any girl who opens her mouth is in big trouble. Any time we spend alone with a master is recorded. There are bugs everywhere here.

'Let something like that slip and you end up with a tongue that no longer works. Not only that, I get the feeling you won't have done the particular visitor any favours, if you know what I mean?'

Mary nodded solemnly and made a gesture with her finger across her throat.

'Exactly,' Kelly said. 'We get treated OK, so long as we stick to the rules, but these people are right bastards when they want to be. You tell a VIP that he's screwing what amounts to an android clone and it's odds on he won't get off this place in one piece.

'Of course, his body will almost certainly turn up three or four hundred miles from here. They're not stupid enough to do anything to raise suspicion.'

Mary shuddered. 'I almost wish they'd left me to die,' she said quietly. 'To think that I'm supposed to stay here and perform like some high-class tart for the next God knows how many years, earning money for a bunch of murderers who may well be descendants of some lost Aztec tribe, isn't exactly cause for singing and dancing, is it?' She lowered herself stiffly on to the edge of her bed and sat for several seconds in contemplation.

'It seems fantastic that these people could have developed so differently, just because they did it separately from the rest of the human race,' she mused. 'And you reckon the men live as long as us in their normal bodies?'

'So I've been told,' Kelly said. 'I never press for information, but it's surprising what you can pick up over twenty years, especially if you get the chance to talk to someone like Jessie, who's been here even longer.'

'And have they always had this Jenny-Anne technology?' Mary asked.

Kelly nodded. 'Sort of,' she said. 'Jess reckons that one of the trainers told her, years ago now, that they've been developing it since the South American days. Apparently, it all started as a means to keep their adult females alive longer. Why they should have been dying so young, none of us knows, but the idea was that they made new host bodies like these.' She indicated herself.

'Unfortunately, the clones they made from their original bodies didn't last much longer themselves and their early attempts to clone hosts from the indigenous women were complete failures. However, Doctor Lineker then found a way of cloning European women in a form their own males could breed with.

'They were then able to clone from the resultant offspring and use those hosts to carry the brains of their own women afterwards.'

Mary shuddered in horror. 'That's awful!' she cried. 'It's

using us like livestock. What happens to the children afterwards, the ones they clone from?'

'Well, they only need a handful of them and they aren't harmed in the cloning process, so they grow up normal and healthy. Of course, they never get out into the big wide world – they're kept on another island, I think – and they have no idea about their origins, not until they're a lot older.

'Then they're trained as servants, or sometimes they even get to join the hierarchy. You can always tell who they are. They still have that lizard look around the eyes and nose, but it's not so pronounced. The male kids live a long time too, though they haven't had time to tell if they last as long as their fathers, and the females – well, they choose the best ones to breed on from and then they all end up in new bodies so they don't pop off prematurely.'

'It's like something out of an Ursula Le Guin book,' Mary said. 'If I didn't have the evidence of myself, I'd never have believed any of it was possible. A super-race from the jungles – crazy!'

'I know,' Kelly agreed. 'But then Jessie's got an even crazier theory. She reckons they came from outer space in the first place!'

For Helen Montgomerie, now Helen (Type AG-Three), the introduction to her new life on Ailsa Ness had been considerably less traumatic than for Tommy MacIntyre, for at least her new body retained the same sexual characteristics as her old one, but she was not so lucky in her appointed mentor.

Not that Julia was cruel, nor even unpleasant to her, but she was far less intelligent than Kelly and had not had the benefit of a good education prior to her own arrival on the island. Consequently, her attitude seemed to be that the girls complied with the regime under pain of suffering and that they owed their masters an incalculable debt of gratitude in any case.

In addition, even in her current body she had retained certain predilections that she had had in the old one and to Helen, the only thing worse than submitting herself to a male was the thought of any intimate contact with another female. The fact that this new body, however, appeared to have a mind of its own where these things were concerned served only to make things even worse.

Twice a day Helen was taken to a small exercise area, arms bound behind her back in tight leather sleeves, where trainers – male and female alike – put her through what they described as her 'paces', forcing her to run, jump obstacles, bend and stretch and perform acts with the males that she would never have contemplated prior to her initial indoctrination.

By shutting off all but a tiny part of her mind, she was quite quickly able to come to terms with this and the presence of the whips and straps – while their application did not cause her any real pain – helped even more, for she was able to view these people as pure evil and the presence of the constant bondage, often including variations on the discipline mask in which she had first been broken, made it easy to absolve herself of any feelings of guilt.

However, the trainers continued to hand Helen back to Julia still in this state of helplessness and her supposed mentor was not slow to take advantage of this. Her skilful kitten-tongue probed nipples through the strategically placed zip openings, prised between Helen's exposed loins as soon as the leather gusset strap was removed and drove her charge to paroxysms of helpless lust, during which Helen became oblivious as to the gender of her partner.

Afterwards, when Helen had been fully sated, she was immediately overwhelmed by feelings of remorse and disgust and Julia rewarded her periods of sulky silence by immediately replacing her bondage, forcing her into even more cramped positions and then taunting her by bringing her halfway back towards her previous state of abandonment and then leaving her to suffer, usually in gagged silence.

'Please,' she had begged, after being released from her latest torture, though not daring to remove the dildo from her vagina until Julia gave her permission to do so, 'why do you keep treating me like this?'

Julia simply shrugged at this. 'I'm doing you a favour,' she said. 'Before long, you'll be available to both masters and guests, male and female. Up there, if you act the way you'd like to with me, you'll pay heavily for it. The sooner you get wise, the better for you.

'We no longer have any rights – none at all – and these bodies are only ours until they decide otherwise. We belong to them now, completely. Those tits, that cunt – they're not yours to decide who uses them and how. It's the same for me, too.'

'So you're getting your own back by taking it out on me?' Helen said and earned, for her pains in suggesting such a thing, a further two hours gagged inside an eyeless leather helmet, bent double over a steel frame, with a tiny vibrating device inserted in her rear that had been programmed to operate for just a few seconds at a time and at completely sporadic intervals.

After this, she had been almost eager to lie with her head between Julia's sleek thighs, her tongue lapping at her roommate's clitoris while she enjoyed orgasm after orgasm to the accompaniment of ear-splitting shrieks and screams.

The woman had a cloned body, but there was no need of the tell-tale flat nose bridge and wider-spaced eyes for Mary to know immediately that she was one of *them* and not just another Jenny-Anne. It was not just her mode of dress, but the way in which she stalked into the room that set her apart and immediately Mary leaped to her feet, as Kelly had instructed her. Kelly herself had been dozing, but some sixth sense brought her immediately awake and her feet landed on the floor only a second or two later.

'So, this is Mary Three?' the woman said. Her inflexion suggested it was a question, but the rest of her attitude made it a statement. She raised the small device in her right hand, thumbed some keys and studied the results. While she did so, Mary studied her in turn.

She was very tall, much taller than Mary and Kelly, her heels just as high to prevent any loss of differential in their heights and her dark hair was swept back and up, giving the appearance that she was taller still than she already was. Dark eyes, olive skin, high cheekbones, all suggested Mediterranean or Hispanic origin, but her accent was flawless Oxford English, even if the shimmering leather jodhpurs, black silk blouse and tightly cinched corset belt were not exactly Home Counties *de rigueur*.

'Yes,' she said, after a few seconds. 'Very interesting. You are a university graduate, Mary?'

'Yes, I am – or *was*,' Mary added, emphasising the past tense deliberately.

The dark eyes flashed a warning. 'You will address me as "miss" at all times,' she snapped. 'Kelly already knows me. I am Amaarini Savanujik, though I am known by the name of Amanda Savage in the presence of outsiders, so you may call me Miss Amanda if it will help prevent any slips. Kelly may have told you that I am Chief Assistant to our Head of Training, Miss Selina Major?'

'I – I think so, miss,' Mary said, trying to recall the names, though without any success.

Miss Savage cut short her uncertainty. 'Unfortunately,' she continued, 'I have to tell you of the tragic death of Miss Selina. The helicopter in which she was returning crashed during a violent storm and there were no survivors. As a result of this sad event, our leader has seen fit to appoint me as his daughter's successor.'

'I would congratulate you, miss, but –'

Kelly left the sentence unfinished and Amanda nodded. 'Yes,' she said, 'it is not the way I should have chosen to succeed to the position. However, what is done is done and Miss Selina would expect for me to continue the programme without interruption. Which is why I am here to see you now, Mary.' She glanced down at the electronic gadget again.

'I see that you have already experienced a short session as a pony-girl,' she said. 'Apparently, for a complete novice, your performance was deemed as very promising, although of course that was only an exercise session and lasted but a few hours. The real thing may show us a different side to your character.

88

'Bearing that in mind, I was tempted to move your full pony-girl initiation forwards and I still shall, though I think it unwise to start it immediately. Although Kelly has been teaching you a few basics, you have not yet been tested in any real way, nor have you undergone any of the induction therapy courses.

'We have several of these, selecting them according to our evaluation and assessment of the individual newcomer. Some require quite extreme therapy; others less so. It is my opinion that you fall into the latter character.'

'Thank you, miss,' Mary replied demurely, although she was not sure whether Amanda's statement should be regarded as a compliment, or rather as an indication that she, Mary, was considered 'easy meat'. Silently, she cursed her inability to control herself during that session with Jessie, certain that she could have prevented herself from reacting so obviously, if only she had shown just a little more willpower.

'I have therefore decided that you will go to what we call our "think tank" this evening. Kelly will help prepare you, but please do not ask her questions concerning the session. She is forbidden to tell you anything in advance and knows the penalties for breaking such a rule.'

She turned to Kelly. 'Take Mary to the preparation room for Tank Nine in one hour,' she instructed. 'When she is ready, you will sleeve her. You may remain with her until it is time, to help her remain relaxed.'

'And, of course, they'll be monitoring us now, won't they?' Mary said, when Amanda had swept from the room. 'So there's no way you're going to tell me a thing.'

Kelly gave her an apologetic look. 'You heard what Amanda said,' she replied, 'and believe me, they have some very unpleasant ways of punishing disobedience here. I've experienced one or two over the years. What I can tell you, though it's not much, is that it won't harm you in any way. It might seem just a bit scary at first, but the rest . . . well, you'll see for yourself soon enough.'

Too soon, Mary thought grimly and realised that at least three minutes of the hour had already elapsed.

* * *

'I think you're chasing shadows here, Alex.' Detective Inspector George Gillespie stroked his prominent jaw and shook his head, staring out of his office window at the nearby harbour and at the approaching sea fret that would soon, he knew, engulf it.

'You've said yourself, you and Walker haven't been able to find a thing on these Healthglow people and the only links you have are a couple of phone calls. As far as the pathologist is concerned, there is no evidence of foul play in either of your sudden deaths and the crash investigators haven't turned up anything with the helicopter, so it was either engine failure or pilot error.'

He leaned further back in his chair and sighed. 'You might as well leave it alone, lass,' he said sadly. 'I'm not saying you're wrong, but there's no evidence, is there?'

'Somewhere there will be,' Alex Gregory persisted. 'There's no such thing as a perfect crime, so they'll have made a slip-up, I know they will.'

'Assuming "they" have actually committed a crime in the first place,' Gillespie pointed out. 'As I said, your hunch might be right, but we need more than copper instinct before we can go any further.'

'I could always go out to Carigillie and ask a few routine questions,' Alex suggested. 'Until the inquest, every death is entitled to be treated as suspicious.'

'Maybe, but what sort of answers do you think you'll get? Even if they were involved with either of these doctors, they'll have perfectly plausible answers ready for you and if you push it, they'd have every right to start making nasty noises.

'From what you've told me, Healthglow is part of a pretty big operation and their guest list includes some powerful names. They aren't going to take kindly to Mr Plod – sorry, Ms Plod – clumping all over their little health retreat.'

'If it *is* a health farm,' Alex retorted. 'I'd like to get a closer look at the place and going over for a few simple questions would give me the chance. Do you know, I can't find anyone local who has ever set foot on the place?'

'So?' Gillespie shrugged. 'There are over a hundred islands up here, as you very well know, and lots of them are private property. These millionaire types value their privacy and guard it jealously, so there'd be no reason for any of us humble locals to get an invite.'

'Maybe not,' Alex agreed, 'but several of these places employ locals to tend the grounds, keep house and such. These people seem to have imported all their own staff.'

'It *is* supposed to be a health farm,' Gillespie said. 'That would require special skills, trained personnel, medical types and so on, and these islands aren't exactly bursting with that sort of talent. Maybe that's where your doctor chappie came in. Perhaps he was acting as a consultant and he was a local, which rather shoots a hole in your theory.'

'He's also a *dead* local,' Alex replied, 'which doesn't count – and maybe he's not the only one. I've got Geordie checking back through records to see if we can tie any other deceased persons in with the place.'

'Well, let me know if you find anything,' Gillespie said, 'but in the meantime, I can't authorise you to go out there. Now, if one of the drug runners was to get wrecked on the rocks there, it might be a different story.'

'Oh, I'll just make a couple of phone calls and see if I can get one of them to oblige, then, shall I?' Alex snorted, turning for the door.

Despite the administration of regular doses of sedative, his guards evidently thought Tommy could not be trusted to remain passive, for they laced stiff leather sleeves over both his arms, pulled them around behind him and joined the two with snap catches at wrist and elbow. Even in his dazed and shocked condition, Tommy was still able to register surprise at how close together they were able to force his upper limbs, for in his old body he could never have hoped for such suppleness.

He was half-led, half-carried to a small cell room, where the only furniture comprised two narrow bunks and a small chest of drawers. A metal partition, bolted to the wall, offered a sparse degree of privacy for anyone forced to use the primitive toilet in the corner, but, arms bound and the catsuit and gusset sealing him effectively, that facility was beyond Tommy's reach. Thankfully, his new bladder did not seem to be in imminent need of emptying.

It was the only comfort he could take, however, for although the guards had deposited him on one of the bunks, his strict bondage meant that he was forced to lie on one side or the other and even the act of shifting between those two choices required a lot of effort. Time began to drag and eventually he fell into a half-doze, head filled with myriad images and questions to which he had not the faintest hint of an answer.

He was brought back to full awareness by the opening of the cell door and, as he struggled to regain a sitting position, two imposing female guards entered, followed by an even taller male, the latter's features reminding him a little of a lizard, or snake. The women took up position to either side of the doorway and it was the man who addressed him.

'They tell me you are quite fit and well,' he said, 'though understandably distressed at your new condition. No doubt you are wondering just exactly what has happened, so I am here to put you out of your misery, in a manner of speaking.' He smiled, but it was not a reassuring gesture.

'My name is Doctor Lineker,' he continued, 'and you, no doubt, are aware that this is the island of Ailsa Ness. They tell me you are local to this area and that your boat was sunk the other night, during the storm. By now, of course, you will be presumed drowned, along with the rest of your crew.'

'I tried to tell your people I only got here by accident,' Tommy whined, hating the sound of his new voice. 'I just wanted to get back home again. Whatever you were doing here is no concern of mine.'

'Quite so,' Lineker said, 'but we cannot afford to take chances.'

'So why not just lock me up, or even just kill me?' Tommy demanded. He nodded down at himself, peering at the prominent breasts that now threatened to burst

92

through the elasticated fabric of the catsuit. 'Why do this to me? Or is this just some elaborate hoax?'

'No hoax, my friend,' Lineker assured him. 'Rather an extension of a development programme on which we have been working for a long time – long before you were even born, in fact.

'No, what you see is what you now are, a very attractive female, in body, at least. It will be very interesting to see how long it takes your brain to come to terms with that and also how much longer than our usual subjects before you are properly broken and trained.'

'What do you mean by that?' Tommy demanded, his eyes widening in alarm.

Lineker sighed, lowered himself on to the edge of the bed opposite and proceeded to tell him and, as he spoke, Tommy's eyes grew wider and wider . . .

'What is this, some kind of wetsuit?' Mary held up what looked like a floppy black skin. It was complete with finger extensions and sockets that would enclose the feet and there was even some kind of hood, or mask, connected to the front of the collar ring, ready to be pulled up and over the head. Her fingers explored the fabric, which was quite thick, yet soft and pliable.

'It feels like rubber,' she said, 'but I don't think it is.'

'It's not rubber,' Kelly confirmed, 'but it's very like it in most ways. I don't know what it's made of exactly, but it's definitely waterproof, though it allows the skin to breathe. These catsuits we wear day to day are made from a thinner version of the same stuff.

'If you've ever worn a latex catsuit, you'd soon appreciate the difference. They make you sweat something horrible and you end up with little pools around your toes.'

'I can't say I've ever had the pleasure,' Mary retorted. 'But I dare say I will.'

Kelly shook her head. 'Not if you toe the line here,' she said. 'They only use genuine rubber outfits as part of a punishment routine. Most of my experience of latex stuff came from before I arrived here.'

'But that was years ago!' Mary looked at her companion in astonishment. 'And you were already –'

'Yes, I know,' Kelly interrupted. 'I was already nearly fifty then, but sex and stuff doesn't stop at thirty-five, young lady. Besides, rubber and leather started to become part of the alternative scene as far back as the fifties and early sixties – earlier than that, in some places.' She grinned. 'And yes, I might have been a schoolteacher back then, but teachers get long holidays, as everybody knows: and idle hands and all that . . .'

'Well, I'm sure I don't know,' Mary muttered. 'To think that people would choose to get themselves togged up in something that made them all sweaty.'

Kelly suppressed a chuckle. 'You shouldn't knock it till you've tried it,' she said. 'Speaking of which, let's get you out of that lot and into this outfit. Lateness is regarded as almost as bad a sin as disobedience here.'

She produced the small key tool that unlocked the fastenings on Mary's corset belt and boots. A few minutes later, Mary stood naked, feeling very cold, despite the fact that the little anteroom was apparently well heated. She supposed it was psychological, being naked in this spartan little chamber, knowing that their every move was undoubtedly being recorded by hidden cameras and microphones. She was almost eager to start struggling into the black bodysuit.

Despite the tightness of its fit, she quickly discovered that its elastic properties offered very little resistance to her limbs. Even the fingers slipped in easily and to Mary, whose pet hates included putting on rubber kitchen gloves, this seemed quite remarkable. As Kelly moved behind her, easing the suit over her shoulders and drawing up the long zip-type fastener at the rear, Mary took advantage of the slight delay to study herself.

The rubbery fabric moulded itself to her large breasts, lifting and shaping them quite exquisitely, even contouring her prominent nipples separately. Her waist, which was now exotically narrow, even without the assistance of the corset belt, emphasised both bust and hips and the shiny black surface made her legs appear even longer than they already were in this new body. Not for the first time was she aware of just exactly how she and the other Jenny-Annes had been deliberately created in a particular image and this was not detracted from by the fact that her hairless sex had been left completely exposed by a strategically positioned oval aperture.

She could not see herself clearly, but Mary could tell, from the way in which the fabric around this opening was pressing into her flesh, that the lewd effect would be increased by the way in which her lower lips were being forced outwards, making them more prominent even than they already were. She sighed and shook her head in a gesture of resignation.

'This goes on next,' Kelly said, holding up a new corset belt that was made from an even thicker version of the same material. 'Of course, it's not going to make much difference to your figure, but it serves a specific purpose, as you'll see later.' She noticed Mary looking down at the hood, which lay crumpled against her front, just above her breasts. 'We can leave that till last,' she said, wrapping the corset about Mary's middle. 'Once it's on, you won't be able to talk.'

True to Kelly's word, the corset, although cinched tight by a number of rear fastenings, did not reduce her waist noticeably, the main suit already having had such effect as her new body allowed for, but it did act to reduce quite a lot of her mobility, at least when it came to bending or turning.

Mary had anticipated boots, but she had assumed that they would be similar in design to those she had been wearing since her arrival, complete with steepling, needle-thin heels. The pair that Kelly produced from the little locker came as something of a surprise, for, although both soles and heels were high, they were moulded as one piece. They reminded Mary of the hoof boots, except that they were not shaped to give the equine appearance that those produced.

Also, she noted, when she tried walking in them, they felt overly heavy, almost as though they were weighted in

95

some way. Recalling Kelly's reference to the fact that the suit fabric was waterproof, she suddenly understood where all this was leading.

'This *is* a diving suit!' she exclaimed. 'It is, isn't it?'

Kelly gave her a half-smile. 'Sort of,' she admitted.

Mary took half a step back. 'But what if I told you I can't swim?'

The smile on Kelly's face grew wider. 'It wouldn't matter,' she said. 'You don't have to be able to swim for this. Besides,' she added, 'you can swim OK. I read your file before I first met you. Anyway, don't panic – I already told you, you won't come to any harm. This crowd are a lot of things, but they aren't wasteful.'

Somewhat mollified, Mary allowed Kelly to guide her to the heavy stool and press her down on to it, allowing her easier access for the tricky process of fitting the all-enveloping hood. Eyeing the black fabric as Kelly stretched the neck opening for her, Mary sighed.

'Don't I get any last requests?' she joked.

Kelly laughed and stooped down to kiss her cheek. 'You won't be needing any last requests for a very long time yet, my sweet,' she said.

And then Mary's world went black, as the hood was pulled over the top of her head and down over her face . . .

There was something familiar about the woman's face, but it took Tommy several seconds to work out what it was. Conscious of how ungainly a struggle it was just to sit up again, he remained lying on his side on the bed, staring up at her in bemusement.

'Yes,' she said, as if reading his mind, 'we are identical in appearance. We're actually type CB-Fourteens, but you needn't worry yourself about that just yet. It just so happened that there was a spare CB-Fourteen at the time they caught you.'

'So what are *you*?' Tommy demanded. 'Are you male or female?'

The woman appeared quite surprised at this. 'Why, female, of course,' she said, 'the same as you are now.'

Tommy gave an exasperated sigh. 'But I'm *not* a female,' he insisted. 'At least,' he added, 'I wasn't when I came here.' He paused, considering this statement. 'In fact,' he went on, jutting out his jaw defiantly, 'I'm not a female now, either – not inside, where it matters.'

The newcomer stepped over to the bed, offering a hand, which he did not try to shrug away and helped Tommy to swing his legs over the side of the bed and sit upright once more.

'My name is Kelly,' she said, reaching behind him for the catches that held the leather arm-sleeves together. 'I have been appointed as your mentor, which means I have to teach you the rules and stuff around here.

'Actually, this is quite unusual, as I'm already mentor to another CB-Fourteen, but she seems to be a quick learner and anyway, she's engaged elsewhere at the moment. Her name's Mary, by the way.'

'Mine's Tommy,' he conceded sullenly.

Kelly laughed. 'I know,' she said, 'but that's hardly appropriate any more, is it? We have to find a new name for you. Usually, a Jenny-Anne gets to keep her original name, but of course, you're not a usual case. In fact, as far as I know, you're quite unique.'

'You mean I'm the first bloke to be given a female body?' Tommy said. 'Forgive me if I don't appreciate the honour. I can't even figure out why they had to do this to me.'

'Well, they guard this place pretty strictly,' Kelly said, 'so, given that they could hardly just let you go, Doctor Lineker probably couldn't resist the opportunity to carry his experiments that one stage further. By the way,' she added, unfastening the first clip at last, 'though I'm taking these things off you, please don't try anything silly.

'For a start, you're going to be weak after the transfer, as your new host body will need several more hours to acclimatise, so I could probably overpower you anyway – especially as your system is still full of tranquillisers and sedatives – but even if I couldn't, everything here is being monitored and there would be guards in here within seconds.'

'Those mean-looking women, you mean?' Tommy said.

Kelly nodded. 'Yes,' she confirmed, 'and they're even meaner than they look, if you upset them. So, I suggest you resign yourself to co-operating with me. In the long run, it will be a lot easier for you and a lot less painful.'

'It's OK for you to say that,' Tommy complained. 'You aren't the one who's woken up in a woman's body – well, maybe you did, but at least you were a woman to begin with.'

Kelly nodded sympathetically as the last clip fell away.

Gratefully, Tommy eased his stiff arms back around to the front.

'Listen,' Kelly said, placing the clips on top of the chest of drawers, 'I've been here a long time; long enough to know that when they say there's no way of escaping from this island, they mean it. That means I'm going to spend a lot more years here, in this body. The same applies to you, so the sooner you start getting used to your new situation, the better and easier it'll be.'

Tommy stared at her, aghast. 'You think I should start thinking of myself as a bloody woman?' he exclaimed. 'No way! It takes more than a pair of tits and a – well, you know what I mean. I'm a bloke and that's the end of it!'

'Not from where I'm standing,' Kelly retorted, grinning. 'And as far as anyone else is concerned – anyone who never knew about the old Tommy MacIntyre, that is – they're going to take one look at you and think the same sort of things they think when they see me. At least, that's what I assume Doctor Lineker has in mind for you. I can't see him keeping you locked away for ever.'

'But that's – that's perverted!' Tommy all but screamed. 'You mean they expect me to –? No, I'd rather kill myself.'

'And just how would you do that?' Kelly replied smoothly. 'Don't you think they've already considered that possibility? Do you think they're just going to hand you a knife or a length of rope? Don't be silly, Tommy. They'll make sure you stay safe, sound and healthy.

'Meantime, I can't keep calling you Tommy, whatever you think. Tommy is a boy's name.' She paused, wrinkling her nose in thought. 'I think we'll just change it to Tammy, shall we? The way you pronounce it, with your accent, it's not that different and it may help you to keep on thinking of yourself as Tommy for a bit longer, at least.'

'I'll *always* be Tommy,' Tommy snapped back. 'And if they think I'm going to let a whole load of other blokes get their rocks off on this body, well, they'll have to tie me down first.'

Kelly started to laugh, but just managed to check herself and he glared at her accusingly. 'What's so bloody funny?' he snarled.

Kelly shook her head. 'You are,' she said. 'At least, that statement of yours was.'

'Why?' he demanded. 'All I said was –'

'Yes, I know what you said,' Kelly cut over him. 'And they will,' she added. 'Believe me, they will.'

Helen Montgomerie was beginning to find it difficult to recall her former existence. Not that she was afforded much time for contemplation and reflection, but even in those quiet moments before she fell asleep, she was aware that something was now beginning to move her further and further away from memories of the outside world and she was coming to resent the few little flashbacks as intrusions now.

She knew that she probably ought to hate herself for what she was becoming and the old Helen certainly would have, but then the old Helen was dead and wouldn't have allowed herself to be taken over by these wild new emotions and sensations in the first place.

Standing before the mirror, the ankle-length rubber sheath-dress shimmering in the reflected light, the assiduously overmade-up face smiled back at her, heavy black lashes fluttering provocatively.

'Slut!' she whispered and the full lips pouted defiantly. A delicious shiver ran down her spine and she mimed a kiss to herself, before finally, reluctantly, turning away from the image, just as the door opened and Julia returned.

The mentor studied her for a few seconds and nodded. 'Delicious,' she said approvingly. 'He'll love every inch of you.'

'Who is it this afternoon?' Helen asked casually, surprised at how the identity of her prospective next encounter did not concern her overly. 'The same one as last night?'

'No, this is a fellow we only see every few months,' Julia replied. 'He comes from South America and he's very rich. Something to do with rubber manufacturing, which is why your outfit is genuine rubber today and not synthetic.'

'Yes, the difference is remarkable,' Helen said. 'I'm already feeling hot and damp, but it's pretty nice, all the same.' She giggled, only just checking herself from adding that the heat and damp were not all perspiration. Indeed, the fire had started up again even as she had wriggled into the tight rubber panties and, by the time she had added the long stockings and fastened them to the rubber corset that Julia had earlier laced her into, her attention was centred on one thing and one thing only.

'His name is Ramon,' Julia continued, adopting her lecturing tone, 'and he will first wish to dine with you. There will be several courses, served by two maids, dressed accordingly: though the portions will not be large.'

'In this corset, that's just as well,' Helen quipped.

Julia nodded. 'Ramon will also be similarly restricted and his costume will keep his face hidden. None of us knows what he looks like, but he does have a very good body.'

'You've been with him yourself?'

'I have,' Julia confirmed. 'In fact, he usually asks for me specially, so you are going to pretend to be me today, at least to begin with.'

'But what if he asks me questions about previous times?' Helen protested. 'I don't know a thing about him, do I?'

'And neither do I,' Julia said. 'But it won't matter. You won't be having that kind of conversation over dinner, believe me.'

'So, what sort of conversation will I be having?' Helen demanded, curious now.

Julia smirked. 'You'll see, soon enough,' she said. From behind her back she produced a long, black rubber penis, which she waved in the air between them. 'And you have to wear this, too,' she said. 'So, work that dress up around your thighs and I'll do the necessary, unless you'd rather do it yourself?'

Helen hesitated, considering the suggestion, but then quickly shook her head. 'No,' she said. 'I think I'd rather you did it for me.'

Julia's smirk grew wider still.

'Yes,' she said softly, 'I thought you might.'

The first feeling of panic had subsided as soon as Mary realised that the hood was not intended to deprive her of vision. The eye holes were covered with darkly tinted lenses, it was true, but she could see clearly enough through them, once Kelly had adjusted them into their intended position.

Having attended to that detail first, Kelly then pulled and stretched the rest of the mask, so that two small tubes slipped into Mary's nostrils and a curiously moulded mouthpiece nestled between her teeth, fitting tightly about them and her lips, holding her mouth open about a central tube section. There were also thickened pads that settled against her ears, immediately dulling even the closest of sounds and forcing her to strain to make out what Kelly was trying to say to her.

As she felt Kelly sealing the hood to the collar of the suit, Mary found that she could breathe easily enough but, as Kelly had warned her, speech was now denied her completely and she felt curiously isolated as she sat there mutely.

'Now,' Kelly said, holding up another black item, from which dangled an apparent tangle of laces, 'I have to put this on you. I'm afraid it's not very comfortable, but you won't have to wear it for long. Someone will take it off you again when everything is ready.'

'This' proved to be a long sleeve, again in a thick version of the same fabric, into which Kelly guided Mary's arms, so that they were now behind her back and, when Kelly tightened the laces, rendered Mary totally helpless and

101

placed an awkward strain on her shoulders. At the same time, this enforced new posture thrust her breasts out even more noticeably, which, Mary guessed, was all intended to reinforce in her psyche her new role as some sort of sex-object.

'You look fabulous,' Kelly assured her, her voice seeming to come from the end of some far corridor.

Mary found this of little consolation. After all, she thought, even without the identity-crushing mask, Kelly herself would look exactly the same in her situation, given that they were the equivalent of identical twins. Not only that, but every single Jenny-Anne in the place had been created to be decorative and decorated, so there was no longer anything special about Mary McLeod. 'Except what's inside my head,' she told herself, staring dumbly back at Kelly through the tinted lenses.

Time seemed to drag now. Kelly remained dutifully by her side, chatting now and then, but it was frustrating for Mary not being able to hear her very well, nor to respond other than by means of nods, and she was almost relieved when the inner door finally opened. The female who appeared had that same bearing and confidence that Amanda Savage had, that certain something that set *them* apart from the ordinary Jenny-Annes. Kelly introduced her as Kara, nodded a salute and, with a final reassuring squeeze of Mary's hand, left by the door through which the two of them had earlier entered the outer chamber.

Kara had not yet spoken, nor, it seemed, did she consider words necessary. As soon as Kelly had left them, the taller woman simply turned on her heel and passed back through the inner doorway, leaving Mary, deprived of the use of her arms to assist her balance, to stand up and totter along precariously in her wake.

Immediately she emerged into the larger chamber beyond, Mary saw the pool, illuminated by fierce overhead lamps, the area about remaining in shadow, and understood, in part, the reference to a 'tank' for, although at first sight it appeared to be nothing more than a slightly smaller version of the sort of swimming pools to be found

102

in many of the gardens in the better-off suburbs, a closer inspection showed that it was very much deeper than would ordinarily be expected. Strangely, however, there was no water in it at all, although the reason for this quickly became apparent.

Access to the bottom of the tank was by means of a tiled stairway against one of the longer sides, a metal rail preventing any chance of Mary overbalancing and falling sideways. Stepping aside for Mary to now lead the way, Kara fell into step behind her, joining her on the white tiled lower floor, something which she would not have been dressed for had the pool contained water.

Still unspeaking, Kara took Mary's arms and led her into the centre of the area, where a coiled cable lay waiting. One end of this was already secured to a heavy staple, the other terminating in a locking clasp that Kara quickly clipped on to a ring at the back of Mary's corset belt. Alongside the cable lay another black item, this time a collar that was fastened loosely about Mary's neck.

From a pouch at her belt, Kara now withdrew a small cylinder, screwed it into a valve in this collar and operated a trigger mechanism. There was a faint hiss and the floppy fabric quickly filled with air, expanding until it formed a close, though not uncomfortably tight fit, forcing Mary to hold her head erect, yet not interfering with her ability to breathe.

As Kara removed the gas cylinder, Mary looked up and around her for the first time proper. The top of the tank seemed a very long way above her, a stark white line against the gloom beyond the illuminated area and the two figures that she was now barely able to discern, moving along the edge, seemed very tiny.

Preoccupied with thoughts of isolation and smallness, Mary did not notice the long tube descending until the odd-shaped attachment on the end of it suddenly appeared in front of her face. She just about had time to realise its purpose before Kara was fitting it to her, the moulded end covering both Mary's nose and mouth openings, a series of tight straps pulling it tightly against her face and preventing any chance of slippage.

As a further precaution, the hose was now looped around behind Mary's neck and she felt Kara fastening it to something near the top of her corset belt, so that now any strain on the air line was taken up there and not put directly on to the breathing mask.

Breathing mask.

Mary suddenly realised she had been holding her breath for several seconds and now, as she inhaled again, she imagined she could smell the aroma of rubber, but knew that that was impossible. It had to be all in her mind, she reasoned, but the sudden jolt of awareness was certainly not imaginary, for her vision, although still monochrome and not helped by the lenses over her eyes, immediately seemed to become much sharper.

Oxygen. That had to be the reason. She breathed deeply again and exhaled noisily into the mask, though most of the sound was the reverberations inside her own skull. Yes, that was it; they probably wouldn't want to risk feeding her pure oxygen for too long, but this mixture had to be easily fifty per cent and rapidly began producing a curiously elated sensation.

Meanwhile, Kara had been occupied with attaching another device, a flattened round box that clipped on to the web of straps that held the mask in position. As soon as she had finished and stepped back, a voice boomed into Mary's ears, filling her head.

'Welcome, Mary,' it said.

She looked around at Kara, but the woman's lips were not moving. There was a delay of a few seconds and then the voice came again, this time much softer.

'Welcome,' the woman repeated. 'You are now ready to begin the next stage in your re-education. Kara will now remove the bonds from your arms, but please do not attempt to remove anything else yourself. Failure to obey in this matter will earn you a severe punishment, as well as possibly bringing most unpleasant repercussions more immediately.

'You are now able to see quite clearly and breathe easily. Very shortly, the tank will begin to fill with water.' Mary felt the laces beginning to loosen at her back. 'The collar, together with special buoyant pockets in your bodysuit, will ensure that you float. However, the line that is attached to you will ensure that you cannot reach the surface. Do not waste your time and effort trying to remove it. You cannot, not without a special release tool.

'You will already be aware of the weight of your boots. Once submerged, you will effectively become weightless, but your footwear will ensure that you largely remain in an upright position. Everything else will become clear to you then.'

There was a dull click and everything went silent once more. Behind her, the bondage glove fell away into Kara's arms and Mary gratefully eased her own limbs back around into a more comfortable position. By the time she had flexed them and eased her aching joints a little, the tall figure was climbing back up the stairway and, as she peered down at the tiled floor, Mary saw that there was already an inch or two of water there.

She closed her eyes, breathed deeply and steeled herself for what was still to come.

'I can't wear this!' Tommy protested, as Kelly began wrapping the stiff rubbery corset about his middle. Peering down, he saw that the cups attached to the top of the garment were hardly cups at all: rather, they were stiffened platforms that offered support and uplift to his new breasts, while concealing nothing of the twin mounds.

'Don't worry,' Kelly soothed him, hooking the front clasps together steadily. 'There's a dress to go over the top.'

'Exactly!' Tommy cried. 'I mean, the bodysuit thing was bad enough, but at least it was, well, I don't know,' he flustered. 'But this sort of thing is completely bloody girlie.'

'It's very flattering, actually,' Kelly said. 'And very sexy, too.'

'That's what I'm trying to say,' Tommy wailed. 'I don't want to be sexy. Being sexy in this body is like asking for trouble. I know what I'd have thought if I'd ever come face to face with a girl wearing something like this. Look,' he pleaded, 'isn't there something else I can wear instead?'

'I'm afraid I've been given my instructions,' Kelly replied. 'I'm to set you to room-cleaning chores for a couple of days, just while you start getting used to being a female, and this is all part of the standard room-maid's uniform.'

'But I can hardly breathe in it!' Tommy gasped, as she began to tighten the laces at the back, pulling in his already slender waist even further. 'And I won't be able to bend,' he added. 'Not only that, but rubber will make me sweat like mad.'

'It might look and feel like rubber,' Kelly said, 'but it's not, so you won't have that trouble. As for not being able to bend, well, I'll show you how to compensate for that by bending at the knees, which is far more ladylike anyway. If you bend over at the waist in these uniforms, you'll be flashing your knickers and just asking for trouble – the sort you want to avoid.'

She finished lacing the corset and handed Tommy a pair of matching panties that looked far too small to accommodate his flaring hips, but the strange fabric proved surprisingly elastic, even if it did hug his buttocks and mound tightly once in place.

'This is disgusting,' Tommy muttered, looking down at himself. The tight panties may have covered his female genitalia, but they did nothing to disguise their outline; if anything, they emphasised what was beneath them and Tommy was in a position to judge only too well what sort of effect the sight of this body clad as it was might have on any man who saw it. He began to feel slightly sick as he realised that the design and selection of this outfit was deliberate.

He needed Kelly's help once more to get into the long stockings for, despite the fact that they, too, were made from the same material as the rest of the ensemble, they also incorporated an openwork design up the outside of each leg and this had to be positioned precisely, Kelly informed him, before being held in place by means of three suspenders on each side, leaving just a narrow band of flesh between their tops and the iniquitous panties.

The long gloves were even more awkward. Once again, the intricate openwork motif was repeated, but there was also the problem of fitting each finger into place, so that not even the faintest hint of a wrinkle remained and Kelly fussed and fiddled for several minutes before she was satisfied.

'Surely all this is a waste of time?' Tommy complained. 'If I'm expected to be a bloody chambermaid, they're going to get mussed up pretty quickly.'

'Not if they're fitted properly,' Kelly said. 'Once we have excluded wrinkles, we've excluded air pockets, which enables this stuff to cling to the skin tightly. It'll move with you perfectly, without slipping, without ruching up and, unless it comes into contact with a sharp edge or very rough surface, without tearing.

'It's also completely waterproof from the outside in and any marks or dirt can be simply wiped off. And it polishes up to a near-mirror finish, which is what we'll do now, before we put your dress on. We'll polish that afterwards.'

Feeling completely stupid, Tommy was forced to stand while she carried out the task, using a small spray can and a soft cloth. To his amazement, the fabric buffed up easily and, if he had thought it shiny beforehand, now it took on a sheen that was truly dazzling. Despite the incongruity of his position, he stared down at the transformation in wonderment.

'I feel like a bloody doll,' he whispered, as Kelly finished and straightened up. 'This isn't right, is it? I mean, I'm just being put on display and I can guess what the final plan is.' He shuddered at the prospect, but Kelly seemed unmoved.

'All we're doing is maintaining standards,' she explained. 'And, of course, getting you used to your new identity. Naturally, you will attract attention from any guests who happen to see you, but you needn't fret over that. For the moment, you're off limits, to be seen, but not touched.'

'You'll be with me, to make sure of that?' Tommy pleaded.

Kelly flashed him her broad smile. 'For a while, yes,' she said, 'but even when I'm not, you'll be wearing a special insignia which will tell everyone the score. You needn't worry – no one dares break the rules around here. Anyone who does regrets it. Inmates get punished and guests get banished – permanently.'

'I hope you're right,' Tommy said, half under his breath, but Kelly was no longer paying him much attention, already shaking out the uniform dress that would go over the bizarre underwear.

As she dropped it over his head and began lacing the back tightly into place, Tommy saw what she had meant about bending over in it, for the hem, which was trimmed with a lace replica of the rubbery material, barely covered the tops of his stockings and, despite the fact that there were two or three layers of white petticoats beneath the black outer skirt, they offered scant protection from prying eyes.

Satisfied that the bodice closely followed Tommy's enforced curves, Kelly turned her attention to the sleeves. They were puffed out around the shoulders, but narrowed just above the elbows, where further lacing allowed them to be tightened over the gloves, thus precluding any chance of those being removed.

However, Tommy had more to worry about than that, for he could see now that the scooped neckline of the dress, again white-trimmed, left an awful lot of his breasts exposed, barely covering the nipples and permitting the twin orbs to move alarmingly whenever he moved. He opened his mouth to protest again, but immediately thought better of it, for it was painfully clear that no one was going to take any notice of him and, he reasoned, the less trouble he gave them, the more likelihood there was of them becoming careless and maybe affording him some opportunity of escape.

Not that he would be running very fast if that happened, he reflected sourly, as Kelly began lacing on the ankle-length boots, for the heels looked impossible: high, spindly things that seemed as though they would snap at the least stress on them.

'Not at all,' Kelly assured him, as she slipped the locking ankle-straps into place. 'There's a thin core of some super-strength metal through each one and you could take a sledge hammer to them without doing more than maybe bend them a bit. Now, stand up again and let's see you walk.'

Tommy obeyed, feeling very ungainly as his feet were forced into such unaccustomed positions. The elevation of his heels made him feel as if he was falling forwards and he automatically spread his arms to compensate for the imbalance.

Kelly grinned. 'It takes practice,' she said, 'but you won't get anywhere until you get your posture right. Get your shoulders back and your knees closer together – and keep them straight. Yes, that's better. Now lower your arms to your sides and point your toes ahead. Good . . . now, take a small step forwards . . . no, keep your arms down and *don't* let your knees bend!'

Patiently, she schooled Tommy for what seemed like hours, making him walk back and forth in the tiny room, turning carefully at the end of each brief promenade, repeating instructions over and over until, at last, miraculously, he began to get the hang of it, although the fact that the boots forced him to take tiny, mincing steps and his hips swayed provocatively as he moved was not lost on him.

Male or female, anyone wearing such footwear had to walk like a cross between a catwalk model and a Glasgow street whore, or risk serious injury. The heels may have been indestructible, but they did not guarantee to stay vertical and a careless move would easily result in a turned or broken ankle. Like it or not, there was no alternative.

'We'll practise some longer walks out in the corridor, before you start your duties,' Kelly said, apparently pleased with her protégé's progress. 'You've done remarkably well,' she added, as if to confirm Tommy's impression, 'but you'll still find it makes your leg muscles ache after a bit, despite our reduced pain responses. Even that'll get better after a few days, but high heels can be murder for long periods, even when you've had fifty years to get used to them.'

'So why can't I wear something more practical?' Tommy suggested, as Kelly fastened the frilly choker about his long neck. He knew it was a wasted question and wasn't even mildly surprised when it drew an amused reaction from his mentor.

'Practical?' she echoed, eyes gleaming. 'Around here, they save "practical" for other things. We're just supposed to be decorative, sweetie, and you most certainly are that. Come and take a proper look at yourself in the mirror.'

Tommy did and could not suppress a groan of dismay. Nor could he suppress the strange flicker of desire that was forming somewhere deep inside the pit of his stomach, despite the fact that he no longer possessed the male equipment to respond in the way he once surely would have, given the image that now confronted him.

Kelly allowed him to contemplate his reflection for several seconds, standing well away from him in motionless silence, as her doppelgänger gazed unblinking at the unbelievable transformation. At last, however, she stepped forwards again to break the spell, taking him by the left elbow.

'C'mon, Narcissus,' she said softly. 'You've got work to do and there are plenty more mirrors in this place, believe me!'

Ramon spoke flawless English, without the slightest trace of an accent and, with his features hidden by the all-enveloping rubber mask, which left only his mouth and eyes visible, there was nothing to suggest his South American origin, other than Julia's word.

The rest of his outfit was as bizarre as his headgear and made from the same fabric throughout. Tight trousers and a jacket cut along the lines of a tuxedo, beneath which he appeared to be wearing a skin-tight vest and a severely laced corset-cum-belt. Cuban-heeled boots and black gloves completed the sinister image and Helen, herself already perspiring beneath the high-necked, long-sleeved rubber evening gown, imagined that he must be just as hot.

The two maids who waited upon them in the private dining room were also patently suffering, beads of sweat trickling down their heavily made-up faces, odd little rivulets appearing on their rubber stockings, obviously escaping from whatever narrow band of flesh was left unsheathed beneath their flouncy little uniforms.

They were identical, of a body type that clearly had been cloned from a middle-eastern source, their jet-black hair and olive complexions suggesting Iran, or maybe even Pakistan. Neither spoke, their dark red lips remaining set in motionless lines as they moved about their duties, but Ramon was far from silent during the meal.

Evidently, he was aware of Helen's condition, even if not her true identity, for he made several references to the dildo upon which she was struggling not to squirm. Deliberately, he kept instructing her to turn from one side to the other in her seat, with predictable results.

'You do not seem very hungry, goddess,' he mocked. 'Could it be that your appetite has moved from your stomach? Perhaps you would prefer a filling of a different kind?'

'I – I am not very hungry, to tell the truth, master,' Helen replied, lowering her eyes. 'I am a little over-full already, I think.'

Ramon's eyes glittered behind the mask. 'Then perhaps we should arrange for a change of diet,' he said, pushing aside his own plate. 'Stand up and walk over there, to the wall.'

Struggling to maintain some sort of dignity, Helen pushed back the heavy dining chair and rose uncertainly to her feet, cursing the rubber phallus for the way in which it seemed to be moving about inside her. The tight skirt and high heels restricted her to tiny, shuffling steps and every one was a challenge to her self-control.

'Turn and face me,' Ramon instructed, 'and then tell me exactly what it is you want of me.'

Taken by surprise, Helen simply stood with her mouth half-open. She saw the corners of his lips twitch.

'We both know what it is,' he said, 'yet still you always like to pretend to me, don't you?' He leaned back in his chair and laughed. 'But Ramon knows you too well, slut goddess, does he not? Beneath all that elegance is the soul of a whore – a rubber whore.'

Helen deliberately avoided his gaze, but this seemed to serve only to encourage him.

'Yes, such a demure little thing, but we both know the truth, eh? So, let there be no secrets between us, my beautiful rubber lady. Speak and ask the favour of me.'

Against the far wall, the two maids waited in dutiful silence, but their eyes never left Helen as they waited for her response. She looked from them to Ramon and back again, knowing exactly what it was he expected from her, cringing at the thought of actually voicing it out loud in front of an audience, yet knowing she would have to do it eventually anyway. Taking as deep a breath as her corset would allow, her breasts swelling against the thin latex, she looked down at the carpet. 'I wish for my master to take me,' she murmured.

Ramon gave a short cough.

'I *ask* my master to take me,' she corrected. He did not reply immediately and Helen wondered whether she was going to be expected to actually beg him.

'But you already have a rubber lover beneath all that finery,' he said, at last. 'Why would you want more? But then, a whore always wants more, doesn't she?' He paused again and Helen risked a quick look up. Ramon remained as he had been, one arm draped over the high chair back, his own eyes riveted on her.

'Of course, a whore is also selfish,' he went on, sensing her uncertainty and Helen wondered how it could be that he had not yet realised that she was not Julia. Surely, she thought, Julia would respond differently, having played out this scene several times before, as she had intimated. Or maybe not, she concluded; maybe the hesitancy was expected.

Ramon turned his head slightly, nodding towards the two maids. 'Have you no thought for these two?' he asked. 'Why should you, who have already been granted one favour, expect more, when these poor creatures have to work without reward? You have not even thanked them. You,' he said, stabbing a figure at the one nearer to him, 'get over there and let the slut express her appreciation for your diligence.'

He turned his attention back to Helen. 'On your knees, slut goddess,' he ordered.

For a moment, Helen was completely confused, obeying only as an instinctive reaction, but as the dark-skinned maid moved closer and reached down, grasping the hems of skirts and petticoats in her hands, raising them to reveal the absence of panties, Helen suddenly understood.

She reached up, placing her gloved hands on the girl's thighs, gripping the band of brown skin above the tops of her stockings. The flesh was damp and slippery to her rubber touch and Helen wondered at what mixture of aromas her lack of a sense of smell was depriving her of.

'Thank her properly, my sweet little whore,' Ramon said, 'and, when you have satisfied them both, maybe I will satisfy you too.'

By the time the water had reached the level of her shoulders, Mary could feel the buoyancy of her bodysuit beginning to take effect and, as it reached her chin, her feet were losing contact with the tiles beneath them. She fought back a momentary rush of panic as the lower half of her face was submerged and let herself relax, floating in an upright position, the weighted boots keeping her from tipping over.

For a few minutes, she continued to float as the water crept inexorably up the sides of the tank, until a slight pressure in the small of her back indicated that the tether line had reached its full extent. A few minutes more and Mary was completely submerged, cut off from the outside wall by a shimmering mirror that continued to move higher and higher above her head.

Carefully at first, she experimented by moving her arms, which seemed to want to float out wide of her anyway, presumably due to some sort of added buoyancy about her wrists, which seemed slightly thicker than usual. She also

113

found that it was possible to turn through three hundred and sixty degrees, though it was largely a wasted effort, as the view was the same in all directions.

Movement up or down was, however, impossible. The combination of Mary's body and the suit had been deliberately combined to ensure that they wanted to float upwards and the line at her back ensured that this was prevented, so that she was held permanently at the same depth, to all intents and purposes weightless. It was a strange and not unpleasant sensation.

The body is now as free as the spirit.

This time the voice in her ears was male and its unexpected intrusion gave Mary a start. She sucked in deeply on the breathing tube, exhaling so hard that a tiny stream of bubbles emerged from what she presumed was some sort of release valve.

The spirit and the body now float as one, Mary. The spirit is yours, but the body is mine. Are you enjoying our new body, Mary? Is it not a wonderful gift you have been given?

It was, she thought, but there was no way she could reply. Instead, she continued to lazily tread water, her arms moving languidly as she drifted in her peaceful limbo.

It is a gift that should be shared, Mary, is it not? Do you not yearn to share your new body?

Yes, she thought, maybe she did. After all, it would be a great shame to just drift here alone, wouldn't it? But maybe that was to be her fate, to be left in her own little private cocoon, as far from the rest of humanity as if she had been marooned on a distant planet.

I have come to you, Mary, the voice continued. It was a very soothing, reassuring voice, gentle, kind and understanding. It seemed to know what she wanted. *Look and see me, Mary. Look, I am here.*

As she slowly turned, the figure came into view, black and featureless, wearing a suit and mask not unlike her own, although there were no airlines attached to it and for a few seconds she thought that maybe the newcomer was able to breathe underwater like a fish. Given what these **people had already shown they were capable of, it would** not have surprised her; but, as he began to circle her, she saw that there was a small cylinder pack on his back.

He remained some distance from her, but there was no doubting his sex, despite the fact that the mask covered his face and head completely, for from the cutaway between the tops of his thighs, an impressive erection projected. Mary's eyes were drawn to it as though by magnetism.

We are alone here, Mary, just we two, here in our private world. He stopped circling, holding himself expertly in the same position, but now slowly drifting in towards her. Ahead of him, the huge phallus moved like the bowsprit of an ancient sailing ship, the deep purple knob almost glowing in the oddly distorted light.

Will you offer me your new body, Mary, for I am your creator and it is only fitting that you should honour me with what I have given you?

Mary could hear her laboured breathing inside her head now, to the accompaniment of a thunderous heartbeat and at the same time her entire body seemed to be catching fire. Every nerve-end, every sinew, every fibre seemed to be screaming at her and she knew only too well what they were demanding.

She forced her hands down and together, placing them over the exposed and denuded mound of her sex, even her own slight touch sending spasms of animal desire coursing up and down her body, so that her legs jerked and danced, causing her to start spinning wildly.

Gently, Mary, gently now. She felt the hands on her shoulders and her helpless pirouette slowed and finally stopped. They faced each other, eyes upon eyes, hands reaching and touching. The fingers of her right hand closed upon his length and she gasped, sending more bubbles scurrying to the surface.

It is my other gift to you, Mary. Will you claim it?

From somewhere, she heard a tiny cry, a guttural, animal noise and was vaguely aware that it had come from her own throat. Hands closed upon her breasts, kneading them firmly yet gently through the suit fabric. Instantly, she responded, her nipples feeling as though they had swollen to many times their normal size and her lower stomach contracted as though she had touched a live cable. She felt something warm down there, but refused to acknowledge its source.

Receive me, Mary. Receive me now as you have received my gift of life and beauty.

Yes, she thought, life and beauty. Painless life, beautiful life, everlasting life.

Her legs moved apart of their own accord and her grip on him tightened, pulling him closer, thrusting the tip of his huge organ against her yearning lips, impaling herself on him and squirming until he was safely embedded within her. Only then did she release him, her hands grasping at his buttocks, muscles straining as she pulled him fully into her.

And, as her head exploded with rapturous release, she knew that she had surrendered her last chance of self-determination forever, drowning in an orgasm from which she never wished to be saved.

Slowly but surely, the numbing shock that had overtaken Tommy from the moment he had awoken in his new body was beginning to wear off, to be replaced by a horrific realisation of the true import of the situation in which he now found himself. If, initially, everything had seemed too incredible to be true and thus induced an almost dreamlike obedience from him, now, as he tottered out into the corridor in Kelly's wake, the dream was fast becoming a nightmare and he realised he ought to be trying to do something about it.

However, he reflected, as he followed his lookalike through the bewildering maze of subterranean passageways, there was a huge difference between realisation and actuation. For a start, just exactly what *could* he do?

Whatever tranquilliser they had used on him had worn off to the effect where he was beginning to think straighter again, but there was obviously some residual effect, for his mind kept wandering off the immediate problem and focusing on the problem he was having in getting accustomed to both his high-heeled boots and, moreover, his new breasts, which bounced before him with every jiggling step.

The presence of the latter was a constant annoyance, their weight and movement uncomfortable and their size obstructive to his downwards view. To think that a lot of women had to contend with this problem permanently . . .

. . . but then so did he, now! The thought struck him like a sledgehammer blow and he almost stumbled with the shock. Even if he did manage to escape, not only from these people, but also from the island itself, he could not escape from this body in which they had imprisoned him. Surgery might reduce his bust size but, as far as he knew, there were no surgical techniques that would alter certain other aspects of his new physique.

'You'll have to wear this, before we go up to the guest level,' Kelly said. She had halted before a steel door that was marked ELEVATOR and was holding up something small and white.

Tommy eyed it suspiciously. 'What is it?' he demanded.

Kelly held it out for closer inspection. It appeared to be made of a rigid plastic material and was shaped like the segment of an orange, with the fruit removed and only the peel and pith remaining. At either side was a T-shaped projection, pointing towards the inner side of the curve and small holes on the outer surface were aligned with these.

'I'm afraid,' Kelly said, 'that you have to wear it in your mouth. It's a gag, you see, as you cannot be allowed in contact with the guests yet, while you have the power of speech. They ignore a lot of curiosities, but a maid claiming to be a male might be a bit awkward to explain. And there might also be a few among the guests who would misunderstand anyway and find you more appealing as a result.'

'That's disgusting!' Tommy cried vehemently. 'I'd never have believed there were such vile people in the world. You can't really be serious!'

Kelly regarded him gravely. 'Listen,' she said patiently, 'I can't even begin to understand what must be going

117

through your head, Tammy, but I remember how I felt when I first woke up here.'

'Yes, but at least you hadn't changed sex overnight!' Tommy spat. 'And don't call me Tammy!'

'You'd better get used to *that* and quickly,' Kelly advised. 'And yes, I was born in a female body to start with, but there were still a lot of things I had to come to terms with, all the same. I didn't like it, any more than you do, but I also had to face the fact that there weren't a whole lot of alternatives.

'I should have been dead – and, but for chance, so should you now. OK, slightly different circumstances, but same end result. We've been given new lives – longer, healthier lives.'

'But for what?' Tommy stormed, stamping his foot in frustration. 'Look at us, Kelly. Just take a good, hard look. We haven't been given these bodies as an act of charity. We've been created for one purpose only, so don't give me that crap about longer, healthier lives. All we've been given is a longer than usual life sentence of slavery.'

'You're trying to tell *me*?' Kelly laughed harshly. 'After twenty years, don't you think I *know* what I am?' Her eyes became very sad and she half-turned away from him. 'Oh, yes,' she muttered, 'I know all right. For the first day or two, I tried to kid myself, told myself that at least I was going to live, at least there would be no more pain – at least, not the sort of pain I'd been living with night and day.

'I even tried to kid myself that being given this body was worth almost anything and, if you'd seen what I looked like before, you might even understand that. Do you know, Tammy, I even got a real kick out of the way men looked at me – I'd never had men look at me like that before, not even before I got sick.'

'But I don't even want men to look at me!' Tommy snapped. 'And I was quite happy with the body I had before. Look, I'm barely keeping my head together over all this – by rights, I should be barking mad, and I reckon I'd be in good company around here, so I don't really need your life story. It isn't going to make me feel any better.'

118

'No, it won't,' Kelly admitted. 'But that's the whole point. *Nothing* will make you feel better, except acceptance of what is and even that is only an act, but resistance is a waste of time anyway, so it's simpler to make the best of things as they are. We can't alter a thing around here and getting away from these islands is impossible.

'And do you know what's worse?' she said, turning back to face him, her shoulders noticeably drooping. 'Do you know what's worse than knowing that you've been created for a life of sexual slavery? Oh, yes, you were dead right on that, by the way,' she added grimly. She placed her hand on Tommy's shoulder and stared him in the eyes. 'Well, I'll tell you what's worse than being a slave to every bastard with enough cash to hire you as a weekend facility,' she said, speaking very deliberately. 'It's being a slave to your own body.' Without warning, her hand moved down and cupped Tommy's left breast, her thumb rubbing across the nipple.

Immediately, Tommy felt a cold shudder shoot up through his body, followed by a small explosion of warmth somewhere in the region of his groin. Instinctively, he pulled away.

'You see?' Kelly said gently. 'That's all it takes to start the motor, Tammy. And it won't matter who does it to you, either, no matter what you might be thinking now. Male, female, old, young, beautiful or ugly, it makes no difference.

'These beautiful, healthy, long-living bodies are a damned trap, Tammy. Don't ask me how they've managed it, but managed it they have. Every normal sexually triggered response, every normal erogenous zone – it's all magnified and multiplied with us. One touch is enough to start it and then ... ' Her voice tailed off and she turned away again.

'Inside your head – deep inside – you hate yourself for it, but usually only afterwards. At the time, all you can think of is ... well, I don't need to draw you pictures, do I?' Tommy reached out and touched her shoulder.

'We *will* get away,' he whispered. 'I promise you I'll find a way. It doesn't matter about what I look like: this body, anything. It can't work the same for me.'

'No?' She turned back, moved closer to him and slipped her arms about his neck, pressing her breasts close to his, their hips touching. Instantly, the little shockwaves began again and, as her lips closed over his, Tommy felt a different sensation inside his panties.

Shaking, he grabbed her arms away and stepped back. 'No!' he cried. 'It can't happen with me!'

Kelly's expression did not flicker, but she sighed. 'I think,' she said evenly, 'you'll find it just did.'

'That's the third body from the *Flora* washed up,' Geordie said, replacing the phone and scribbling a quick note on the scrap jotter alongside him. 'Only one to go now, apparently.'

'Who's left?' Alex asked. She was absently studying her own scribbled notes, chewing on the end of a pencil that had seen better days.

Geordie consulted the pad again. 'Chap by the name of MacIntyre,' he said.

Alex looked up. 'That'd be Tommy MacIntyre,' she said. 'Damned shame.'

Geordie was impressed. 'Do you know everyone in these islands?' he asked.

Alex shrugged and let the pencil fall on to the desk. 'It's not that difficult,' she replied. 'The resident population of the entire Shetlands wouldn't fill half a dozen decent-sized Newcastle streets and I *have* lived here for most of my life. I was at school with Tommy's sister, Lois, and I walked out with their cousin Donald for about a year.'

Geordie couldn't suppress a smile. 'Bit of a quaint expression, isn't it?' he teased. 'Even for up here.'

'We're a quaint people,' Alex said. 'Surely you've heard all the jokes? In these parts, the definition of a virgin is a girl who can run faster than her brothers!'

'I don't believe that,' Geordie laughed. 'Besides, you don't have any brothers, do you? Anyway, I'm sorry about this Tommy – and the rest of the crew. It must be hard when there's a tragedy like this in such a small community.'

'Yes, but it's also a fact of life.' Alex sighed, pushing her chair back. 'Fishing is not an easy way to earn a living and the sea, as they will tell you, is a hard mistress, especially in these waters. One minute a mill pond, the next ... well, you saw that storm the other night. Fortunately, modern technology and more robust trawler design means that we don't have many *Flora*s these days.'

'Which probably makes it harder when they do happen,' Geordie suggested.

Alex nodded. 'I guess so. And I suppose I really ought to go up and call on Lois MacIntyre. This'll be a particularly hard time for her, especially till they find Tommy's body. That'll be the worst part, just waiting.'

'No chance ... ?'

Alex shook her head. 'No, hardly likely. Even if he'd not gone down with the *Flora*, there's no way Tommy could have survived in the water till now. He'd have had to have been washed ashore, or picked up next day. The coastguard will have notified the populated islands in the vicinity and the air-sea searches are pretty thorough.

'No, I'm afraid poor Tommy's as dead as the rest of that crew. It'll only be a matter of a few more days before we know for certain, unless he was trapped below decks, of course.'

Geordie shuddered. 'What a horrible way to go,' he said. 'I can't imagine a worse fate.'

The duties of a room-maid were not arduous, or would not have been under normal circumstances, for they comprised mainly light dusting and polishing of the few surfaces in each bedroom, emptying ashtrays and pulling bedding back to the foot of the bed, ready, as Kelly explained, for the laundry-maids to collect it and leave fresh linen and a fully made-up bed.

However, these were scarcely normal circumstances, Tommy reflected, and the combination of high heels and a bosom that seemed to have a life of its own, especially whenever he bent forwards, made him feel awkward and slow. Kelly remained with him, overseeing his efforts and

121

giving the occasional tip or instruction, but he was unable to respond, for the gag prevented any intelligible speech, while remaining invisible to the casual observer.

It really was a clever piece of engineering, he thought, bending awkwardly at the knees to retrieve a soiled pair of female panties from beside the bed in the third room. The orange peel segment design enabled it to be placed into the mouth, between teeth and lips, the T-shaped extrusions fitting over upper and lower molars on either side. Then, by the simple expedient of inserting a hexagonal key into each of the small holes, Kelly was able to tighten these so that they locked on to the teeth, preventing any jaw movement whatsoever, but also – and more importantly – any chance of Tommy himself removing the fiendish device.

Once in place, he was able to close his mouth over it, the small gap that remained between his lips revealing just a flash of white that could easily have been from his teeth, so that apart from himself and his mentor, no one else need know that he had been gagged and, as Kelly explained, there was no need of an unsightly strap to spoil the appearance of his new features.

The first four bedrooms were empty – two of them looked to be currently unoccupied, anyway – but in the fifth, a dark-haired man in his late forties or early fifties lounged in an armchair, watching television. He was naked, apart from a leather belt and pouch that cupped his genitalia, but he scarcely bothered to acknowledge their entry. Only when Tommy had completed the routine chores and they were turning to go did he speak.

'You,' he said to Kelly. 'I take it you're the senior, seeing the colour of her collar.' Kelly nodded confirmation. 'Well, open that wardrobe over there and get rid of the slut for me, there's a good girl. And tell your bosses I want to book your friend here, just as soon as she's put on to proper service duties. I'll have you, too, just to show her the ropes.'

Tommy stared at the man, too stunned to be truly appalled at his casual attitude, hardly even surprised when

Kelly opened the wardrobe door to reveal the strait-jacketed and hooded female figure standing statue-like within. To Tommy it seemed impossible that one human being could display such a total lack of emotion towards another, treating them like goods on a supermarket shelf, to be ordered, bought, used and disposed of like some mass-produced commodity.

He turned away, not wanting to look at the near-naked brute, not wanting to even contemplate what lay beneath that leather pouch, nor what its owner was intending to do with it when the time came. Tommy moved to the door, opening it and standing aside, as Kelly guided the mute, blind and helpless girl past him and out into the corridor beyond.

The Mariners Arms was generally pretty quiet in mid-afternoon, especially when the weather was fine, and today was no exception. The few early-season holidaymakers would be off sight-seeing and the only local trade comprised a few pensioners and two fishermen whose trawler was awaiting a new engine part.

Geordie ordered a pint for himself and a lager shandy for Alex and they slipped into a vacant booth, as far away from the other clientele as possible. The big Tynesider took a mouthful of the thick ale, tapped a cigarette from the packet, and lit it, waiting for Alex to break the silence.

'It's this Carigillie business,' she said, at last. 'And this is strictly between us, OK?'

'Which is why you suggested coming here,' Geordie said, 'away from prying ears and such. Presumably, you've got something on your mind that the DI might not like, if it got back to him?'

'Maybe,' Alex admitted, 'but it's only an idea at the moment. You see, I'm thinking about going out there to take a quiet look around.'

'To Carigillie?'

'No, actually to Ailsa Ness.'

Geordie furrowed his brow. 'You're losing me,' he said. 'Who or what is Ailsa Ness?'

'An even smaller island, about three quarters of a mile or so from Carigillie itself. I've been doing some more research and I've discovered something quite interesting. Ailsa Ness is owned by the same crowd that run the health farm on Carigillie.'

'So? Nothing suspicious in that,' Geordie replied. 'I imagine several of the islands are owned by the same companies or individuals.'

'One or two,' Alex conceded. 'But in this case they've gone to a lot of trouble to keep it quiet. According to the Land Registry records, Ailsa is supposed to be a wildlife sanctuary. It would be ideal for that, as it's supposed to be almost impossible to get ashore there, other than one little cove and only then in perfectly calm weather conditions.'

'That would make it ideal, as you say,' Geordie agreed. 'Stops twitchers and egg collectors and that sort of thing.'

'But,' Alex continued, 'in this modern age, it is almost impossible to hide anything away forever. There's always something, somewhere, sitting on someone's computer and, if you know what you're doing, it's only a matter of time before you can find a link.'

'So, you're a computer boffin, as well as your other talents?'

Alex shook her head. 'No, but I know a man who is – a guy I was at college with, down south. Peter Fletcher, but his name's irrelevant. We were quite good friends a few years ago, so I phoned him and asked him if he could do a bit of electronic detective work for me, stuff that wouldn't be on our computers.'

'And he came up with something?'

'In a roundabout sort of way,' Alex said. 'It was in some very old government records, dating back to the war. As you may know, the islands up here were very important for the Royal Navy, especially Scapa Flow.'

'But that's down in the Orkneys,' Geordie pointed out. 'Even I know that.'

'True, but there were other bases and, because of our proximity to occupied Norway, there was always the danger of Nazi infiltrators using unoccupied islands as

124

bases themselves. So, in order to guard against that, every single island was given a military garrison.

'I suppose "garrison" is a grand name, as a lot of the time it was only two or three soldiers, probably reservists or older guys, I imagine. They'd be armed, of course, but their main weapon would be their radio. First sign of anything, they'd report in to their main base and summon the cavalry.

'Of course, these soldiers would also rely on the help of any locals and, in the case of Ailsa Ness, Peter dug up a reference to a certain Richard Major. Apparently, his family had bought the title to the island back in the last century and, although he actually lived on Carigillie, he also had a small cottage over on Ailsa, so he took responsibility for it – in fact, he took responsibility for both islands, formed his own Home Guard platoon of six men and was given the rank of Captain.'

'Captain Major,' Geordie mused. 'You could make a joke or two out of that.'

'If you didn't have anything better to do,' Alex agreed sourly. 'But the main thing that interests me is that the current head of this Healthglow crowd is also called Richard Major.'

'A son – or grandson?'

'Probably. May even be a nephew, but that isn't important. What is, is that the Major family own both Ailsa Ness and the lion's share of the company that runs Carigillie Craig and, if Carigillie has been kept private, Ailsa is even more of an unknown quantity. Apart from the original Richard Major and his personal little army, no one else has ever set foot on it, so far as anyone can tell.'

'So what? Surely the same could be said of half the islands around here?'

'Maybe, but there's more. Most wildlife and bird sanctuaries enjoy at least a little support from either government or charity organisations. They qualify for grants. Not much, in the usual run of things, but enough so that no true-blooded Scot would turn down the opportunity for a little extra cash.

'In return, all they have to do is keep records and have the odd fact-finding mission – the anorak bunch, probably – wander around for a few days, taking photographs, counting beaks and so on.'

'And Ailsa Ness doesn't get any grants?'

'Actually, it does,' Alex said. She picked up her glass and took a sip of the lager, wrinkling her nose at the taste. 'Ailsa comes under the wing of a charitable trust set up at the beginning of the century. That trust receives a small government grant and in turn doles out money to a total of six small sanctuary islands – here, in the Orkneys and also in the Scilly Isles.

'They compile all the records themselves, so no other organisation is ever involved, not even the RSPB, which is quite unusual, apparently.'

'So, it's a self-contained organisation,' Geordie said, stubbing out his cigarette and immediately pulling out another. 'Nothing remarkable in that.'

'No, there isn't,' Alex said. 'But Peter discovered a few things that might be. For a start, this trust receives thirty pounds per year from London, exactly the same amount as when it was first set up. No one has ever asked for an increase.

'The rest of its income is derived from donations and fundraising activities. Donations are from a variety of businesses and the fundraising is just entered in the annual accounts as a simple total. Peter did a further search, but couldn't find any evidence of the nature of these activities: just a simple total given to the Charity Commissioners each year.'

'You think there could be some sort of fraud going on, is that it?'

'I don't know,' Alex said, 'but if there is, it isn't for very much. The Trust's total income is only around fifty thousand a year and that's accounted for by warden salaries and odd incidentals, so there wouldn't be much left over to line anyone's pockets, if at all.

'No, the interesting thing is in the list of trustees. One is the present Richard Major himself. Another is a Doctor

Keith Lineker, who also is a director of Healthglow, and a third is a guy who is also a major shareholder of a company based in South Africa – a company which also lists Richard Major as a director and shareholder.'

'All very interesting, I'm sure,' Geordie said, blowing a smoke ring. 'But hardly grounds for suspicion.'

'Oh, no?' Alex held her glass up before her and stared into the amber depths. 'Well, try this one on for size. I asked Peter to find out what he could about Major and about Lineker and, guess what? Apart from the fact that they also appear on a few other company listings, there's nothing.

'No birth certificates, no weddings, no deaths.'

'Well, there'd hardly be death certificates for two guys who are still alive, would there?' Geordie reasoned.

Alex gave him a strange look. 'No,' she said, 'but there should be something for the original Captain Major, as well as for a certain Captain Lineker who was the officer responsible for maintaining security on two other islands during the war.'

Geordie screwed his eyes up, mentally calculating dates and figures. 'They could just be the original pair, this Major and Lineker of yours,' he said.

Alex put her glass down carefully and turned her head towards the window. Outside, the sun continued to shine warmly. 'The original Captain Major was supposed to be in his early fifties,' she said, 'otherwise he would have been called up for active service. And the original Lineker was also supposed to have been about the same age. There's a record of him working for a hospital in Edinburgh, back in the thirties, though he doesn't seem to have stuck at that for long.'

'So, what are you saying? The original pair could just still be alive, even if the Major and Lineker on these company boards are descendants.'

'Only if they were both now over a hundred,' Alex said, 'and I find that hard to swallow. No, I reckon the names are just aliases, passed down over the years.'

'But why?' Geordie demanded. 'Why go to all that bother? It seems to me you're just making a mountain out of a molehill. Maybe the original pair are dead and the records have just got confused.'

'Or maybe you just think I'm getting *myself* confused?' Alex said accusingly. 'Listen Geordie, I know this all seems like a waste of time and a load of very vague connections, but there's something here that makes me twitch.'

'Good old intuition?'

'Yeah, but more than that. I can't explain it.' She picked up her glass again and emptied it down her throat in three quick gulps, banging it down on the table a little too sharply. 'But what I do know is that a quiet little look around out on Ailsa Ness wouldn't hurt.'

'You think they're hiding something out there? Why Ailsa and not on Carigillie itself?'

'Well . . . whoever these guys are, they haven't tried to make any great secret about their connections with Carigillie and, besides, I've been checking flight plans and passenger lists. There are a lot of very well-known bods use that health farm – very respectable bods, too. So, if there is something going on, it's not on that island.'

'So what could they possibly be hiding on a glorified lump of rock that's worth killing two people to protect?'

'I don't know, but there's only one way to find out, isn't there?'

'Except that you've already said it's a bugger to get ashore there and if the DI finds out you've gone against his orders, he'll have your guts.'

'Then we won't have to tell him, will we?' Alex said brightly. 'And as for getting ashore, there's more than one way to skin a cat, as they say.'

Mary had no recollection of being brought back to the room, nor of being stripped of the suit in which she had been submerged and when she first regained consciousness, for several seconds she could not even remember anything of the previous few days. As on the occasion of her first awakening on the island, she looked about her, confused by the absence of tubes and wires, by the lack of pain and by the strangely light-headed feeling.

Then, slowly at first, but all in a rush as the pieces began to fit together, everything came back to her. With a groan, she levered herself into a sitting position, pushing aside the thin sheet and swinging her legs over the side of the narrow bed.

'How are you feeling?'

For the first time, Mary saw Kelly, stretched out on the bed opposite, propped up against the wall, still wearing her regulation catsuit and boots, but holding a dark-coloured bottle, from which protruded a plastic straw.

'Confused,' Mary muttered. She closed her eyes and leaned forward, elbows on knees, hands cupped to support her chin. 'I think maybe I may have blown something in my brain, or maybe a fuse has gone in whatever it is those bastards put inside me.'

'I doubt that.' Kelly smiled. 'You're just a bit wrung out, that's all. The tank does that to people.'

Mary opened her eyes wide and stared at her. 'It does more than that!' she exclaimed. 'I . . . well, I can't believe what I did back there.'

'I know,' Kelly said. 'I remember my first time.'

'First time? You mean I'm expected to go through that again?'

'Was it really so bad?'

'Huh?' Mary sat upright again, her hands falling down beside her. 'No, it wasn't *bad*,' she said, 'but then that's the point. I just sort of lost it. I can't believe myself, I really can't!'

'Because you wanted – really *badly* wanted – exactly what they knew you'd want?'

'Yes!' Mary looked down, suddenly not wanting to meet Kelly's earnest gaze. 'Yes,' she repeated more softly. 'Exactly because of that. And I shouldn't have, should I? I mean, they've turned me into something I shouldn't be, abducted me and all the rest and yet, when it came to it, I think I'd have died if he hadn't . . .'

'Fucked you?' Kelly grinned. 'It's OK,' she said. 'That may be a crude way of putting it, but it's the truth and it isn't your fault. I tried to tell you earlier – these bodies aren't subtle, not when the chips are down. We can sit and moralise, theorise and every other "ise" you can think of, but a few cunning touches and that's it.'

'We become nothing more than bitches in heat,' Mary moaned, trying to shut out the memory. 'And that's awful.'

'Is it?' Kelly stood up, put aside her bottle and crossed the room to sit beside her. Carefully, she put her arm around the younger girl's shoulder. 'OK, we could get all moral about it and there'd be plenty of arguments against, but in the end, wasn't it just amazing?'

Slowly, reluctantly, Mary nodded. 'Yes,' she muttered. 'It was. And a part of me is already wanting to go back and do it again.' She took a deep breath, sat up and shook her hair vigorously. 'And that's the really awful part about it all,' she added, her voice no more than a whisper.

After three hours of room-cleaning duties, the final one spent working alone, the opportunity to sit down came as a blessed relief to Tommy, though the fact that his break involved going above ground meant that there was no chance of the awful gag being removed.

On their way up in the elevator, Kelly, who had finally returned to collect him after taking away the hooded girl, tried to explain. 'They think that until you've been here long enough to understand exactly what they're capable of doing, you can't be trusted not to say the wrong thing,' she said. 'The J-A rest area is actually quite private, but occasionally guests are given tours, so we're not allowed to take any chances.

'Later on, you'll be allowed to swim in the pool. It's man-made, but looks like a natural rock pool and the water is always nice and warm.'

The elevator door slid open and they stepped out into a short corridor, at the end of which stood another door, controlled by an electronic panel on the side of the frame.

'Actually,' Kelly continued, pressing in a sequence of digits, 'it can be quite a pleasant life here. It's not all work and satisfying quirky guests, otherwise we'd probably all go a bit mad.'

To Tommy, it seemed that Kelly was already quite mad, with her easy acceptance of her chattel-like situation, but he could not make any comment on this. Besides, he reasoned, fifty years was a very long time and if she really had been here for that long, her cheerful resignation was not to be wondered at. He wondered whether he would be the same in another fifty years, but then angrily thrust the thought from his mind. There was no way he was going to be here that long, no way he was going to . . .

The door slid open and they emerged into a small garden area, a well-cultivated lawn bespotted with small shrubs, four large and very mature trees, several rustic wooden benches and a ten-foot-high perimeter fence of fine and almost invisible wire mesh, supported by steel uprights that looked far too slender for the job. Any hope that might have been trying to raise itself in Tommy's head, however, was quickly dashed by Kelly's next words.

'Don't bother trying to break through the wire,' she advised. 'The mesh will cut through even your gloves, right to the bone, and the posts may not look like much, but they're a special alloy which has a breaking strain of tons and tons.' She led the way over to the nearest bench, which sat in the shade of one of the trees. From beneath the seat, she withdrew a length of fine chain, at the end of which, Tommy saw, was a steel fetter.

'And this is just in case you don't believe me about the fence,' she said, pushing him down on to the bench and opening the manacle. Stooping, she quickly fastened it about his left ankle, just above the boot, closing it with a solid click.

'You can stay out here in the fresh air for about an hour,' she said, standing up and stepping back. 'Usually we bring a book or magazine with us, but you'll just have to enjoy watching the birds. If you look through there, to the right, between those big trees on the other side of the fence, you can see down to the shore, but it isn't that interesting, I suppose,' she admitted.

'I'll be back for you myself and nobody will interfere with you in the meantime. Your collar shows you're a novice, so even if anyone else does come out here, they'll leave you alone.' She smiled disarmingly. 'You really do look sweet, Tammy, sitting there with those big sad eyes.

'Do try and cheer up. It really won't help to go around the place with a face as long as the queue for the beer tent at the Highland Games. It's all down to making the best of things, you know. Whatever you may be thinking, there's no chance of anyone getting off this island. I expect you already know it's almost impossible, even with a boat – and they never leave boats here.

'In fact, I don't think we've seen a boat here in twenty years, anyway, not since they finished the tunnel over to Carigillie. And don't even *think* about getting out that way. The doors at each end are electronically operated from a single control centre on the other side and the Carigillie end goes through a checkpoint that would make a Russian border-crossing look like open house.

'I know it must be harder for you than for any of the rest of us,' she said, 'but try to accept that it's too late to change anything now. You're a Jenny-Anne, just like me and a whole load of others. You've been given a body that most people would die for, so what if you do have to share it occasionally?

'Look upon it like giving someone a lift in your car.'

Tommy stared up at her, hardly able to believe what he was hearing. A lift in a car? The woman was definitely mad, no doubting that any more. He looked down at himself, at the shimmering black uniform, the long legs and their ridiculous boots, the fingers trapped inside tight gloves, and drew in a deep breath.

He knew that in normal circumstances he'd probably rather die than submit to what Kelly was suggesting was the inevitable, but then these circumstances were anything but normal and death was a very final option. He remembered those last conscious moments in the water, the seconds before he had passed out and the thoughts that had crowded through his reeling mind then.

No, he resolved firmly, he wasn't going to die. But then he wasn't just going to sit back and play the part of obedient and obliging little maid either. OK, he would

132

have to stomach some very unpleasant moments, but at the end of it, he knew he would come out of it OK. Kelly seemed convinced there was no escape from Ailsa Ness but, in even his limited experience, Tommy knew there was seldom anything that was truly impossible.

Not if you were determined enough.

'I do hope you're just pulling my leg, Alex,' Rory Dalgleish spluttered, when Alex Gregory had finished explaining to him. 'Apart from the fact you could do yourself a serious injury, from what you've told me, this is really no more than a wild goose chase.

'You want to risk jumping out of a plane at night, trying to hit an island the size of my back garden, and for what? All you'll find out there is a whole load of scruffy and very unsociable birds, plus a whole heap of bird shit.'

'In which case,' Alex said, quite unperturbed, 'I'll ring you on the satellite phone and you can bring your chopper over and take me off again.'

'So why don't I just take you in with the chopper in the first place?' Rory suggested. 'Or maybe we could just fly over the place and take a few pictures. I can get hold of a really powerful camera.' He leaned back, scratching the stubbly beard he had been trying to cultivate since he and Alex had been friends at university several years before.

'Because,' Alex said, 'we'd lose the element of surprise. Your chopper is hardly the quietest thing in the air, which is why you need to use Terry's Piper. You can cut the engines and glide in and I can bale out at around fifteen hundred feet. Even without a moon, Ailsa will be easy enough to see from that height.

'If you bank around and fire in the engines, putting yourself between me and Carigillie, there'll be no chance of them spotting me on their radar.'

'You're sure they've got radar?' Rory asked.

Alex gave him a dismissive look. 'They've got a helicopter pad, haven't they?' she said. 'So they're bound to have some sort of radar. Jesus, even the trawlers carry surface radar nowadays.'

'I suppose so,' he said. 'But how about a surveillance run first?'

'Waste of time,' Alex snapped. 'If they have got anything to hide out there, you can bet your life it'll be mostly pretty well camouflaged and, assuming they are up to something, they'll be on their toes for any low-flying air traffic. By the time we get over the island, anything that wasn't already hidden most certainly will have been.'

'But won't their radar pick the Piper up, too?' Rory pointed out. 'Especially if I come in at fifteen hundred feet.'

'Not if you switch your engine in and out as you pass over Carigillie. Let it cough and splutter a couple of times, then give it the gun and climb up again. They'll hear you and assume you were having engine trouble.'

'Very cunning, I'm sure, but jumping in the dark, at that height – I don't know.'

'Rory, trust me!' Alex exclaimed. 'We've jumped together dozens of times, right from when we joined the club at uni, and I've still got both my own chutes.'

'And when was the last time you used them?' Rory demanded.

Alex smiled at him very sweetly. 'About a month ago. I still belong to the "Manics" and we had a rally then. I did four jumps that weekend and I always repack my own chutes, same as you would. I haven't had much chance for free-falling lately, but I do keep my hand in.'

Rory's craggy features remained set in an anxious expression, but already he knew he was fighting a losing battle. He had never been able to refuse Alex anything and there had been a time when there was nothing she would have refused him. In fact, he was pretty sure that even now, if he . . .

He stopped himself, just in time. 'OK, so I borrow the Piper and you pay your midnight visit. Don't you think it might just be a bit dangerous, going in there on your own?'

'Not really. I'm fit, fast and very light on my feet. If I wear dark colours, once I've stowed my chute, I can just lie low until I'm certain I haven't been spotted, then have a nice quiet snoop about.'

'And when were you thinking of doing this?' Rory said.

'Friday night,' Alex said. 'I've got the weekend off, so I don't need to make any excuses at work. That way, if I do find anything suss, I can stay out of sight during daylight hours on Saturday, have Saturday night to carry on snooping and then call you to take me off again at first light on Sunday.

'Mind you, if I find anything really interesting, I'll be staying 'til the cavalry gets there.'

' "If" is a big word, young lady,' Rory said. He stood up, stretching his arms wide. 'However,' he yawned, 'I can see you won't be talked out of it, so I'll agree, so long as you pay me for the fuel for both machines. Business hasn't been that good, this spring. It'll also cost you for me to fly over Ailsa in the chopper this afternoon.'

'And why would you want to do that?'

'Well, whatever else they might hide, they can't do much with the natural geography of the place and it might just be a good idea to have a couple of photographs of the ground, just so you can identify any awkwardly placed trees or rocks that would be worth avoiding.'

'Fair enough,' Alex agreed. 'You work out what I owe you and I'll give you a cheque. Meanwhile, I'm going to go and check out both my chutes.'

'Mad lady,' Rory sighed, as the door closed behind her. 'And I must be almost as mad to go along with you!'

When Helen finally left Ramon's room, it was with a mixture of emotions. Primarily, it was a relief to be able to wriggle herself free of the latex outfit, stagger into the shower that was part of the facilities adjoining the room she shared with Julia and let the torrent of warm water sluice the perspiration from her skin.

However, as she languidly soaped herself, grateful for the moment that she no longer possessed a sense of smell, the satisfaction of her immediate physical needs gave way to a far deeper need, that of trying to make some sort of sense out of what had just happened, both to her and inside her.

135

Two hours of enduring Ramon's stilted mannerisms, mixed with his dismissive and even contemptuous way of talking to her, had not had the effect on her she might once have expected. Rather, as she sat squirming with the huge dildo inside her, body temperature rising to an almost unbearable degree, so that, when she had been ordered to her knees before the two maids, she had rushed to comply with a haste that was more than just indecent.

She knew that she had needs that required satisfying and if the price for that was first satisfying the two mute girls, then so be it, she had thought. Feverishly, she had worked her tongue in and out of the hot little slits, seeking the swollen buds within, drawing them out, sucking, teasing, anxious to bring both maids to the expected climax with as little delay as possible.

As soon as she had accomplished that, she reasoned, Ramon would turn his attentions to her: but, to her surprise, he seemed content to remain a spectator. The rubber-clad servants seemed to know exactly what was expected of them for, without a word of command, they quickly pulled Helen to her feet, guided her across to the long chaise and stretched her out along it.

Before she had time to realise what was happening, her arms had been pulled out over her head and stout leather manacles locked about her wrists, rendering her completely helpless and at the mercy of whatever they had planned for her.

She did not have to wait long to find out what that was.

As one girl concentrated her efforts on Helen's breasts, sucking greedily on her nipples through the thin latex, until the teats were actually forcing the fabric out into twin cones, the other quickly began easing the confining rubber skirt up Helen's legs, rolling it until it passed over her hips and settled into a tight belt about her waist.

Parting the helpless girl's thighs, she then drew aside the gusset of her panties, but made no attempt to withdraw the dildo. Instead, she crouched between Helen's legs, extended her neck and took the flanged base of the phallus between her lips, whereupon she began to work it in and out, her head bobbing obscenely back and forth. Within seconds, the black monster was producing a series of squelching noises that should have reduced Helen to a state of acute embarrassment, but instead served only to heighten her urgency.

Thrusting her hips in time with the maid's efforts, she heard herself screaming out, begging for more, pleading, crying, laughing, arching up as though electrocuted when the girl, still without removing the invading shaft, managed to locate her clitoris and suck it into her mouth as Helen had done to both maids earlier.

Orgasm followed orgasm, each growing in intensity and duration, until the climaxes merged into one impossible exploding vortex of abandonment and it was only as she was finally descending from this plateau of debauched fulfilment that Helen realised that the two girls had been replaced by Ramon.

Holding himself on his arms, he was thrusting in and out of her flooded tunnel with long, unhurried strokes, gazing down at her black-sheathed form with eyes that burned intensely. Arms still bound, Helen could only lie there, trying not to respond again, but finally unable to re-establish any semblance of control.

Gritting her teeth, she ground her hips to meet each thrust, her internal muscles squeezing him hard and drawing a satisfied little moan from his lips.

'Slut!' he hissed, redoubling his efforts. 'Rubber slut!'

Helen shivered and another orgasm, this time more controlled, yet no less intense, rippled through her body. Her breasts seemed to have swollen to an even greater size, her nipples felt like hard rods inside their rubber sheaths and she groaned ecstatically.

'Ye-es!' she heard herself crying out. 'Oh, yes, master! Oh, fuck this rubber slut . . . please!'

In the hard light of the bathroom, her body stripped of the hot rubber cocoon in which she had so willingly and easily, it seemed, thrust aside everything she had ever thought she believed in, the memory of Ramon's room was not exactly distant, but it did seem unreal.

Could that really have been her, saying and doing those bestial things? Of course it had been and she knew there was no point in trying to shut the images out, but surely there must have been something in the food or wine? Otherwise, what explanation could there possibly be for such animal behaviour?

Tossing aside the towel, she stooped and picked up the crumpled heap that had been the sheath dress. The inside was still wet with her perspiration, dank and slimy now and probably stinking the place out to high heaven, she guessed. She turned the thing over in her hands, shaking it out into something resembling its former shape, and studied it in silence for several seconds.

'It's just a dress,' she said out loud. 'That's all you are,' she told it, aware of how silly it might seem if someone walked in and found her talking to an inanimate piece of clothing. 'You're nothing but a dress, so how come?' She looked away from the dress and down to where the rest of her discarded ensemble now lay, including the massive dildo, which Ramon had insisted was replaced inside her before she was dismissed from his room.

'Just a load of rubber,' she whispered. 'So it has to be this body, surely. I'd never have reacted like that before, would I? I don't even like rubber, usually. It's horrible, smelly stuff.' Except, she reflected, that she no longer had a sense of smell.

She remembered the little mini-dress that an old boyfriend had bought for her, years ago now. She had agreed to wear it to the disco with him, but only because she knew it had cost him a lot of money. Afterwards, as she had carefully washed it in the bath and hung it up to dry out, she had known it would never see the light of day again, even though she had dutifully dusted it with talcum powder before consigning it to the back of her closet.

With a sigh, she dropped the long sheath dress into the empty bath, added the stockings, corset, gloves, panties and dildo to the slippery pile and reached over to turn on the mixer taps.

* * *

Andrew Lachan sat in the high penthouse which served as both city dwelling and office for his infrequent visits to London, ignoring the pile of paperwork on the semi-circular mahogany desk at the far end of the room, instead gazing out over the grey and black rooftops of the capital, the shimmering heat haze under which they sat testimony to the unseasonably high temperatures that made any parts of the city not fortunate enough to have been fitted with air conditioning an unappetising prospect.

Andrew hated London, but then he hated all big cities and was impatient for the completion of his company's new computer system, which would enable him to carry on most of his work from the calm sanctuary of his remote Highlands house, a house that might better have been described as a small castle.

Set on a remote hillside, overlooking a long, meandering valley which Andrew had succeeded in purchasing only four years since, it was an uncomfortable hour's drive from the nearest tarmac-surfaced road – and that itself a winding test of even the most experienced driver's skill and nerve. He had briefly considered having that access track relaid – he could certainly afford it easily enough – but the inaccessibility of the place was the larger part of its appeal to Andrew.

Instead, he had spent money on installing a generator that relied for its energy supply on both the swift-running river that bisected the valley floor and on the two wind turbines that had been almost totally camouflaged among the trees on the opposite hilltop. A helicopter landing pad assuaged the need for constant spine-jarring terrestrial commuting and every door and window in the old building had been carefully replaced with modern, draughtproof versions, though to the casual observer the place looked as though it had not been touched in two hundred years.

The barns and other outbuildings remained, largely, in their original condition, or rather the condition to which two centuries of harsh Highland winters had reduced them, though there was one exception to this general lack of repair.

The stable block had been lovingly restored, complete with discreet heating and a small bedroom complete with bathroom and shower, hidden behind the primary stall. Andrew was not supposed to know about Jess's secret retreat, but he had done for a good while now and he knew he could not reasonably expect his favourite thoroughbred to be happy with round the clock straw and water trough.

Indeed, the television he had provided came complete with satellite channels, surround sound and a multiple recording facility and the bath would have been large enough to accommodate a real mare, complete with a couple of foals. Nothing was too much, so far as Jess's long-term comfort and happiness was concerned, and money no object.

There was just the one – and, to Andrew, totally unforeseen – stumbling block. Major would not agree to sell Jess to him. Not under any circumstances and not for any figure. Not even the exorbitant offer Andrew had made for the pony-girl, a sum which would have bought many an inner city office tower block, or a fair-sized luxury yacht.

Andrew was totally unused to rejection, but he had managed to put a brave face on it, accepting instead Major's offer to reserve Jessie for his exclusive use, not batting an eyelid at the annual fee proposed, nor looking overly disappointed that his favourite would have to remain up there on the island.

'It'll save you having to take on a groom yourself, old boy,' Richard Major had pointed out. 'Could be a mite delicate for you, finding the right fellow and being able to trust him to keep his mouth shut. At least this place assures discretion.'

Andrew had nodded and agreed, but discretion would be, he knew, his least problem. He already 'owned' two enthusiastic slave girls he had found on his various foreign excursions and they were now permanently installed on the estate, so Jessie's care and exercise would be taken care of diligently during his frequent absences.

The 'rental' arrangement would suffice as a temporary arrangement – Andrew likened it to a racehorse owner stabling his champion thoroughbred with a top trainer – but it would not do on a permanent basis. He had to have Jessie completely to himself, in *his* stable, on *his* estate. He allowed himself a grim smile at the prospect and sighed as he remembered their most recent encounter.

Yes, Jessie. Sweet, obedient, beautiful, dutiful Jessie, tall and resplendent in her gleaming harness, champing on her bit, those wonderful lips distorted by its sheer girth, little specks of saliva trickling down either side of that perfect jaw, high breasts rising and falling, her tanned flanks gleaming under the faint sheen of perspiration.

Jessie, always smelling of warm leather and damp girl flesh, those huge, doe eyes so trusting, willing. Jessie, with those firmly muscled legs, strong shoulders, tiny waist and flaring hips. His Jessie.

Perfect Jessie.

Perfect Jessie, groaning and whinnying beneath him, as he rode her after the drive, hoof-tipped legs splayed wide, arms caught up in those ridiculous little slings that made them look like stunted chicken wings and gave her such an appearance of helplessness, as they waved and fluttered and her eyes grew big around the gagging bit.

'Aye, Jessie,' Andrew whispered and his hand dropped unconsciously to the front of his trousers, pressing against the bulge beneath the expensive Savile Row cloth. He turned back to the desk, regarding the three telephones and wondering if he should postpone the overnight trip to Florence, or maybe just hand it over to his ever-efficient deputy, Sara.

He smiled at the thought. Sara, bustling, businesslike, immaculate in her tailored two-piece suits, make-up light and flawless, organiser and mobile phone in the expensive leather shoulder-bag that was never more than a few inches from her. Sara Llewellyn-Smith, three degrees, family money, cut-glass accent – she could certainly handle the Italians on her own, but . . .

Deciding, reluctantly, against postponement or delegation – he would be back inside twenty-four hours anyway – Andrew amused himself instead with picturing how Ms

Sara Llewellyn-Smith might look, bitted and harnessed, running in tandem with the perfection of the wonderful Jessie beside her.

Tommy's sojourn in the fenced-off rest garden was uneventful and uninterrupted. The ankle-chain permitted him to walk a few metres in any direction, but no more and he still had to take care that the fine links did not become snagged around his heels. After a few experiments, he decided it was not worth the effort, especially as it seemed likely he would be spending more than enough time on his feet in the immediate future.

As Kelly had predicted, the unaccustomed arching of his insteps had indeed succeeded in promoting a dull ache in both calf and thigh muscles and he found himself wondering just how much more unpleasant that might have been, without his new body's partial immunity to pain. Worse than the aching, however, was the way in which the high heels seemed to deprive him of the feeling of being in control of his movements.

In order to avoid overbalancing, he was now forced to adopt a completely alien pose, thrusting his bottom forwards when he walked and willing his knees to remain straight. Turning quickly was a challenge, too, and he wondered why any woman would ever choose to wear high heels when she did not have to. Vanity, perhaps, he thought, or a foolish urge to please men.

Pleasing men, that was what it all seemed to be about and now, he was only too grimly aware, he was also expected to assume that role. The thought repulsed him and brought a cold knot of dread to his stomach. Surely they wouldn't push things that far, he told himself: but then why wouldn't they? He had only to look down at the body he now inhabited, if he wanted evidence of just how far these sick maniacs were prepared to go.

It was a relief when Kelly finally returned to interrupt his dark broodings and an even greater relief to be back in the room, where she finally removed the hateful gag.

'What about the rest of this stuff?' he demanded, indicating the maid uniform.

Kelly looked surprised. 'What about it?' she replied. 'There's no reason why you shouldn't keep it on for the time being. You'll be on room service this evening, I'm told, so it'd just be a waste of time changing and then having to change back.'

'So, I'm just an unpaid skivvy, is that it?' But it could have been worse, he told himself, and undoubtedly would be, unless he could think of something fast.

'We all have to work for our keep,' Kelly replied brightly. 'Besides, you won't be working on your own this evening. You just sit there, or maybe stretch out on the bed for a little while. I have to pop next door and get your new partner suitably dressed. You haven't met her yet, of course, but I'm sure you'll get along well. Her name's Mary and the two of you have so much in common now.'

Rory Dalgleish spread the eight-by-ten prints out on his desk, pushing aside the dog-eared files, ashtray, racing form guide and the draft of the letter to his bank manager he had been trying to compose for the past three days.

There were eight photographs in all – he had shot a full reel of thirty-six, but the majority had been back-up duplicates and four had not come out very well anyway – and they showed the unremarkable little outcrop that was the island of Ailsa Ness, taken from four different angles as he'd hovered just over a thousand feet above it. He had considered dropping lower, but the place was listed as a bird sanctuary and there were rules about that sort of thing; besides, the camera he had borrowed from Colin McLeish was fitted with a powerful zoom that made the risk of an irate phone call from the RSPB totally unnecessary.

After ten minutes' careful study, Rory sat back, lit up a cigarette and reached for the phone.

'Alex? Rory. Done your recce for you.'

'What's the verdict?'

'Well, I still reckon you're mad, but it doesn't look too bad. There's a hill at one end of the island, but the rest is pretty flat. There are trees – plenty of 'em for such an exposed place, but there's also a fair bit of flat ground.'

'Anything interesting on the ground?'

'Nothing much, but then you didn't expect there to be anything visible from the air, did you?'

'No. They'd have seen you coming a long way off.'

'Always assuming there was anything to hide,' Rory cautioned. 'You don't seem to have much to go on – certainly not enough to warrant jumping out of a kite in the middle of the night.'

'Well, it'll brighten up my boring existence, won't it?' Alex chuckled. 'So, you reckon there's enough leeway for me to get down safely?'

'As long as there's no real wind, I reckon. There's actually an area that looks as though it's been deliberately cleared. It's hard to tell from the photos and I was too high to make it out with the naked eye, but there seems to be some sort of oval track down there.'

'You mean like a race track?' There was a short pause from the end of the line. 'How big? Big enough for cars?'

'Wouldn't have thought so. More like a running track. Maybe they send some of their health freaks over from Carigillie, get them to run off a bit of excess fat.'

'Maybe. Any signs of life?'

'Not while I was there. But there was one other possibly interesting thing.' He reached across the desk and picked up the print on which he had written the number seven. 'Again, the photo isn't brilliant. It's good, but it isn't the sort of quality we were used to in the RAF.'

'Well, lucky I don't want you to bomb it, then, isn't it? Stop hanging it out and get to the point, will you?'

'Well, like I said, it isn't that clear, but there's an area that's largely wooded, close to the foot of the hill, loads of undergrowth and stuff. You could hide a lot there, especially if you rigged up camouflage netting.'

'Camouflage netting?' Alex's voice took on a new note. 'There's camouflage netting out there?'

It was Rory's turn to chuckle. 'Steady on, old girl, don't jump ahead,' he said. 'Like I said, the photo's not that good, but there's a couple of areas where I'd swear the carpet isn't natural. I can't explain, but it's something we used to look for.'

144

'Bit like my copper's intuition?'

'Something like that,' he agreed. 'Of course, there could be a perfectly reasonable and legitimate explanation . . .'

'Of course,' Alex said. 'But there's only one way to find out, isn't there?'

'You could take someone else with you, though?' Rory said, his tone almost pleading.

He heard Alex's derisive snort down the line. 'Like who?' she said. 'Geordie's already told me he thinks I'm wasting my time and ought to drop it unless we get more evidence, so he won't want to know. Besides, this needs someone who knows how to use a chute properly.

'There's always you, of course, but the damned plane isn't going to fly itself, unless you can persuade your mate, that is.'

'If he knew what I was intending to do with his precious kite,' Rory said, 'he wouldn't lend it to me in the first place.'

'There you go, then,' Alex retorted. 'That just leaves me. Anyway, don't fret so, you great lummox. I'll be perfectly OK; you know I will.'

Helen stood morosely staring at the locked stall door, shuffling her feet in frustration and chewing on her bit angrily. It wasn't fair, she thought, to leave her like this, not after everything else they had done to her. After all, she had tried, eventually – tried to please as she knew they wanted; driven by the unfamiliar sensations that coursed through her, it had been surprisingly easy in the end and it had almost been a disappointment when they finally called a halt to the proceedings.

Hot, sweaty and physically almost exhausted, she had expected a bath, or a shower, some food and then perhaps a rest, but instead she had been brought down here, to this cavernous subterranean stables area, where her costume had been almost torn from her and then a hosepipe turned on her, cold water knocking the breath from her. She had tried to dodge it, eventually turning to run, but the grooms to whom she had been handed over were far too quick and experienced for her.

While one kept the icy jet unerringly on her, the other sent his long whip snaking about her ankles, the thin rawhide coiling itself about them like a serpent, the sharp crack of leather on flesh followed by a searing pain in her legs as she toppled headlong on to the stone floor.

They had not bothered to dry her first, simply hauling her to her feet and forcing her arms into the odd little chicken-wing restrainers and then proceeding to buckle on the rest of the cumbersome harness whilst she just stood there, breathless, defeated and dripping.

She was not sure which was worst, the heavy hoof boots, with the added weight of the steel horseshoes, the foul bit that forced the sides of her mouth back so painfully, or the tail and the anal plug by which means it was attached to her. In the end, she thought, it didn't really matter about the individual components of her degradation, for it was the overall effect of being reduced to and treated like a mere animal that she would remember for the rest of her life.

They hadn't even wanted to use her, despite the fact that her denuded sex was forced out and opened so lewdly by the thin straps that were drawn so tightly to either side of it, or that her breasts were thrown out so enticingly by the cunning harness that encircled them, the nipples pushed through the rings so that they looked even larger than ever. No, they were simply carrying out a duty, following instructions and nothing more.

And they hadn't even spoken to her in a manner that acknowledged her humanity, simply pointing at the small metal water trough and then at its companion, with the unappetising gruel mixture. The one lad had gone so far, then, as to tell her it was all she would get while she was here, but he didn't even bother to explain to her how she was supposed to eat or drink whilst the thick bit remained in her mouth.

Alone now, her new stall closed against all other contact, the silence pressing in on her, Helen, the newest Ailsa Ness pony-girl, began to weep . . . only no tears appeared to roll down her pale cheeks and dampen her bridle tack.

* * *

The reappearance of what could easily have been two Kellys instead of the one did not surprise Tommy at all. He was by now, he reflected, past the stage of being surprised by anything here and still more concerned about the prospect of being stuck in a female body for the rest of what promised to be a very long life.

'This is Mary,' Kelly said. 'She's almost as new here as you and, as you can see, she's now dressed as you are, ready for your evening duties. This is Tammy, Mary. Tammy was originally Tommy, as I was explaining to you. She's still a bit upset about that –'

'I can imagine,' Mary said. 'Poor you, Tammy.'

'It's Tommy,' Tommy growled, though the effectiveness of his attempt at surliness was somewhat ruined by his lack of an effectively male voice with which to make his point.

'Tammy is being just a little bit silly,' Kelly said, sounding exactly as Mary imagined she might once have done in front of a class of unruly schoolchildren. 'She knows very well that if she doesn't respond to her new name, she'll end up being severely punished and she could well get me into trouble as well, which is very selfish, as I'm only trying to make things easier for both of you.'

'The only thing that would help me,' Tommy snapped churlishly, 'is if you could persuade these lunatics to let me have my own body back and let me go back home and somehow I just don't think that's going to happen, is it?'

Kelly gave him a look of deliberate patience and the sigh was just a little too theatrical. 'I wish I could tell you different,' she said, 'but unfortunately, I can't. Your old body wouldn't be much use to you by this time and, by now, what's left of it will probably have been washed up somewhere, minus the head, I'm afraid, to save any awkward questions.'

'And that'll be blamed on the fish, I suppose?'

'Or the propeller of your trawler, or some other passing ship,' Kelly said. 'Either way, as far as the outside world is concerned, Tommy MacIntyre no longer exists. I doubt even whether letting you go would do you much good, either.

147

'If you turned up over on the mainland, claiming to be Tommy, they'd just lock you up in a padded cell somewhere and throw away the key, so why don't you just try to make the effort, Tammy?'

'A padded cell over there, or a cell and God knows what over here – what's the difference?' Tommy muttered, gritting his teeth, but Kelly took his question the wrong way entirely.

'Exactly,' she said, 'so you'd be better off trying to be a good girl here and enjoy the perks that go with that. Just to give you some idea of how good things could be here, if you both work well this evening and I don't get any complaints, I've got a nice little surprise lined up for you both.'

Part Three

Beneath the canopy of trees and netting, Jessie wandered happily, enjoying the filtered sunlight and the gentle sea breeze, drinking in the aroma of heather, moss and ozone as she had done so many times before. They had restored her sense of smell some fifteen years ago now and she remembered how amazing it had been, how she had forgotten the simple joys to be had in the air of a fine spring or summer morning.

The modification to her eyesight – a modification she had been told she must keep a secret, even from Andrew – had not been such a success. It had given back an element of colour vision, but the shades were not quite right and reminded her of those early American technicolour films that she had watched at the local Gaumont on a Saturday evening, back between the wars, when there had been another world beyond the shores of Ailsa Ness and a life that did not involve harnesses, buggies, stables and near permanent hooves.

But, if it was not perfect colour vision – and it was now so long ago that Jessie could not quite remember what perfect colour vision was like – at least it was better than seeing things in black and white. Black and white reminded her of the flickering newsreels, footage of those poor men in mud-filled trenches, footage of huge steel killing machines and barbed wire, footage later of more men going off to a different war, with more killing machines, screeching, whining death from the skies and then more barbed wire and images that were too horrible to believe.

Jessie had not been sorry to leave behind a world that could treat itself so badly, a world in which man was prepared to slaughter fellow man in exchange for a few square miles of mostly useless territory, or for the right to take a percentage of what a few more poor, struggling peasants had grubbed from it. Jessie remembered the last war, the bombs falling through the night, skies lit up with orange and red, the anger of a mechanical god that had no face and no name, save for yet more flickering monochrome images of a few strutting tyrants with armbands and corrupted symbols of peace.

And it was one of those bombs that had led to Jessie's arrival on the island, though not during an air raid and not even during the war itself. The bomb had fallen in nineteen forty-one (how she had found that out, she didn't know for certain) but had failed to detonate, choosing instead to burrow its way into the rubble of a building that had already suffered one losing encounter with another delivery of high explosive. And there it had lain, unexploded and undetected, safe and warm as all well brought-up bombs like to be, for nearly a decade, until, eventually, the site of its new English home finally caught the eye of the developers.

The bomb itself caught more than an eye; it caught the blade of a bulldozer, a glancing blow that rudely awoke a timing mechanism that had somehow, in nineteen forty-one, forgotten its function. An hour or so later, the bomb caught the eyes of several people in the vicinity. It also caught arms, legs, heads and two thousand window panes in the brand-new housing estate opposite, leaving a crater more than thirty feet deep and a trail of rubble and dirt that was to take a month to finally clear.

Nine people dead, including the driver of the bulldozer, who had just returned from his mid-morning teabreak, with a sure-fire tip for the greyhound meeting that evening, and more than forty more injured, many seriously. Including Jessie, who had been cycling by the high wooden perimeter fence just as the explosion ripped it from its mountings.

It was a miracle that she hadn't been killed outright; she remembered them saying that, over and over, voices in a misty world of white coats and blue uniforms, voices that were firm and kind, efficient and cheery. Voices that occasionally became muted and spoke in whispers that Jessie could not hear, though she knew exactly what they were talking about.

Miracle or not, she was going to die, but she hadn't really minded. Even without the morphine, there was little pain. Her body, beneath the sheets and beneath the swaddling of daily changed dressings, was burned beyond hope of repair, shattered beyond healing, ripped and torn, one leg and half an arm gone already, the remainder useless, even if the bones had remained intact, for it is as impossible to use fingers, wriggle toes and flex knees, as it is to feel pain, when your spine has been broken in three places, including at the neck.

And then one morning she had woken up and thought that death had finally claimed her, for surely she was in heaven. The beautiful new body was surely the body of an angel, although there were no wings and the rooms in heaven were not so unlike the hospital room in which she had lain during her final days of mortality.

The truth, when they told her, should have shocked her, but it did not. The miracle – the impossible scientific miracle – she neither understood, nor questioned, accepting without demur the simple answer, that she was alive, she was whole, there was no pain and they had promised her it would be a very long time before her mortality was ever brought into question again.

It had never really troubled Jessie that her salvation had not been an altruistic act on the part of her saviours. After she had been brought to the island – the big hospital complex underground here had not been built then and Doctor Lineker performed his medical miracles in a secluded sanatorium somewhere near the Welsh border – it hadn't worried Jessie that this beautiful new body had been created more for the benefit of others than for her own.

Jessie had never married. It was hard to find suitors when you have a face that is misshapen and badly marked because of the incompetence of a doctor too drunk to be allowed in a pub, let alone the back bedroom of the two up, two down in South London where a screaming little Jessie first entered the world. It was not even easy to get a decent education, given the particular cruelty inherent in all children when faced with oddity and deformity, and Jessie finally left the school which she had rarely attended anyway, to find simple, menial work in a succession of sweatshops where the shape of your head was not important – just so long as you kept it down and worked.

The thought that men would now not only look at her without pity or revulsion, but could and would actually desire her was one that appealed to Jessie greatly. Her old body had died virgin, but the new one was soon showing her what she had missed, including childbirth.

The baby had been a girl and fathered by one of Doctor Lineker's closest assistants. They had named her Marylin and Jessie had been allowed to keep and care for her until she reached the age of five. They had parted mother and daughter gently, promising that Jessie would be able to see Marylin regularly, but that the child needed to be educated in the organisation's own school.

Later, as the years passed steadily by, Jessie learned a lot more, especially from Marylin, who indeed came to visit her every few weeks or so and who, as she grew older, was able to pass on the pith of what she was learning. It all seemed very complicated to Jess's simple mind, but Marylin seemed to find the whole thing quite straightforward and reasonable.

There were women in the organisation – Marylin referred to it as the 'colony' – who died prematurely, either after childbirth, or by their mid-twenties if they remained childless. However, Doctor Lineker was able to perform a miracle with them similar to the one he had performed with Jessie and the other girls that they called 'Jenny-Annes', except that the new bodies these women needed could only be made by what they called 'cloning', using the living tissue of the child born from the union of a male member of the colony and what they called a human Jenny-Anne.

Jessie did not pretend to understand any of this, but it was plain to see that Marylin was inordinately proud of her role as a donor for these 'third-generation hosts', as she patiently explained to her mother.

If anything saddened Jessie at all – and very little did – it was that she hardly ever saw Marylin now. As the child had grown into a woman, it was clear that there was a difference in their status and, while Marylin enjoyed ranking privileges through her father, Jessie remained little more than a chattel and, when she finally asked to be moved to the stables permanently, she also requested that her daughter be allowed to visit her and see her true nature and position.

If Marylin had been shocked by the sight of her beautiful mother standing between the shafts of a glittering sulky, bridled and bitted, perched upon her high hooves, she had not given any indication of it. Accompanied by the tall lizard-browed man who was her father, she had walked slowly around pony-girl and cart, examining everything in minute detail.

Finally, at her father's behest, she had climbed up into the driver's seat and fingered the long whip which sat in its clip.

'Take her for a little drive, why don't you?' the man had suggested.

This had, finally, seemed to have some effect on Marylin. 'But she's my mother,' she protested.

Her father shrugged. 'She's a pony-girl first,' he said. 'She's been trained for this and it's her request that she now does it full time. The fact that she gave birth to you is now immaterial. You are *my* daughter and that is all that really matters. You may still visit her, of course, but when she is out here in harness, even you will treat her accordingly.

'Now, drive her down to the cove and back, or else I'll call the grooms and you can spend a couple of days between the shafts yourself.'

Out of sight, Marylin had reined Jessie to a halt, jumped down and run around in front of her, unclipping the bit and pulling it from between her teeth, apologising, trying to hug her.

Jessie had simply smiled. 'It's all right, my darling,' she had soothed. 'I'm not unhappy now, not at all. You're a grown woman and have things to do that I never could. We both know that but for this place, I'd have been dead a long time ago, or if not for the explosion, I'd be a rickety old crone.'

'But they can't expect me to treat my own mother like some kind of animal!' Marylin protested. 'I know what goes on here, but I won't be a part of it myself – at least, not with you.'

'Then be prepared to be between these shafts yourself,' Jessie had warned her. 'He meant what he said and I don't think you would like this the way I do.'

'But how *can* you like it?'

Jessie shrugged and smiled. 'It's a long story,' she said quietly, 'and I don't even think I can explain it myself. Now, put my bit back in, climb up in your seat and let me show you how a champion pony-girl performs.'

The function at which Mary and Tammy were serving was a special party hosted by one of the more exalted guests, Kelly explained. Apparently, he was not only a multi-millionaire, but was also well known throughout the western world, though there was no opportunity for either of the maids to confirm this, as all the guests wore all-enveloping masks of either rubber or leather.

The host, who everyone referred to as Jay, was tall and well built, though Mary suspected that without the assistance of the broad belt about his middle, he would have been seen as beginning to go to fat slightly. However, the leather band was drawn tightly about his waist, so that his figure, clad in a body-hugging catsuit of some pale-coloured, elasticated material, was still very impressive.

From the lower edge of the belt, two thinner straps descended to form a V shape, holding in position a leather pouch above his genital area; it seemed to be a popular idea among the other male guests and the only one among the six men who had not chosen to dress similarly was a stocky, fair-haired individual, whose mask had also been designed so that it left the top of his head exposed.

Apart from this mask, the blond man wore only a leather breechclout and, where the other men all wore boots, he had selected a pair of Grecian-style sandals, with criss-crossed thongs running up to his knees. From the belt that held his loincloth in position, a short, heavy whip hung in a coil and Mary found her eyes drawn to this throughout the early part of the evening.

Apart from the six males, there were four female guests, whose costumes were as varied as they were bizarre. They too were all masked, their head adornments ranging from complete leather hoods to, in one case, a bland anatomical face mask, atop which was the most incredible wig of curly red hair.

It was a curious phenomenon, Mary realised, that although not one of the people in the room was displaying any flesh remotely in the regions of what would be described as their erogenous or erotic zones, they nevertheless appeared far more as sexual beings than they would have done had they been completely naked.

If the combination of the deviant, flamboyant and outlandish in the costumes was not enough, the room itself had been designed and lit to create the ultimate gothic atmosphere. Black walls, heavily draped, red and green lighting casting sinister shadows and ominous arrays of straps, whips, canes and paddles and, as a twin centrepiece, the darkly polished horseshoe-shaped dining table, facing the open end of which stood a huge timber wheel, from which hung an array of stout leather manacles.

In addition to Mary and Tammy, the waiting at table was attended to by three males, all of whom had been rendered blind by the eyeless hoods which had been laced tightly over their heads. On their feet were locked heavy boots with thick platform soles and high, chunky heels and their flaccid organs had been laced into tight leather sleeves. About their wrists they wore wide studded leather bands, but apart from that they were naked, their oiled bodies shining in the curious light.

They moved slowly, but nevertheless their skill at navigating about the chamber when they could not see the various obstacles was quite incredible. Nor did they seem at all surprised or put out when an occasional slap from a guest landed on their unprotected buttocks. Mary's first reaction was that there had to be some sort of openings for their eyes which weren't immediately obvious to the casual observer, but in the small adjoining room, from where the food was being served, she was quickly disabused of this theory.

Kelly, who along with two dark-haired and non-identical Jenny-Annes, was supervising the offloading of the food from a large dumb waiter, quietly whispered the truth to her two protégés.

'They're actually guests,' she said, 'and, believe it or not, they pay for the privilege of being treated even worse than we are. They come here and stay for anything up to a month at a time and are kept in cells, chained up, or even put out with the pony-girls.'

'Weird,' Tammy muttered, staring at the shuffling waiters. 'Why would anyone want to be treated like that?'

Kelly shrugged. 'Who cares?' she said simply and returned to the task of organising the serving of the next course.

If the majority of the guests lost no opportunity to torment the three blind men, they treated the two maids almost as though they were invisible. The one exception was the shortest of the four females, whose choice of costume was not that different to what Mary and Tammy were wearing, except that her skirt was a little longer and cut in a slightly straighter line. Unlike the maids and in common with her fellow diners, she wore a full face-and-head mask, from the top of which, via a short rubber tube, her pale blonde hair emerged into a flowing ponytail.

The other guests referred to her as 'Fee', which Mary presumed was short for Fiona; but, whatever her real name, she was giving both rubber maids plenty of attention. Apparently as blind to the three men as they were to her, Fee hardly took her eyes off Mary and Tammy, beckoning each of them to her side at regular and frequent intervals under some pretext or other and taking advantage of their proximity with a blatant lack of concern for either them or her companions' reactions.

At first, she contented herself with surreptitious stroking of knees and buttocks, her gloved hands remaining above the girls' skirts and petticoats; but, as the proceedings gathered momentum, she became more bold, fingers stretching up to inner thighs, bare flesh and, ultimately, to tautly gusseted rubber crotches.

The effect on Tammy was complete confusion. His/her male ego was instantly affronted, though the fact that this personal assault had been committed by a female went some little way to assuaging what might otherwise have been an extreme reaction. At the same time, her growing attentions were having a disturbing effect on some part of his/her system hitherto only briefly demonstrated by Kelly. When the prying digits caressed the narrow band of bare flesh between stocking-tops and panties, Tammy was mortified to discover that the treacherous Jenny-Anne body was reacting in a way that was totally at odds with his brain's instinctive reaction.

Back in the side room, he protested to Kelly, but the older Jenny-Anne was not impressed. 'A few stray hands are nothing to worry about,' she said dismissively and insisted that Tammy stand obediently whilst the internal gag was put back in place. 'It's for your own good,' she said, tightening the second clamp. 'If you say something to insult a guest, you'll be in more trouble than you'd ever want to know about.'

When Fee's fingers ultimately sought to pull aside the crotch band of Tammy's panties, he did not need the power of speech to make his aversion of such an invasion obvious. With a grunt, he drew sharply back, only just avoiding spilling the plates from the small silver tray from which he was serving cheese. His assailant considered this reaction hysterical, spluttering into her wine goblet, and made no attempt to call Tammy back when he retreated to the side room sanctuary yet again.

For the next ten minutes or so, Tammy contrived to keep to that side of the table furthest from where Fee was seated, leaving Mary to suffer her advances. Mary, however, did not seem that disturbed by the repeated intimate intrusions and made no attempt at swapping positions. Tammy heaved a sigh and started to relax once more, but the reaction was premature and the relief short-lived.

In the dining room, the atmosphere was now becoming quite boisterous, yet with an air of expectancy. Clearly the meal was only the first course in the evening's entertainment and, as the maids and waiters began taking round bottles of spirits and clearing away dishes, another side door opened and two dark-garbed masked women emerged, flanking a smaller female, who was naked except for a single leather glove that held her arms tightly compressed together behind her back, a broad leather collar and heavy leather ankle-cuffs, joined by a short chain that forced her to walk in awkward, shuffling steps. In her mouth was a large, red rubber ball-gag, which held her jaws wide open, the retaining strap that prevented her expelling it buckled so tightly that her cheeks bulged above and below it.

Her guards led her towards the wheel, where she was positioned with her back to it, facing the dining area, and stepped back into the shadows, obviously waiting for further instructions. The girl stood motionless, only the slow rise and fall of her impressive breasts betraying any indication that she was anything other than a lifeless statue.

Tammy's gaze went from her to the wheel itself and then to the rack of implements behind it and he/she shuddered. The guests, meanwhile, continued to drink and chat as though the helpless girl were not there.

So concerned with the poor creature's fate was he/she that Tammy was completely taken by surprise when she next went out into the side room. There was a pile of empty plates on the side that required stacking into the dumb waiter and, seeing a perfect excuse for staying out of the way, Tammy began carefully moving them. Behind her, the two guards who had escorted the naked girl slipped into the room without attracting her attention and the first indication she had of their presence was when they grabbed her arms from behind and twisted them up into the small of her back.

While one held them there, forearms horizontal and close together, the other worked a soft leather bag up over them, a sack that fitted so closely that her elbows were thrust into the opposite lower corners. Thin straps passed over Tammy's shoulders and buckled swiftly into position ensured that she would not be able to wriggle free of it, so that while neither her wrists nor arms were actually bound, they were nevertheless held immovably, just above the small of her back.

Eyes wide with terror, Tammy struggled furiously, but either one of the amazons on her own would have been more than a match for her and against two of them, and once her arms had been so efficiently immobilised, it wasn't even a contest. As they dragged her back towards the main chamber, she lashed out desperately with her feet, catching one of the guards a glancing blow with her heel that would have ripped most ordinary fabrics, but the dark material in which the two women were clad did not even seem to mark. Nevertheless, they forced Tammy down, first to her knees and then on to her face and, while one kept her pinned there, her companion deftly locked leather cuffs about each ankle, the chain joining the two so short that any chance of Tammy using her feet as weapons again was summarily removed.

'Up!' the first guard commanded, placing her hands under Tammy's shoulders and hoisting her easily into a standing position again.

Mutely, Tammy glared at her, but the woman merely laughed in her face.

'Stupid little bitch,' she sneered. 'No one's going to hurt you here, but if you keep struggling, I'll personally see to it that you get a dozen punishment lashes tomorrow!'

'And I'll give them to you myself,' her companion said. She bent her head closer to Tammy's, her hand tightening on the frightened creature's upper arm. 'Just calm yourself down and do as you're told,' she whispered. 'We know all about you, but I'm sure you've had your tongue between a girl's legs before now, haven't you? Now, get out there and behave yourself.'

Andrew Lachan had renamed the sixty-four-foot motor cruiser after his beloved Jessie a year since and he even kept aboard several photographs of her in full racing harness, although they were always safely out of sight in the sturdy safe beneath the bunk in his private cabin and only he knew the correct combination for the multi-levered security lock.

There might be those among the Ailsa Ness regulars who would chide him for honouring a mere pony-girl in such a way, but Andrew was untroubled by that possibility. He could buy and sell any three or four of them, of that he was confident, yet it irked him that his money could get him no more than what amounted to a lease on his beloved Jess.

Now, as the *MV Jessica* rode gently at her sea anchor, less than half a mile off the shore of the island, her cabin windows blacked out, the only illumination on the bridge coming from the instrument dials and the flickering radar monitor, Andrew had arrived at his personal Rubicon. He would have a banker's draft delivered to Richard Major afterwards, of course – after all, he was not, and never had been, a thief – but nothing now was going to stand in his way in his determination to have the beautiful Jess safely back in his own lovingly prepared stables.

For Andrew did love Jessica, in his own curious way, even when she was standing there so placidly while he whipped her wonderful buttocks and flanks. Nothing would be too good for her, not once he finally had her to himself. The discreet specialist saddler was already working on a complete new set of harnesses, fur-trimmed straps, gold-plated buckles and an interchangeable set of bits that incorporated chrome-plated flanges and disciplining probes. He had even found a tattooist who would soon give Jessie a distinctive black blaze that would run down from her forehead to the tip of her nose. He knew how much that would please her, how proud she would be to carry such a permanent mark of her ownership by the master she so clearly adored ...

Standing Tammy so that she was facing the wheel, the two black-clad amazons turned their attention to their earlier prisoner, who had remained exactly where they had left her, rigidly at attention, eyes staring straight ahead. Even when they released her from the single glove that had pinioned her arms, she made not the slightest attempt at resistance, simply moving backwards between them and, when one of the guards grasped her waist and lifted her, she obediently spread her arms high and wide, so that the second woman could fasten them to the appropriate cuffs on the wheel.

It took them less than two minutes to finish securing her. Cuffs at ankle, knee, thigh, waist, chest and elbow were added and the collar about her neck was clipped back to a waiting ring, so that when they stepped away from her finally, the poor creature was held rigidly spread-eagled, unable to do more than wriggle her toes and fingers and turn her head a few inches to either side.

Staring at the deep pink gash at the apex of her thighs, Tammy shivered, but only partly through fear. Her own sex felt hot now and an unaccustomed dampness was spreading inside her panties. She groaned in shame, but the heat in her groin refused to be damped down.

Behind her, she felt a soft body pressing against her bound arms and, a moment later, gloved arms encircled her, hands cupping her breasts through the fabric of her uniform. She heard the woman, Fee, chuckle close to her ear, as the first touch on her nipples sent a shock wave ricocheting through her body.

'That'll be you up there pretty soon, baby,' Fee sneered, her voice a rasping whisper. 'We're not allowed to do it tonight, but you won't wear that novice collar for ever and I'll be waiting for you when it comes off. Now, let's have that gag out of your mouth and see it do some real work.' She had the allen key in her hand and within seconds was pulling the curved plastic segment from between Tammy's teeth.

'C'mon, bitch,' she urged, propelling Tammy towards the waiting sacrifice. 'I'll even make it easier for you, see?' She reached out one foot and pressed down upon a raised button, set in the floor just to the side of the wheel. There was a click, followed by a low hum and very slowly the wheel began to revolve in a clockwise direction. Another push, another click and it stopped again, so that now its burden hung precisely upside down, her gaping yaw just a few inches below the level of Tammy's frozen face.

'Use your tongue, maid-girl,' Fee snapped. 'I want to see the cow overflowing before we start fucking her. Pretend it's a nice juicy cock there, if you've never done a girl before. It's all the same thing, in the end!'

Suddenly, Tammy realised that this malevolent witch didn't know the truth, even though the two guards evidently did, which meant that the remaining guests were probably also in the dark. Seeing the first opportunity to present itself so far, she rounded upon Fee, teeth bared.

'I'm a man!' she snarled. 'Don't you realise what's going on here! I'm a man!'

Fee's only response was a delighted laugh. 'Attagirl!' she roared. 'Now you're getting in the spirit.' She turned and shouted over her shoulder, to where the other guests were now forming a semi-circular appreciation society. 'Miko,' she shouted, eyes searching the anonymous masked faces, 'see if you can't find a cock to strap on this slut. She wants to think she's a man; she can join the queue with the rest of you pigs.

'But first,' she said, turning her attention back to Tammy, grasping her by the back of the neck and forcing her head downwards, 'you're gonna do it girlie style.'

And suddenly, as the hot warmth of the waiting tunnel touched against her nose, Tammy needed no further bidding. With a little moan, she buried her lips against the girl's gaping orifice, her long tongue snaking out for its prey.

'Remember,' Andrew Lachan said, 'I don't want anyone hurt, if at all possible. Those weapons are just for show and to frighten people back, if it comes to it.'

Across the cabin table, on top of which was spread a large-scale map of Ailsa Ness, former Lieutenant Nigel Hawkes gave a curt nod of his cropped blond head and tapped the holstered pistol at his belt.

'Understood, boss,' he said. 'We're only loaded with rubber bullets anyway, just to be on the safe side.'

'Good.' Andrew jabbed a finger at the centre of the map. 'The doors are here,' he said, 'but they're well camouflaged. There is heavy foliage screening the area to begin with and the doors themselves look exactly like the rock face when they're closed. What's more, from what I've seen of them, they're pretty well immune to anything other than armour-piercing shells.'

'What about guards?' Hawkes said. 'You reckon they aren't armed?'

'As I told you before we set out,' Andrew said, 'the only weapons I have ever seen them carry are whips and riding crops. They rely almost entirely upon the fact that attempting to effect a landing on the island is widely regarded among the locals as suicidal and, under most circumstances, that would be correct.

'Even if they detect our presence here now, it won't cause any suspicions. They'll just assume we're another trawler, anchored to sort out our nets. There are two in the vicinity at the moment, or there were. The radar's playing up at the moment, so I'm told.

'However, there is one small inlet where it is possible to navigate a small craft, such as your inflatables. That's here, as I explained before also.' His finger moved across the surface of the map and stopped again. 'I've been able to survey the spot in detail during the past few months. When I take Jess out for a few hours, no one bothers to monitor what I get up to, privacy being what we pay for there in the first place.'

'The place sounds intriguing.' Hawkes smirked. 'Maybe I'll spend some of this bonus you promised me on visiting it myself before long.' He fingered the balaclava helmet that lay in a crumpled ball on the edge of the table. 'After all, they won't recognise any of us.'

'That may not be necessary, Nigel.' Andrew smiled. 'Once I have Jessie safe, I intend to add to my little stables and you would, of course, be most welcome. You are, after all, one of my most trusted employees.' If only because I pay you such an astronomical salary, he added to himself, but then, he knew only too well, the former Special Services officer had proven his worth on several occasions already and, in doing so, had also placed himself in Andrew's hands when it came to trust.

This particular operation, however, was like nothing else Hawkes had ever been asked to carry out. For a start, the four men he had recruited for the raid were not from his regular staff, as a precaution to preserve Andrew's identity, and they had remained in the cabin aft since boarding the *Jessica* some hours earlier.

The only other person aboard who knew Andrew personally was the skipper, Giles Ashley, whose loyalty and discretion were as beyond question as Hawkes's and who, in any case, knew very little of the intimate details, including the true nature of what went on at Ailsa. Bringing aboard one sedated female would not arouse his curiosity overly. He was well paid – exceptionally well paid, like Nigel Hawkes – not to ask questions about matters that were not his direct concern.

'The timing of the exercise sessions,' Hawkes said. 'You're absolutely sure this never varies?'

'Absolutely,' Andrew confirmed. 'First trots are at oh-six-hundred, usually the temporary ponies. The regulars don't come out until oh-eight-hundred. I did consider waiting until then and grabbing her once she's outside, but that means trying to remain hidden for two hours extra and it would only need a chance discovery to ruin the whole thing.'

'I agree,' Hawkes said, 'especially if the stables themselves are only just inside the entrance.'

'Just that short tunnel and then it opens up into the large hitching-up area I told you about. If we wait in the undergrowth to either side of the doorway, once the first ponies have been taken out, there'll only be one or two grooms left on the inside, sweeping out and getting tack ready for the girls who come down to polish it.'

'And they never close the doors after the early ponies are outside?'

'Not in the early morning, except in the very depths of winter,' Andrew said. 'Although there is a very efficient ventilation system, having a direct open access to the outside for a few hours is even better and enables the air to be refreshed more thoroughly.

'However, they are very quick at getting those doors closed if any low-flying aircraft are spotted in the area, so we need to secure the control panel – there.' He jabbed a finger again and Hawkes nodded.

'Roger, will do,' he said. 'And this Jessie woman will be where?'

'Here,' Andrew said. He moved his finger an inch or so. 'There are rows of stalls down either side of this far end and hers is on the right from our approach viewpoint. It is the eleventh we come to and it also has her name on the door, but I shall be with you and go in first. She is unlikely to panic if she sees me and I can administer the sedative without any problem.'

'OK, but it'll take a minute or so for that stuff to work,' Hawkes warned, 'and sometimes it can knock a person out completely, so we may have to carry her.'

'I doubt that,' Andrew smiled. 'Jess is extremely fit and healthy and has youth on her side, too. She'll still be on her feet and, as long as she is bitted, will follow where I lead her without question, even without being sedated.'

'Fine, well I'll leave her to you, but sing out at the first sign of problems, 'cause we shan't have much time. When we go in, I'll leave one man to hold the approach to the outer door, one more will secure the door controls and the

165

remaining two, plus myself, will deal with any of these groom lads. Then those two will hold the inner corridor until we are outside and fall back to the outer door while we make it back to the inlet. A few smoke grenades is all it should take.'

'You make it all sound very easy.'

Nigel let out a little snort. 'If everything goes according to plan, it should be,' he said. 'At that hour there will only be the grooms exercising the first ponies outside, you say, and a couple of shots over their heads should make them stay well back, even if we run into them between the doorway and the cove.'

'Which we probably won't,' Andrew said. He traced another imaginary line across the map. 'They take the ponies down to the track straight away. There aren't many places they can give 'em a decent workout, apart from there, and it's well screened by trees from where we'll be. We should be back on board here before they even know anything's wrong.'

'Then we're all set,' Nigel said, picking up his balaclava. He held it up. 'Don't forget to wear yours,' he warned, 'and don't forget to take it off when you go into the stall, otherwise you'll frighten this little pony-girl of yours half to death.'

'I know,' Andrew said, though he smiled inwardly, for the last thing to startle Jessie would be the sight of a masked figure entering her stall. He turned away and opened a small locker on the bulkhead, taking out a silver flask. 'Drink?' he invited.

Hawkes shook his head. 'Not 'til it's done,' he said. 'And I'd suggest, if you don't mind my saying so, sir, that you don't either. We'll need to be at our sharpest in an hour or so.'

If she wasn't exactly completely mad, Tammy thought, the woman Fee was certainly dangerous to be around and completely wrapped up in her own warped little world. The rest of her 'crowd' were obviously far from being saints, but it was she, always safely anonymous behind her mask, who was the ringleader and she, also, who once the girl on the wheel had been reduced to a shuddering wreck by Tammy's tongue, picked up a wicked-looking tawse and began to systematically beat the hapless creature until her entire body had turned what Tammy presumed was a bright pink.

When she had finished, she turned to Tammy once more, taking up a hideously fashioned head harness and pulling it over the startled she-male's face, thrusting the stubby gag between her teeth and buckling the straps so that the long penis extension jutted out crudely from her bulging mouth.

'Right, little maid-girl,' she leered. 'You reckoned you wanted to be a man, so give the bitch some of *that* cock!'

Afterwards, Fee seemed to lose interest in the bound slave-girl, but not so where Tammy was concerned. Taking hold of the protruding phallus, she used it to pull Tammy's face close to her own, opening her mouth and running her tongue over the bulbous end of the dildo.

'Wouldn't you just love to put your face cock into me?' she taunted, eyes glittering. 'Or maybe you'd like me to do it to you?' she suggested. 'All you whores here are the same. Trouble is, you all seem to think you're something special.' Her words were sounding slightly slurred now and it was clear that the alcohol she had consumed throughout the evening was beginning to take its toll.

One of the male guests stepped forward. He too was masked, but Tammy recognised him from his clothing as the one called Miko.

'Why don't you show her, Fee?' he challenged. 'Show her anything these paid island sluts can do, you can do better!'

'I don't have to prove anything!' Fee retorted, thrusting Tammy off at arm's length. 'I mean, look at this stupid little bitch, with her cock-face. What could she do that I couldn't do a hundred times better? Has she got bigger tits? Better legs? Is she prettier?'

Without warning, she pushed Tammy roughly again, sending her sprawling on to the ground, then, reaching behind her head, began fumbling with her own mask and finally, with a flourish, ripped it off, exposing her face.

'She's not even as pretty as I am!' she stormed. 'And these are supposed to be the best-looking slaves money can buy!'

'But that's the whole point, Fee,' Miko said. 'She's a slave; they all are. They get off on all this, same as we do by being able to control them for a while.' Tammy hardly heard his words, for her eyes were riveted on Fee's unmasked features and she could scarcely believe that she was now staring at the face of one of the country's best-loved television presenters. The woman saw the recognition in her stunned reaction and stooped over her threateningly.

'Think you could do my job?' she said. 'Reckon you could earn the money I do, you pathetic little cock-sucker? Not a fucking chance, baby. I'm the damned best and don't you forget it!'

Tammy cringed before this outburst, expecting at any minute that Fiona Charles was going to strike her in the face, but another of the female revellers pushed forward and stepped in between them.

'Steady, Fee,' she cautioned. 'The poor bitch is only doing what she's supposed to do. She hasn't done anything wrong.'

'No? Well, I don't like the way she looks at me. They're all just as bad, can't you see that? We pay fucking good money for all this and they despise us for it. Don't swallow all that bollocks about them being genuine slaves – that's bullshit. Major and his crowd pay them bloody good money to put on an act, that's all!'

'So what if they do?' the second woman said. 'This is the best place of its kind in Europe – we all know that, or we wouldn't keep coming back.'

'Of course it's the best,' Fiona snarled. 'It can afford to be, that's my point: yet this little trollop and her kind are laughing at us. This one's not even been properly trained yet and still she thinks she's better than me, because no one's supposed to touch her pristine little cunt until that collar's off!'

'Well, that's more bollocks. It's coming off now.' She reached down, seized the reinforced band about Tammy's neck and pulled at it fiercely, but all she succeeded in doing was almost choking Tammy. For a few seconds, Tammy thought she would end up being strangled to death, but Miko grabbed Fiona's wrist and prised her fingers free.

'Get the fuck off me!' Fiona screamed, aiming a back-handed slap at him. Miko ducked and the blow went sailing harmlessly wide of his shoulder. For a second or two, it looked as though Fiona might launch herself at him, but the voice from the outer doorway had all heads turning at once.

'I must say, this isn't the party atmosphere I normally expect to find with you people,' Richard Major said smoothly, stepping into the centre of the room. His eyes flicked up to the girl on the wheel and then down to Tammy. Turning to Miko, he smiled.

'Take the gag off the maid, please,' he instructed, in a tone that made it clear that the 'please' was merely an observance of good manners. He shook his head at Fiona. 'Really, Miss Charles, I thought you understood the house rules better. The girl's collar is supposed to indicate that she is a new recruit. Only when the new girls have had the chance to get accustomed to everything are they available to guests. Until then, they clean and wait on table, yet I understand you gave two of my handlers instructions to the contrary.'

'They weren't two of your women,' Fiona replied sullenly. 'They were two of our crowd. We borrowed a couple of uniforms from the staff area. Don't worry yourself, Dickie; I'll pay for them and for the use of the slut.'

'You don't seem to have a very high opinion of this poor creature,' Major said, nodding down to where Miko was removing the harness from Tammy's head. 'Yet, as far as I have seen, she's done nothing apart from obey your instructions.'

'I just don't like the way she looks at me,' Fiona snapped. 'She's too damned impertinent by half. Look at her, the stupid-looking cow, good for nothing but what she does here, yet she thinks she's better than us.'

'Well, we all have our talents,' Major said, amusement gleaming in his eyes. 'You have yours, she has hers – they are different, obviously, but both have their value and their place.'

'Talents?' Fiona thrust her hands on her hips and laughed out loud. 'You call what she does talented? Oh, do me a favour, please! Any simpleton could take her place, as long as she was passably good looking and fit. All your girls are, are ... well, we all know what they are,' she finished lamely.

'And we all know what *we* are, too,' Major said. 'Our girls are a valuable asset, no less valuable to us than you are to your employers.'

'Well, I'd like to see this dumb bitch perform in front of a camera three evenings a week, with an audience of ten million out there waiting for the smallest cock-ups so they can enjoy my embarrassment.' Fiona Charles was, Tammy realised, despite her fame, money and apparent power, a very shallow and insecure person beneath the façade, a bully *and* a coward: which was a common combination.

'Perhaps not,' Major conceded, 'but then, equally, I'd like to see you do some of the things our girls do here.'

'I wouldn't choose to do most of them,' Fiona said, turning and looking pointedly at the girl on the wheel, who everyone else now seemed to have forgotten. The poor thing was watching the events from her elevated position, eyes round with apprehension.

'I'm not suggesting you'd want to change places with Elsa there,' Major said, following the direction of Fiona's eyes. 'And while we're on the subject, perhaps a couple of you would be good enough to take the girl down – if you've finished with her for the moment, that is?' He turned back again, looking first at Fiona and then around the other guests.

'However, there are other talents – skills, even – that I doubt you could match.'

Still sitting on the floor, Tammy held her breath, amazed that the great Fiona Charles couldn't see what was coming. It was obvious that Major was goading her, deliberately leading her on, but the drunken bitch was so full of herself that she was walking right into his trap.

'Oh, yes?' she sneered. 'And what sort of talents might those be, Dickie baby? Being able to take three cocks at once, maybe? Well, that only goes to prove my point, doesn't it?'

'And what about pulling one of our racing buggies in a race?' Major suggested almost off-handedly. 'I suppose that doesn't take any skill, does it?'

'Nothing that an intelligent woman couldn't learn in ten minutes flat,' Fiona replied. 'OK, I'll grant you there are one or two in the stables who are a class above the rest, but as for the others . . .'

'So you think you could take on and beat someone like Tammy here?' Major smirked.

Fiona's top lip curled derisively. 'Easily,' she said.

'Then why not prove it?'

Fiona's expression became somewhat confused. 'What?' she said uncertainly. 'You want me to lower myself to competing against *that*?' She jabbed a forefinger at Tammy, who instinctively recoiled, even though there was now several feet between them.

'Why not?' Major said calmly. 'If you are so certain of your own abilities, why not back your words with actions? Of course, I wouldn't suggest you compete against an experienced pony-girl, even against one of the short-term girls, but with young Tammy here you'd be starting even. She hasn't even seen the inside of a harness yet, so she wouldn't have an unfair advantage, would she?'

'You must be kidding!' Fiona laughed nervously.

The man, Miko, still standing alongside Tammy, nodded his head. 'Why not, Fee?' he said. 'After all, you said it yourself, she's only some salaried trollop and that collar proves Dickie here isn't lying about her lack of experience. Unless you think she'd show you up, of course?'

Tammy looked down, not daring to let Fiona see her face for, despite the circumstances, she was now finding it difficult not to smile. The arrogant Fiona wasn't being set up by just Major, now; even one of her own supposed

171

friends was joining in on the act. Apparently, Miss Superstar Charles was not quite as popular among the members of her set as she seemed to think she was and her reaction was completely predictable.

'*Her*? Show *me* up?' she almost screeched. 'I could run her into the ground. I ran for the county when I was a teenager and if I hadn't gone into television, I'd have been good enough for the Olympics: my coach told me.'

'Then why not show us?' Miko said.

Richard Major had removed all traces of the smile from his face now, watching Miko make all the running for him.

'Yes, go on, Fee,' another of the women urged and there was a general chorus of encouragement from among the others.

Fiona let out a little 'humph' of derision. 'Well,' she said, 'does anyone want to bet against me? Might as well make it interesting, mightn't we? I've got two grand in cash says I hammer the little bitch. Anyone want to cover that?'

'I will,' Richard Major said quietly.

Miko's head snapped round. 'No, I'll take the bet,' he said.

Fiona gave them both a look of contempt. 'I'll cover both of you,' she said. 'I've only got two grand and some loose change with me, but I'm sure my IOU will be good enough. Besides,' she added, grinning maliciously, 'I shan't be the one paying out anyway: not when I've won.'

'Your IOU is good enough for me,' Major said, 'but perhaps you'd prefer to stake something other than money?'

'And what do you suggest?' Fiona said.

He shrugged and pursed his lips. 'Well, I'll stake five thousand pounds on our girl, which you get if you beat her. If she wins, however,' he said, 'you remain in the stables for a week.'

There were several sharp intakes of breath and a couple of muttered comments. Only Miko spoke out loud. 'That I'd like to see,' he chuckled.

Fiona glared at him. 'Well, eat your heart out,' she snapped, 'because the bitch doesn't stand a chance.' She looked down at Tammy, shook her head again and then turned back to Major. 'Get your money ready, Dickie boy,' she said. 'You've got yourself a bet.'

'Very well, then,' he said, a flicker of a smile returning. 'I suggest we meet in the stables area in one hour from now.' He reached down, put one hand under Tammy's armpit and lifted her to her feet with apparently no effort at all. 'I'll need to organise some grooms to prepare the contestants and they'll need time to get dressed. We don't usually have night racing here, either, so they'll have to organise some temporary lighting.'

Turning Tammy, he steered her towards the door through which he had entered. 'One hour,' he called back over his shoulder as they went out into the corridor; then, as they turned right and set off back the way Kelly had brought Mary and Tammy earlier that evening, he chuckled to himself.

'Human nature,' he said, almost under his breath, 'is so appallingly predictable. And as for you,' he said, slightly louder now that the distance between themselves and the party was growing, 'you must be the trawlerman they told me about, but don't worry. You won't be racing tonight.'

'I won't?' Tammy said weakly.

Major laughed. 'No. For the rest of tonight you can be Mary and Mary can be Kelly. Kelly can then be you.'

'What?' Tammy said, and then the penny dropped. 'Oh, I see.'

Major's laugh was even louder this time. 'Exactly,' he said. 'I never bet money unless I can tip the odds in my favour first.'

'This is your last chance to put your sensible head back on,' Rory Dalgleish said over his shoulder. 'I'm just going to bank around, get another couple of thousand feet and then turn for the final glide approach.'

Far beneath the little twin-engined aircraft, the dark water was barely visible as a black carpet upon which the odd ripple of lighter strips rippled and died, the scudding clouds passing over the starlit sky allowing very little illumination to penetrate for long.

'And another thing I don't like,' Rory continued, pulling back on the column, 'is this damned radar playing up the way it is. The screen's almost completely fuzzed whenever we get anywhere near that island. There's some sort of interference coming from down there – a strong radio signal, or a beacon maybe.'

'Or the set's on the blink,' Alex suggested. She was sitting in the rear seats but, despite the fact that the space was intended for two people, room was at a premium, thanks to the bulky parachutes she wore on her back and chest and the smaller pack she wore attached to her left hip by a short canvas strap. 'It could also be electro-magnetic activity from an approaching storm. There was something on the forecast about localised thunder.

'Anyway, you don't need the radar for this. Even without the moon, the island's been clearly visible both times we've passed over it and, once I jump, the radar won't do me any good anyway.'

'Maybe not,' Rory said, 'but I also had some radar problems when I came over here in the chopper to take those pictures. Not so bad, but then I was a lot higher up and I only made the one pass directly overhead.'

'Look, Rory, stop being an old woman.' Alex laughed. 'Just point this crate in a straight line and tell me when to jump. I'll be perfectly OK and the darkness will be useful. My main chute is dark blue and the emergency is dark red, so I won't be easy to spot from the ground.

'So be a love and let's get on with it, please. If it's going to piss with rain any minute, I'd like to be down on the ground and tucked away in those trees we saw on the photo. As long as I can find a wee space, I can have this pup tent up and wait it out, but I'd rather not get soaked before I start.'

Fiona Charles was still drunk enough not to be having second thoughts about her wagers with Richard Major and Miko, but when she was confronted by the line of grooms waiting in the stables area for the two contestants, her stomach gave a little lurch, for they all possessed the

174

slightly flattened features and hooded eyes of what Fiona always thought of as the 'locals'. Centuries of in-breeding, she supposed, though Major himself was clearly of the same stock and his sharp mind was not what informed thinking would have expected as the product of that sort of bloodline.

Miko and the rest of their party had gone ahead up into the night air, ready to enjoy the moonlit spectacle, although apparently Major had arranged for more of his staff to organise lighting for the race track as well. Fiona stood, uncertain for a moment, looking from the grooms to her intended opponent, to Major himself, who stood behind her and then back to the grooms.

'Why are there so many of them?' she demanded.

Major gave her a smile that never reached his eyes. 'Two for each pony-girl,' he said. 'One of them will then drive you to the track, where two female drivers, chosen from among our more senior and experienced girls, will take over the reins. I will toss a coin to decide which will drive whom, so there will be no favouritism. In any case, their skill levels are about the same and neither will know the identity of their particular pony. Pony-girls usually race without masks, but your grooms have been instructed that that will not be the case tonight and will fit special masks that we reserve for occasions when the anonymity of our ponies is essential.'

'But it won't need two of them to help me get into one of those harnesses, will it?' Fiona persisted. 'I've seen enough of your pony-girls to know what's what.'

'Ah, but that's not the way things are done here,' Major said. 'I know it may sound silly to you, my dear Miss Charles, but we have a strict code of rules and ethics governing competitive races. All entrants – in this case there are only the two of you, of course – are treated and prepared exactly the same, which includes showering and a basic veterinary check-up to ensure that you are fit to race.'

'Of course I'm fit to race,' Fiona stormed, 'and I don't need a shower, either.'

'Rules are rules, Miss Charles,' Major said firmly. 'You accepted a legitimate challenge, which must now be contested properly, otherwise you forfeit your stake money and I suppose I could, if I were of a mind to, insist that you undergo your week in these stables.'

'You wouldn't dare!' Fiona snapped.

Major shrugged. 'Perhaps I would, but there would be little in winning by default, just because you were not prepared to play by the rules, would there?'

Fiona hesitated, her brows furrowing in concentration. 'What you're suggesting is that I let these – these oafs – treat me like they treat your paid sluts,' she said. 'I think I'm a little above that, don't you?'

'I thought that was what you wanted to prove here,' Major replied easily. 'Tammy here will be prepared in the regulation manner, especially as this will be her first time and we don't want to teach her bad habits from the word go, and you wouldn't want to seek any unfair advantage, would you? For my part, I have done everything to ensure that the contest will be scrupulously fair.'

Fiona still appeared undecided. 'How do I know I can trust you?' she said. 'After all, you stand to make five thousand pounds if I lose this race.'

'I can assure you that five thousand pounds is a mere bagatelle, my dear.' Major chuckled. 'I've gambled ten times that much on one of these races before now – and lost it,' he added, apparently unconcerned at the fact. 'Now, are we to stand around here until dawn, or do I tell your friend up there that you will pay him the two thousand instead? As I said, you can forget our wager, if you like.'

'No!' Fiona said fiercely. 'I won't give that pig the satisfaction. OK, so I get to play pony-girl for an hour, so what? Seven grand for an hour's work – I earn more than that in London, of course, but this could be a lot more interesting.' She turned to face the line of grooms. 'Which are my pair?' she asked defiantly.

'Now, remember,' Mary said, 'that you are supposed to be me. That shouldn't be too hard, as I've not been here that long myself, but say and do as little as possible anyway. Just stand next to me and I'll hold this leash, so they'll think I'm Kelly. In fact, it'd probably make sense if I put your gag back in.'

Tammy looked confused. 'Why couldn't Kelly and I just swap places?' she said. 'That would have been a lot easier, surely? I mean, all Major wants to do is make sure that Fiona woman gets beaten, obviously.'

'Of course,' Mary agreed, 'but the one thing I have learned in my short time here is that nothing is taken for granted. Kelly is a senior J-A and has a lot of experience, which sort of shows in the way she conducts herself, I guess. I'm not saying I could pass myself off as a senior indefinitely, but I can do it for an hour or so, whereas you wouldn't have a clue.

'And if we mess this up, you can be sure we'll be punished, whatever else. I've seen some of the things they can do to us and you wouldn't like them any more than I would, take my word for it.'

'That woman will suspect something anyway,' Tammy said.

Mary shook her head. 'I doubt it,' she said. She had exchanged costumes with Kelly and was carefully adjusting the wide belt as tightly as possible. 'She's so arrogant, it wouldn't occur to her that Major would swap us around. I wouldn't mind betting she hasn't really noticed that there are three of us. The way she was drinking earlier and with all that confusion and noise at their party, all she'll have seen is you and I serving and probably not even noticed our faces, not until she picked on you.

'By that time, Kelly had pulled me back out of the firing line and Kelly herself was never out there in the main room for more than a few seconds at a time, if you remember.'

'I'm having trouble remembering anything here, it seems,' Tammy said morosely. She stared down at her rubber-sheathed legs and at the high-heeled boots that she appeared to have been wearing forever now. 'I *seem* to remember being a man, *once*,' she said. 'Doing a proper man's job, as well: and now look at me.'

177

Mary placed a hand on her shoulder. 'It must be harder for you,' she said gently. 'It was bad enough when I woke up here, but at least I was able to think myself lucky to be alive.'

'So was I, after a fashion,' Tammy said. 'I mean, fair enough, I was alive when they captured me, OK, but the one memory I'll never forget is being in that sea: waves as high as houses and higher, the cold, the darkness, the noise. It was terrible. I remember starting to pray – at least, I tried to pray, but it was hard to think of a god, right then.

'I remember thinking, if there's anyone there at all, please help me. Get me out of this alive and I'll do anything, anything at all. I think I'd have sold my soul just then. Maybe I did at that.' She shrugged, stood up and swayed across the floor, pirouetting to turn back to face Mary. 'Seems like I've sold my body, anyway,' she said, with a grim smile. 'Trouble is, I don't get the money; I just pay the price.'

'Have you – have they . . .?' Mary started, but hesitated. Tammy looked down at her toes.

'With a man?' she finished for her. 'No, not yet. I've still got that to come, obviously, and I'm not sure I can go through with it. Trouble is, there's something about this body that sort of takes control, I think.'

'I know,' Mary said. 'So try not to even think about it, at least not 'til the time comes. And you may be surprised when it does. I know I was.'

'But you're a female anyway,' Tammy said.

Mary raised her eyes in a gesture of frustration. 'Tammy,' she said, 'that's the whole point. I *was* a female and still am, but I'm not the sort of female I was in my old life, believe me. I'm now something totally different and I'm going to keep changing, the longer I'm here. So are you, sweetheart, and there's no getting away from that fact.

'OK, you *used* to be a male – though from where I'm standing it's pretty hard to imagine that – and now you're not, so you've got to come to terms with that.' She moved forwards, drew Tammy close to her and placed her hand under the layers of the uniform skirt. Even through the

178

latex layer that still covered Tammy's crotch, the intimate contact triggered an immediate reaction.

Gasping from the shock, Tammy staggered back.

'You see?' Mary said. 'And yes, OK, I'm a woman, so it's not the same, is it? Wait and see, my lookalike friend – I suspect it will be, and sooner than you expect. Now, let's go and watch this race.' She turned to the table, picked up the plastic internal gag and held it towards Tammy. Reluctantly, the latest Type CB-Fourteen opened her mouth.

The speed of events, once she had entered the stall with the two grooms and stripped off her evening outfit, took Fiona completely by surprise. One moment, she was wriggling out of the black rubber leggings; the next, her wrists were seized, pulled behind her back and secured with cold metal cuffs. Then, without further ceremony, she was hustled back into the main stable concourse, half-dragged across to a white tiled cubicle, pushed against the far wall and a metal collar snapped about her neck. From this, a short chain ran back to a hefty staple so that, until the metal band was released, she could not get out of what was clearly a shower unit. She peered upwards, searching for the shower heads.

The shock of the icy jet from the hosepipe took her breath away and almost toppled her headlong with its force. She opened her mouth to protest, but merely ended up swallowing a mouthful of water and, by the time she had finished coughing and spluttering, it was all over and she was being led back to the stall, her hair hanging in lank, sodden strands about her streaming face, cursing the two grooms, whose only reaction was to completely ignore the torrent of abuse.

They used rough towels to dry her off, brushing out her hair once they had removed the worst of the effects of its soaking and then pulling it up into a high ponytail, where it was secured with a narrow leather strap. She glared at the groom standing in front of her.

'I suppose you bastards think this is bloody Christmas and Easter rolled into one!' she spat. His face showed absolutely no emotion. 'Well, buster,' she said, 'have your fucking fun. When this is all over, I'll offer Dickie baby enough readies to have you two cunts as my personal whipping-boys for a week! Then we'll see who's boss!'

It was her last opportunity to vent her anger verbally, for the bridle was thrown over her head, straps adjusted and tightened and the hard rubber bit thrust between her teeth, one of the grooms gripping her nose and lower jaw to prise her mouth open, whilst his partner did the fitting. As the small retaining straps were drawn through their buckles, the rubber rod pressed awkwardly back, distending Fiona's mouth, but it was the hard metal plate fitted to its inner edge, holding her tongue immovably against the floor of her mouth, that was even worse.

Now, when she tried to talk, all that came out was a series of snorts and gurgles, not very equine-sounding, but certainly a long way from anything even close to coherent speech. Fiona was beside herself with anger and frustration, kicking out at the two handlers, but succeeding only in stubbing her bare toes against their thick boots and, despite her best efforts, they quickly had separate leather reins clipped to the rings at either end of her bit, which they paid out and took hold of one apiece, so that she found herself trapped between them, unable to reach either.

'Now then, Missy,' one of the grooms chided her, 'this is all very stupid. A normal pony-girl would earn herself a sound thrashing for this sort of misbehaviour.' He stared pointedly at the rack alongside the stall door, from which hung a selection of whips, crops and switches. 'Perhaps that's what you need now, to calm you down a bit, eh?'

Frantically, Fiona shook her head, her eyes bulging with terror and immediately she forced herself to stand totally still. The grooms exchanged knowing glances.

'Well then, if you're going to be sensible,' the same groom said, 'perhaps we can finish putting on your tack.'

Despite her fear of being whipped, Fiona nearly rebelled again when they tightened the wide main girth strap, for she was convinced they were deliberately trying to compress her waist further than necessary to get back at

180

her for trying to kick them. However, at the first sign of renewed resistance, the second groom slapped her hard across her naked buttocks. He used only the palm of his hand, but he struck with enough force to bring tears to her eyes and convince her that her best course was to co-operate, get the race over and then afterwards make sure that these two beasts received their come-uppance.

Harness straps were passed over her shoulders, around her breasts and tightened to make them stand out from her chest to a far greater degree than they did usually and then the crotch strap was fitted, but not before the first groom had taken considerable delight in first showing her the huge dildo and then plugging her sex with it. While Fiona was still reeling from the humiliation of this invasion, she was forced to bend over and have her tail fitted, the slimmer phallus greased first to overcome her natural reluctance to allow it into her rear orifice and then, once her sphincter muscles had settled back around the tapered end from which the horsehair cascaded down, another cunningly crafted strap was attached to ensure that it could not be ejected again.

They took longest fitting the thigh-length hoof boots, tightening the laces meticulously as they worked their way up Fiona's legs, so that the thick but supple leather became like a second skin. The sensation of embracing support was not unpleasant, she had to admit to herself, but the fact that the exotic footwear ended in splayed hooves, beneath which heavy steel shoes weighed her every step, rather than the imperious heels she was accustomed to, rather detracted from the potential pleasure effect.

She was still pondering on this and on how she was going to manage to run under such a handicap, when they released her wrists from the cuffs and quickly folded her arms up at the elbow and slipped the triangular leather pouches over each limb in turn, buckling the tops over to keep her hands hidden and prevent the sheathes from slipping off.

'Right, Missy,' the first groom said, addressing her for the first time in several minutes, 'the Chief says you're to

181

be masked, so we'll have to take the bridle harness off again. Frankly, if you'd behaved yourself from the first, we'd have left it 'til the end anyway, but you didn't.

'Now, we can do this easy, or we can do this hard and I ought to warn you there isn't anything you can say that either of us ain't heard before, so you might as well save your breath. Besides, if you start shouting your mouth off again, we have a special bridle with a spiked tongue plate that we use for rebellious fillies and we haven't had any instructions to say we can't use it on you, OK?

'As far as we're concerned, we've been told to treat you the way we'd treat any other new pony-girl, which is exactly what we've done. Do you understand what I'm saying?'

Despite the overwhelming urge she felt to see the superior and condescending grin wiped off his face by means of a good thrashing – preferably with herself wielding the crop or whip – Fiona nodded. In any case, she now reasoned, she would be shortly involved in a race, so it made sense to conserve her energies for that and deal with any other matters later, when it was safely won and Major's and Miko's money was safely tucked in her bag.

However, as the bit was removed from her mouth, she could not resist one question, although she fought to keep the tone of her voice as reasonable as possible, lest they went ahead and replaced the mouthpiece with the threatened punishment version. 'Tell me, please,' she asked, shuffling her leaden feet slightly for emphasis, 'how am I supposed to run in these things? They weigh a ton.'

The first groom chuckled and gave her what he evidently thought was a reassuring pat on her left breast. 'Don't you worry, Missy,' he said, 'it'll be the same for both of you. Now, hold still while I get this thing here over your head. Yes, your hair's just about dry now, so you won't start sweating up in it.'

'Just do what you must,' Fiona sighed, her shoulders slumping resignedly. 'But must you keep calling me that – Missy, I mean?' The groom looked genuinely surprised.

'But that's what we've been told to call you,' he said. 'All ponies have to have a suitable name. Sometimes it's a shortened version of their own, sometimes it's different and anyway, if the two of you are to remain anonymous until the race is over, the drivers have to have something to call you that won't tip them off as to who it is they're driving.'

'So what's *her* name, the little rubber-maid slut?'

'I couldn't rightly tell you, Missy, that I couldn't,' he said. 'Joel and I were just told what to call you. They'll probably call her something like Tessie, I should think. We used to have a Tess here in the stables, but she was transferred out a while back now.'

He stretched the fabric of the rubber hood and eased it down on to the top of Fiona's head, feeling inside the crown opening until he located her ponytail, which he carefully drew out through it. Presumably, Fiona concluded, as both she and the rubber-maid were both fair-haired and both had hair of similar length, it did not matter that it was left on display.

It took the groom several minutes before he finally had the masking hood in the correct position, by which time Fiona was staring out through two almond-shaped eye-pieces, which appeared to be covered by slightly tinted lenses, and breathing through her nose with some difficulty, due to the restricted size of the steel-ringed holes beneath her nostrils.

The lower part of the mask was cut away to leave both mouth and chin uncovered, but the lower collar at the back extended into two bands that were drawn around and fastened at the front of her throat. There was something about the mask that made her head feel slightly unbalanced now it was in place, but she could not tell what it was, not until after they had replaced the bridle harness and bit and led her across to the wall opposite the doorway, where Joel drew aside a length of sackcloth to reveal a long, narrow mirror.

Fiona grunted in horror when she saw what she now looked like, for the thick rubber helmet had pointed horsy ears attached and the part that covered her nose was padded out in some way to make her look uncannily equine. She closed her eyes and shuddered at the thought of the reaction her appearance would cause among Miko and the rest of the crowd out there. The sight of that long tail flowing down between her legs was the worst thing of all, she thought, but the grooms had not quite finished with her and, by the time they led her from the stall to be harnessed to the racing buggy, two heavy little bells jangled from her bulging nipples, held there by wickedly serrated circular clips that bit into the tender flesh.

Thank God, she told herself, as they buckled the straps from the shafts to her girth, that she only had to endure such humiliation for another hour at most and later, she promised herself, she would make a note of the little rubber bitch's name. There would come a time when the insolent little slut would no longer be able to hide behind her novice status ...

The ground underfoot was soft and springy and Alex landed with little more impact than if she had jumped off a footstool, running for a few metres as she began to haul back on the chute on which she had glided in so silently. It was a well-practised routine and within less than a minute she had the billowing fabric compressed down into an untidy package little more than the size it had been inside its release pack.

Staying in a low crouch, she headed for the screen of trees away to her left, which was the area she had memorised as offering the best potential cover and a base that she might require for several hours. Overhead, the clouds were still fairly broken, but Alex had lived long enough in these islands to know that a torrential downpour could materialise in minutes from much less and she was eager to set herself some temporary cover before doing anything else.

Although little more than a scrap of rock sticking out of the North Sea, Ailsa Ness would still take some time to investigate fully and whilst darkness would make an excellent ally, Alex knew she would see or find little without the aid of daylight, which would necessitate moving about carefully and keeping alert for signs of other human presence.

The undergrowth among the trees was patchy: in places impenetrable, in others non-existent and it took half an hour before she found a site she considered suitable. After pushing her way through a particularly unfriendly screen of gorse bushes, she found herself standing in a clearing, although clearing was far too grandiose a word for an area only about six feet square, she thought wryly.

However, for Alex's purposes, the small piece of ground was ideal. Thrusting the folded-up parachute, still half-hanging out from its pack, together with the unused emergency chute, underneath the foliage on one side, she unhitched the third package from her belt, opened it and withdrew the tiny one-man pup tent, together with the small metal thermos flask, the polythene wallet in which she had placed her mobile phone and the final package in which she had earlier wrapped some sandwiches, a few biscuits and some boiled sweets.

It was even darker among these high bushes, but Alex could almost have pitched her tent blindfold and in less than ten minutes, her base camp was ready. Sitting between the zipped end opening and the overhanging leaves, she took out a boiled sweet, placed it into her mouth and, as she began slowly to suck on it, reached inside the thick battledress-style jacket and drew out a tiny penlight torch, together with the rough sketch map she had drawn from Rory's photographs.

Lulu's initial resentment at having her first off-duty night for nearly a week interrupted so arbitrarily had largely dissipated by the time she arrived in the stables area. It had been several weeks since she had been given the opportunity of showing off her driving skills and she had never before taken part in a night race.

The groom they all called Higgy beckoned her towards one of the stalls that were usually kept for the occasional pony-girls and she followed him into it, already unfastening the belt of her tunic. Higgy, a lanky fellow with a shock of unruly black hair, grinned at her as she began to strip. Lulu glared at him.

'What's the matter with you?' she demanded.

The grin did not waver. 'Nothing,' he said. 'Not now you're here, anyway. You know I like you little 'uns.' Lulu turned away to hide her own smile. She should have known, she told herself. The grooms up here were almost a law unto themselves and while they were very strict at observing the proprietary rights of the selected permanent pony-girls, any other female flesh that ventured here, guests excepted, was viewed as fair game. She finished undressing and turned back to face him, hands on hips, legs planted defiantly astride.

'Want to get it over with now?' she demanded.

Higgy's grin grew even wider and he shook his head. 'No rush, princess,' he said. 'We'll get you dressed first, shall we?'

Lulu shrugged. It didn't really matter either way to her and she knew that the different grooms had their individual preferences. Higgy's clearly hadn't changed since her last encounter with him.

He passed her the synthetic rubber catsuit and she sat on the small three-legged stool and began easing her feet into it, while Higgy assembled the rest of her outfit. By the time she had wriggled her way into the one-piece, working her fingers into the attached mitts and stretching the dark fabric over her shoulders with some difficulty, he was ready. Stepping behind Lulu, the groom drew up the rear fastening as far as the collar, leaving the attached hood to hang limply above her small breasts.

The corset belt was as strictly confining as those they used for the pony-girls but, with her already slim figure, the only real difficulty it presented for Lulu was that it deprived her of the ability to bend properly at the waist and she stood unmoving as Higgy laced her into it. That task completed, he motioned for her to sit again and began easing the first boot up the length of her leg, waiting for her to arch her instep so that her foot was forced over into the *en pointe* position of a ballerina.

Lulu smiled at the top of his head as he worked the laces tightly up to the tops of her thighs, for she was one of the minority of Jenny-Annes who could manage such extreme footwear with relative ease. Most, given the deliberately modified nature of their bodies, together with long periods of training, could stand and walk in this design of boot, but they nevertheless more often than not contrived to look clumsy. Lulu, on the other hand, was able to spring about as if she were dancing the lead role in *Swan Lake*, a feat which had endeared her to more than one visitor in the past.

'Up you come then, my little beauty,' Higgy said, standing up himself and offering his hand. Although she did not need it, Lulu took it to help herself into an upright stance. Despite the additional height of her enforced new posture, the top of her head still came well below Higgy's chin.

She peered up at him, licking her lips provocatively. 'I suppose you want your little dumb dolly, as usual?' she said, her eyebrows twitching.

Higgy bent forward and kissed the top of her nose. 'You know me too well, princess.' He chuckled and brought the penis-shaped rubber gag round from his back pocket. 'Open wide, little Lulu.'

Lulu rolled her eyes in mock desperation, but parted her lips dutifully, sucking the cool rubber into her mouth like a large baby's dummy. Higgy kissed her nose again and took hold of the limp hood, stretching it up over her face, over the top of her head and down at the back, where, with a few deft adjustments, he closed it about the collar of the suit, so that the entire ensemble became as one shiny skin.

Lulu peered through the tinted lenses, wondering how she was ever going to be able to see in the darkness up above, hoping that whatever lighting they had organised would be adequate for the task. She held out her hands and Higgy drew the leather over-mitts on to them, buckling the heavy straps at the wrist and then inserting the handle of the long whip into the slot provided in the right palm. The left mitt ended in a stout ring, to which the driving reins would be clipped in due course, the whip then being used to direct the pony, if she was too stupid to think for herself on the track.

'Pretty as a picture, as usual.' Higgy smirked. He reached down and unclipped the triangular section that covered Lulu's sex, letting it drop down between her thighs, revealing her gaping lips, already moist in anticipation. They would be securely plugged again before she was taken up to the track, she knew, but for the moment Higgy had other uses for them.

He stepped back, dropping his breeches around his ankles and kicked them aside, revealing a rapidly thickening erection. Lulu shivered and daintily stepped forwards, reaching out with the attached whip and letting the stiff braid slide down his length. Higgy closed his eyes in ecstasy and they stood in silence for several seconds as she teased him.

'Now!' he whispered hoarsely. Grunting against her gag, Lulu closed in on him, reached up and around his neck with her near-useless hands, locking her wrists together with sheer strength, and leaped into the air. At the last second, Higgy caught her beneath the buttocks, and she spread her legs about his waist as he lowered her on to his throbbing shaft, filling her with one steady thrust. Lulu groaned and flexed her inner muscles and she heard him gasp with appreciation at their strength.

'Sheeeesh! Princess!'

Lulu pressed her rubber-covered head against his chest and squeezed again. Instantly, she felt him erupt within her, filling her womb with a torrent of sticky warmth, but this was Higgy and Lulu knew from experience he was far from finished with her yet.

'Jeez, where are all these people coming from?' The hooded figure crouching behind Nigel Hawkes at the edge of the undergrowth shifted his position awkwardly.

Hawkes held up a cautionary hand. 'Just wait,' he hissed over his shoulder. 'They're obviously headed down to watch whatever's going on at that track, so they can't be much longer. Just keep quiet for a bit, Jerry.'

'But look at them,' Jerry whispered. 'Have you ever seen such a weird bunch in your life? Look at that big blonde

188

one over there, for a start. How the hell did she ever get into that little dress thing? And how can that one there walk in those boots? Bloody hell, boss, what is this place?'

'What it is doesn't concern you, Jerry,' Hawkes snapped, keeping his voice as low as possible. They were fifty metres at least from the route the little knots of people were taking, and well hidden in the thick foliage, but he never believed in taking chances. He turned, his eyes narrowing. 'All you need concern yourself with is what you're supposed to be doing when we move in, OK?' he said. 'You're getting a big pay packet out of this caper, so don't fuck it up because your cock's getting itchy, or you won't have anything to wank with, and that's a promise.'

'Fair enough,' Jerry mumbled. 'Just seems a shame we couldn't maybe just take *one* extra passenger back for the ride, that's all.'

'Like the big blonde, you mean?' Hawkes grinned. 'Forget it.'

'Already forgotten, boss.' Silence descended and Hawkes returned his attention to watching the broken column through his night-glasses. 'Nice idea, though.'

'Shut it, Jerry.'

'Yes, boss.'

Silence again.

Fiona Charles had temporarily ceased to exist and, in her place, Missy the pony-girl trotted out into the cool night air, racing cart and groom driver behind her. It was, Fiona thought, the best way to handle the situation, by forcing herself into the role she herself had been forced to emulate – except she had not been forced at all, not until she had agreed to the race of her own free will without realising the full implications of that situation.

She had run the full gamut of emotions in a very brief space of time – from anger at being handled so impersonally and crudely, through frustration that she could not be seen to back out of the wager and to near terror, followed by a feeling of helplessness when the bit was replaced for the final time and she knew that she could no longer back out, even if she wanted to. And finally had come resignation, mingled with a determination that this humiliation would not be in vain.

Besides, she reasoned, there was nothing else to come that could be any worse than that final inspection after she had been harnessed between the long, slender shafts. Whether the fellow had been a genuine vet or doctor, she had no idea, but he had certainly been thorough, taking blood pressure, pulse and temperature, the latter being achieved by means of a large thermometer which he had thrust dispassionately into her unresisting sex, although he had been less professional when it came to removing and replacing the monstrous dildo, his fingers making more than a passing contact with her clitoris.

Finally, however, he had passed her as fit to race, though she doubted there had ever been any real likelihood that the outcome of his examination would have produced any other result. It was almost certainly done just for effect, one more little way of emphasising to her that her status now was, if only temporarily, subhuman. That knowledge, however, served only to stiffen her resolve.

Let them mock me out there all they want, she thought, as she struggled up the short gradient, the heavy boots dragging at her every step, but I won't let them have the satisfaction of thinking they can get to me. The rubber slut wouldn't be any competition, Fiona knew, just as long as she stayed calm and focused and anyway, there was now absolutely no alternative available to her other than to prove her original boast.

That knowledge brought with it a curiously calming effect. Fiona Charles had always been in control, not just of herself, but of most of the people who surrounded her in both her public and her very private lives, but now she had surrendered that control, albeit unwittingly and, for the first time since being a little girl, she was completely at the mercy of others. It was almost a safe feeling, she thought, being Missy, something Fiona had forgotten could exist and she began to relax, trying to forget everything else except the coming race and her determination to acquit herself well in it.

190

She had watched these pony-girls run on several occasions and had even driven in a couple of events herself and it had astonished her how proudly they carried themselves and the efforts that they made during the actual race. Harnessed like beasts, sometimes dripping with ornamental rings and jangling bells, they still seemed to think that they owed it to their drivers – and to themselves – to give of their best and the whips were scarcely called into play, except by novice drivers who could not bear to pass up the chance to thrash a pair of so conveniently presented buttocks.

Gripping the bit firmer than ever between her teeth, head now erect, Missy the filly was beginning to look forward to the next hour now. Eyes gleaming behind the protective anonymity of the ludicrous horse-head mask, she slowly began to pick up her knees and was soon moving along over the slightly uneven ground at a passable pace.

'Looks like we might not have to wait 'til oh-six-hundred after all.' In the still darkness, Nigel Hawkes's whisper sounded unnaturally loud and Andrew Lachan flinched. They had come ashore easily enough, as planned, in three inflatable dinghies, paddling between the rocks in the curved approach that Andrew had earlier memorised, and scrambled easily enough up the steeply inclined and heavily overgrown path to an area of trees that was also thick with undergrowth that offered excellent cover.

While Andrew and three of the men waited, masked and crouching in the almost total darkness, Hawkes and the fourth man had slipped away to reconnoitre and confirm that there were no guards wandering around unexpectedly.

'What do you mean?' Andrew hissed. He had just checked his watch for the fifth time in as many minutes and was starting to become anxious, knowing that the short summer night would very shortly be starting to give way to the pale northern dawn. 'Hadn't we better get under cover by the stable entrance?'

'Doesn't look like we'll need to,' Hawkes said. 'Look over that way, to your right and tell me what you can see.'

Andrew peered towards the trees and for the first time noticed a faint glow in the distance above them.

'That's your race track over there,' Hawkes said, 'and there seems to be a bit of a do going on. They've got torches and lanterns and a couple of lasses hitched up to these little cart things. There's fifty or more of them over there.'

'Night race,' Andrew said, almost to himself. 'Don't have too many of 'em and usually they're all over and done with by midnight.'

'Well, from where I was looking,' Hawkes said, 'this race is only just about to start. How long do they usually take?'

'Depends. Could be anything from ten laps to fifty, but twenty is usually the minimum for a two-pony contest, especially at night, when the visibility isn't too good for the sprinters.'

'So how long would a twenty-lap race take?'

Andrew considered for a second or so. 'Forty to forty-five minutes, I'd say. A bit less for a real thoroughbred champion like Jess, but then they wouldn't risk the top ponies after dark.'

'Then this is going to be rather easier than we thought,' Hawkes said, his eyes gleaming against the black of his balaclava, 'because Joe's just come back from scouting out the entrance and he tells me the doors are wide open and there's just one bloke sitting outside, making a big dent in a bottle of something or other.

'If we move now, we can take out anyone else who might be inside, grab Jessie and be back aboard before that race is half run. They don't have some sort of night cleaning staff in there, I suppose?'

'Not at two-thirty in the morning,' Andrew replied. 'They'll just have roused enough grooms to prepare the ponies and they'll probably be over at the track with them now. The guy sitting outside will be the night duty groom. Everyone else will be either sleeping, or at various parties deeper down in the complex.'

'Then let's go get ourselves a free pony-girl,' Hawkes said. 'We'll probably even have enough time to grab ourselves a spare, if you want. Be company for this Jessie of yours!'

On previous occasions when Lulu had been selected as a driver, a specially adapted buggy had been employed to carry her and her fellow charioteers to the track, saving them the effort of having to make the walk in the towering ballet-toed boots that were invariably part of their uniform, but tonight there was no spare pony harnessed for the purpose. Instead, Lulu and her opponent had to make their way as best they could, escorted by Higgy, who strolled easily between them.

The other driver had arrived in the stables either before or after her and Lulu's first sight of her was when they came out of the respective stalls in which they had been dressed, by which time she, like Lulu, was securely fastened inside her mask and her mouth gagged, so she could have been any one of about seven Jenny-Annes of the smaller type. One thing was certain, however, Lulu saw, and that was that the girl was not as comfortable walking on tiptoe as she was herself and needed Higgy's arm to steady herself on several occasions.

Lulu would have smiled to herself, had the stumpy gag permitted, as she saw the big groom move his hand down to stroke the rubber-sheathed buttocks, the sight reminding her that her night's activities would not be over with the end of the forthcoming race. She squeezed on the fat dildo that Higgy had inserted into her just before leading her from the stall – the bastard had deliberately chosen one of the thickest phalluses available – and felt the heat that was still there.

'Just so you remember, princess,' Higgy had said, zipping the crotch panel tightly back together. 'I'll be waiting for you when the race is over, win or lose. Got my own trophy for you, too.'

Lulu had grunted at this, unable to make any other comment, and hoped that come the morning someone would remember that she had been out of bed for most of the night.

She liked Higgy, though. Most of the other grooms appeared almost completely detached from their charges, treating the pony-girls like animals and the Jenny-Anne drivers little differently, presumably on the basis that they had also spent time in harness and would do so again. Few of them were especially harsh and their whips and crops were carried as much for effect as for serious use, although there were one or two of the lads who could be very spiteful and for no justifiable reason.

Higgy, on the other hand, was invariably cheerful, spoke to the girls as individuals and handled them with surprising gentleness, although few escaped the attentions of his prodigious manhood during their stay, no matter how short the duration. Just thinking about it again caused Lulu's lower stomach muscles to contract fiercely and, for once, she nearly lost her balance.

Word of the nocturnal pony-girl race appeared to have spread very quickly throughout the small island, for there were easily a hundred spectators gathered by the time the two contestants were trotted on to the oval track and more were arriving all the time. Richard Major, who had evidently decided to assume total charge of the proceedings, seemed in no hurry to get the contest itself started.

Lit by a series of flaming torches, which stood on poles thrust into the ground around the outer edge of the entire track, the small crowd, assembled alongside the right-hand straight, was buzzing with anticipation and although they did not encroach on to the track itself, the arrival of the pony-girls brought them pressing forwards for a better view. Peering through the eye-slits in her mask, Missy could see that her opponent had indeed been prepared in the same way as herself, except that her helmet, boots and tail were white, not black, presumably as a means of identifying which was which once the race got under way.

As promised, two drivers stood waiting to take over from the grooms who had driven the girls down to the course, small and sinister-looking females in featureless black rubber, which covered them from head to toe, leaving openings only for the eyes and nostrils, even their mouths hidden away and, Missy saw, as she drew closer to them, apparently gagged beneath the tight latex.

Moving easily on their steepling heels, the two figures stepped forwards, the only distinction between them being the large white figures stencilled on to their foreheads and, when they turned to display them, their backs. Whoever, or whatever were inside those figure-hugging cocoons, for the purposes of the contest, they were now simply Number One and Number Two. Number Two came towards Missy, taking a light hold on her reins, just below her face. Number One did the same with her opponent.

'As you can all see,' Major said, turning from left to right, ensuring that he quickly captured the attention of the entire gathering, 'both entrants have been prepared in identical fashion. Their hooves are of the same weight, as are the horseshoes, and both buggies are standard competition design.

'There is actually a height difference of half an inch between them and one is four pounds lighter, but they are remarkably well matched. They have both been renamed for tonight's entertainment,' he continued. He pointed first to the other girl. 'This is Jasmine,' he said, 'and this is Missy.' He indicated Fiona.

'At the moment, driver number two is with Missy and number one with Jasmine, but in a few moments I will toss a coin. If it lands on heads, they will remain as they are; if it is tails, they will swap places. Of course, if anyone else would like to toss the coin,' he said, looking along the small sea of faces, some expectant, some masked, 'then that is perfectly all right. As long as everything is completely unbiased, there can be no complaints afterwards.'

'I'll toss it.' Missy recognised the muscular bulk of Miko pushing through to the front of the throng. Now only a few metres from the track, he peered from her to Jasmine. With an effort, she managed to keep her head pointing straight forwards, only her flickering eyes moving to watch him. Although most of his face was still obscured by his mask, Miko's mouth was curling and twitching in amusement. He almost certainly could not tell which of them was which, but he was definitely enjoying the fact that one of these two erotically subjugated figures was one of the few women he himself had never been able to conquer.

'Very nice turn-out,' he smirked, taking the coin from Major. 'And if the maid girl wins, I'd like, here and now, to make it known that I am prepared to top any bid for the services of the other one as my personal pony-girl for the duration of her week in the stables.'

'Your bid has been noted,' Major replied impassively. 'Should the occasion arise, bids will be accepted after the race and the filly available for inspection by prospective drivers. Now, the coin please, if you will?'

There was a flicker as the small disc spun into the air, curving upwards into the gloom and then re-emerging to land only a foot or so in front of Miko. Both he and Major bent forwards.

'A head,' Major announced. 'The drivers will stay as they now are.'

'Heads it is,' Miko confirmed. 'Anyone else wanna take a look?'

No one moved.

'Drivers will now mount their buggies and make three parade circuits of the course at a slow trot,' Major instructed. 'I will then call them under orders, the grooms will fit competition vibrators in place of the ordinary dildoes the ponies are wearing at the moment and, at my signal, they will race for a total of thirty laps. The winner will be the first past the post, or the filly who keeps going the longest.' He smiled and his eyes rested on Missy for a few seconds.

She felt a tightening in her stomach muscles and the phalluses in her two throbbing orifices seemed to grow larger.

Amaarini Savanujik was mildly surprised to find the security chief, Boolik Gothar, at her door at such an hour, but she made no reference to the fact and stood aside to admit him. He wasted no time in getting straight to the point, for he had never been one to skirt around the edges of a problem.

'The Chief is amusing himself with some challenge race at the track,' he said, 'and I don't want to disturb him if this is just me being overcautious, but I need another opinion on this and, with the doctor busy in the lower levels tonight, that leaves you.'

'I'll try not to feel flattered,' Amaarini said, with a tight smile. 'So, what's your problem, Boolik?'

The big man paced back and forth across the thick carpet, his feet scarcely seeming to rest on the ground. 'A couple of things,' he said. 'None would be cause for too much alarm on their own but, put together . . . well, I'd rather be safe than sorry.' He stopped, turning to face Amaarini.

'First of all, the day before yesterday a helicopter made a couple of circuits of the island, prior to making a pass directly overhead. It stayed quite high, but there was little doubt that we were the object of at least passing interest. Apart from our own machines, nothing else has come this way in months.'

'They don't need to,' Amaarini agreed. 'We're too far-flung for the regular island-hoppers. What's the other thing that's worrying you?'

'Well, two things, really,' Boolik said. 'An hour or so ago, a light aircraft made a couple of similar circuits. It showed clearly on our screens at Carigillie and the duty guards could hear it clearly from up top here. It then made a low-level pass, but with its engines switched off. There were a couple of splutters later, before they cut back in, but I doubt it was in any genuine trouble.'

'Where is it now?' Amaarini asked. 'Still in the area?'

'No, it flew off in the direction of the mainland immediately afterwards and went off our radar.'

'So, what do you think they were up to? Was this while the race was going on up top?' Her tone betrayed her concern, but Boolik quickly allayed this.

'No, it was some time before anyone went up, and the race is only just about to start, but we're watching in case it returns and I've got a man up there in direct micro-link with the duty operators. We'll have enough warning if he does return, whoever he is.'

'So you don't want me to back you to recommend they postpone whatever this race is?'

'No, not yet, at least, but there is one more thing. The surface radar shows three vessels quite close in-shore. Two are currently heading very slowly westwards; the third, which at one stage was within less than half a mile of us, is now on an apparently random zig-zag course, though it would appear that it is determined to remain within four or five miles maximum of our northern shore.'

'Trawlers, I should imagine,' Amaarini said. 'They often come in fairly close on their way back to the main islands and they travel slowly because they are generally bringing their nets aboard at that stage and our radio screen affects their radar equipment anyway.'

'Yes, I know that, of course,' Boolik replied testily, 'and the first two craft fit the pattern.'

'But not this third boat, you're saying?'

'I don't think so. It's around the right sort of size and it's moving pretty slowly, but there'd be no reason for any trawler to waste fuel by going around in circles.'

'I don't suppose it might be a sailing yacht? No,' Amaarini corrected herself, 'you wouldn't be here now if you thought that, would you? So, what is it you want me to do?'

'You hold an executive pass card now, I believe?'

'Since I took over from poor Salinia, yes,' Amaarini said. 'Why?'

'Because it needs two separate exec-IDs to open the door on the main armoury and I want to issue weapons to as many security personnel as I can round up in the next ten minutes.'

'But you have weapons in your office, surely?'

It was rare that either Boolik or his guards carried arms, but Amaarini could not fail to notice the small holster at his waist now.

The security chief grunted. 'I have a total of four hand-weapons in my safe,' he said, 'which have now been issued, but I want to put up a cordon of at least twenty men in total. This island may be small, but there are a lot of places to hide.'

'But none where a safe landing could be made,' Amaarini reminded him.

He grunted again. 'Maybe not by fair-weather amateurs,' he conceded, 'and the local fishermen wouldn't risk the currents, but a trained professional, given the right craft, could get ashore in at least three places, maybe four, in calm weather and it's like a pond out there tonight.'

'But why?' Amaarini demanded. 'No one's tried that in years, surely?'

'The letter we intercepted from that stupid doctor,' Boolik said. 'How do we know there wasn't another copy somewhere? I do know that someone has been putting traces on our telephone calls. It was done from down south, but I have an excellent network of informants.'

'Indeed you do,' Amaarini agreed, 'but surely you can't really believe that someone is trying to get ashore here? If the authorities had any suspicions, surely they would have come openly, armed with the correct paperwork?'

'In the normal course of events, yes,' Boolik said, resuming his pacing, 'and I may well be overreacting to the situation, but a helicopter, a plane running with its engines off and now this vessel lurking around tonight – I'd rather be safe than sorry.'

'You're right, of course,' Amaarini said. She probed inside the tight hip pocket with her long fingers and withdrew the tiny oblong of glittering metal, the executive pass key that only three other people on the island held copies of. 'But be careful, Boolik,' she warned, as she strode past him to the door. 'We have a lot of guests here at the moment and a lot of them are up there now, so we don't want any nasty accidents. Preferably, we don't want any shooting at all.'

'My men know what is expected of them,' Boolik growled. 'And hopefully, I'm wrong anyway.'

* * *

'We have to hold off,' Andrew insisted, 'at least until I've been across to the track and checked out what's happening?'

'You said yourself,' Hawkes retorted, 'it'll be a night race. Why waste time when we've been given such an opportunity? All we need to do is hang on a bit longer, until we're sure there's no one else coming out of there and then make our move.'

'But what if Jessie is at the track and not in her stall?' Andrew said.

Hawkes stared at him in the near darkness. 'Isn't she supposed to be reserved for your exclusive use?' he argued. 'That's what you told me, wasn't it?'

'Yes,' Andrew hissed, 'but I wouldn't trust any of this crowd, otherwise I might not have gone to all this trouble to get her away from here. Besides, if they just had one of the grooms drive her down there, that wouldn't necessarily be breaking the agreement, would it?'

'But there were only two of these pony-girls there, weren't there?'

'Only two that your man *saw*, but I need to be sure and I'm the only one who could identify Jess,' Andrew persisted. 'Just hold everybody here and keep watching the main entrance. I'll skirt around and come up on the far side of the track, away from where they'll all be. There are a couple of narrow pathways through the woods that hardly ever get used, so they're pretty much overgrown and make good cover. Don't worry, I know my way around here blindfold.'

'You'll bloody well need to,' said Hawkes, but Andrew was already gone.

Alex pressed herself against the tree, staring in utter disbelief at the scene that was unfolding less than a hundred metres from her shadowy hiding place. What these freakish, outlandishly garbed figures had to do with the deaths that had originally prompted her interest, she had no idea, but their mere presence here, on a supposedly uninhabited nature reserve, was enough to confirm to her that she had been right to trust her intuition.

'Tell me I'm wasting my time, would you, Geordie boy?' she whispered to herself. 'Well, we'll see about that.' She reached inside her jacket and brought out the small camera, squinted through the viewfinder and considered the flickering torchlight illumination around the clearing ahead.

'Damn!' she hissed. It was unlikely that the lens was of good enough quality to capture anything approaching a distinct image with the current light level. The Japanese-made camera had a built-in flash feature, but Alex knew she was too far away for it to make any difference and besides, she had no intention of using it and betraying her presence so stupidly. She ducked back behind the bushes as another small group of people made their way along the nearby pathway.

She counted six of them and a further twenty metres behind them came another four, making around a hundred in the crowd so far, half of that number having arrived in the ten minutes or so she had been observing the scene and there was no sign of any immediate slackening in the rate of increase. Crouching low, she backed into the bushes, crawling between low branches until she found herself on what appeared to be another track, though much narrower than the one these people were using.

'Got to get closer,' she muttered, peering in the direction which this new pathway seemed to be taking. The thick overhead canopy of leaves made it very dark here, but she moved forward slowly, feeling her way at every step and made about fifteen metres before the undergrowth closed in again. She felt to the left and then to the right, but it was a natural dead end. Standing on tiptoe, Alex could just make out the burning brands ahead, much closer now than before, but still a long way off under the circumstances.

To her right, she could still hear more voices passing in the darkness. They sounded further away now and she calculated that this track to nowhere had not run completely parallel with the main pathway, so that the direction she was facing would take her, ultimately, out to the left of the small field in which they were all gathering.

Dropping to her knees, she pushed an arm ahead of her, testing the density of the undergrowth at ground level.

There seemed to be just enough room for someone to crawl between the main root clumps, but it was impossible to guess how much further that state of affairs would continue. She pushed the camera back into her pocket and took out the penlight. Risky or not, she would have to take the chance. Shielding the narrow beam with her other hand, she pressed the button and directed the shaft of light into the gap she had discovered. Two seconds later, she switched it off again and dropped on to her stomach, ears alert for any indication that the light had been spotted.

Slowly, she counted to twenty and then flicked the beam on again, counted to three and switched it off. It was not long, but it was enough to tell her what she wanted to know for the moment. Ahead of her, the roots of the bushes were spaced far enough apart for her to crawl between them, at least for another twenty metres. Beyond that, both the irregular pattern in which the undergrowth grew, plus the limited range of the torch beam, made it impossible to tell.

'Well,' she whispered, easing the torch into the breast pocket of the jacket and buttoning it safely, 'beggars can't be choosers.' She prayed that she wouldn't have to worm her way all the way back again and began to wriggle forward.

Kelly stole a sideways glance as her opponent was trotted up alongside her at the starting line and would have smiled, but for the bit that distorted her mouth, for the once haughty television star now looked every inch the prize pony-girl. Except, Kelly reflected determinedly, her status was some way short of even that yet, as the arrogant bitch was about to find out.

Although not a regular stable-dweller, Kelly had spent many months in harness during her long years on the island and had acquitted herself more than passably in scores of races, beating some quite fancied runners in the process. If Fiona, now Missy, thought she was in for an easy run against a fellow novice, she was due one horrible surprise. Kelly laughed to herself. And if Fiona also thought that Richard Major would relent in the matter of her forfeit if she lost, then she clearly didn't know the man. She was a valued client, true, but only one among hundreds and Major also knew that there were few, if any, other places where she could exercise her own specialised predilections.

The drivers – both experienced Jenny-Annes themselves, Kelly knew – would be equally matched, as promised, but then there were few drivers who could genuinely claim to be skilled enough to affect the outcome of a real race. The guests might be allowed to think differently, but every inhabitant of Ailsa Ness knew that, once the parade laps were out of the way and the flag went down proper, it was purely a contest between the pony-girls themselves and this was one contest Kelly had no intention of not winning.

A hundred metres from the entrance down into the stables, Andrew Lachan dragged the black balaclava from his head and stuffed it into the pocket of his trousers. So far, he had not encountered a living soul, but there was bound to be a groom on night duty inside the stables themselves and the sudden appearance of someone masked other than as part of one of the elaborate costumes prevalent among the guests on Ailsa Ness would have him sounding the alarm instantly. On the other hand, Andrew reasoned, if he just strolled in normally, whoever it was would recognise his face – for although he invariably remained masked in the presence of other visitors, he never bothered concealing his features among the stable staff – and assume, quite naturally, that Andrew was just calling in to check on his beloved Jessie.

To his relief, the familiar figure of one of the younger grooms, Jonas, rose from the bench at the bottom of the corridor and the groom seemed quite unperturbed at his sudden appearance from that direction, nor at the fact that he was dressed quite differently from the way he usually did when on the island.

'Got fed up with the race, sir?' Jonas asked. 'Only a couple of novices, anyway. Well, one novice, at least and the other gal ain't a patch on your Jess. Want to see her? Only I wasn't expecting you, so she's not quite prepared.'

Andrew held up a hand and gave him a reassuring smile. 'I had some unexpectedly free time on my hands, Jonas,' he said, 'so don't worry about it. And I already know about Jess's inner sanctum. She doesn't keep any secrets from me, you know.'

'Of course not, sir,' the groom said, straight-faced. 'It's just that some of the owners . . . well, you know how it is, sir, don't you?'

'I do, Jonas,' Andrew said. 'But then, I'm not them.' A new plan was forming rapidly in his head, a plan that might save the need for a show of force, and he was angry at himself for not having thought of it before.

'Jonas,' he said, 'I think I'd like to take Jessie out for an hour, maybe run her down to the track. It's a pleasant night up there and I think she'd enjoy the fresh air. I'm not exactly dressed for it, but maybe you have something suitable I could borrow?'

To her relief, Alex found that the twisted roots and brambles did not become any thicker; after twenty metres or so, the going actually became a little easier and, after five minutes' arduous crawling to the accompaniment of a lot of huffing and puffing, she found herself on the far edge of the clearing, almost directly across the track from where the crowd was concentrated.

She judged the distance and swore softly as she realised it was still too great for the little camera to have any chance of capturing a usable image but, as she studied the scene from this new angle, she began to understand what seemed to be happening. She stared at the two figures harnessed to the identical buggies, trying not to laugh as she realised the truth.

Pony-girls! Alex had read a couple of articles that had touched on the subject, but she had dismissed them as sensationalism on the part of the writer concerned, not prepared to believe that women could be prepared to go to such extremes. Pulling carts, yes, maybe even a bit of naked flesh and a few bits of harness for effect, but not this. This was incredible. These women had been dressed up to resemble ponies as far as was possible, given the basic differences between the human physique and its equine counterpart. They even seemed to be wearing bits and those whips in the hands of the humanoid-looking drivers were no stage props!

Alex turned slightly on to her left side and reached into her jacket for the cellular phone. She depressed a button and the time display came up a pale greyish green. Geordie would be fast asleep in his bed by now, for certain, but no matter. Whatever else might be going on here, what she was witnessing was certainly sufficient to justify a visit in greater numbers and the sooner the better, before the evidence dispersed again.

She flicked another button until she arrived at the preset number, depressed another and waited, the phone pressed close to her ear, but after two minutes nothing had happened. Cursing, she tried again, but the result was no different. All that she could hear was a faint hissing sound. The third time, she put in the number manually and when there was still no activity, she tried two other numbers, Rory's and the coast-guard. All came up dead and a nasty suspicion began to form in the back of Alex's mind.

The cloud cover was becoming thicker now and visibility was growing steadily worse, but Boolik Gothar's eyes were keener than most. He raised a hand, placing it on Amaarini's upper arm in a cautionary gesture and pointed with the forefinger of the other.

'Down there,' he said, his voice scarcely audible. 'Can you see? Two of them, I think.'

'I can't see a thing,' Amaarini whispered, peering into what seemed to be an inky black blanket, broken only by the odd pale outline where a tree had been stripped of a piece of bark and was catching what little light there was from the one star that remained visible far above them.

'Keep back against the bushes,' Boolik urged. She heard the sound of his holster being unbuckled. 'There's definitely two of them and there may well be more.'

'Are you sure they're not your men?' Amaarini suggested. 'You must have a dozen or more wandering around up here now.'

Boolik gave a little cough. 'If they were my men,' he said, 'they'd either be walking along openly, or else even I wouldn't see them. Besides, none of the sentries should be in this section. I've put extra bodies up by the stable entrance, two at the main entrance, and sent two men to each of the potential landing points, just to keep watch.

'No, whoever those men are, they're not here legitimately.' He adjusted the single headphone over his left ear and spoke quietly into the microphone that hovered just below his mouth and, three hundred metres away to his right, four more of his security guards melted invisibly into the undergrowth, weapons at the ready.

Fiona or Missy, she was already beginning to fear that even completing the race might be beyond her powers of endurance, let alone winning it, for not only was the gently buzzing vibrator that had been secured inside her making it increasingly difficult to maintain a proper level of concentration, the additional check-rein that she had never seen in use before was threatening even worse problems.

These reins had not been fitted to the respective ponies until the drivers were safely strapped on to their narrow race seats and their incredible boots hooked over a transverse bar in front of them. It was to this bar that the check-strap was attached, running between the ponies' thighs and up to a point at the bottom of their girth straps, adjusted then to a precise tension.

Now, by applying pressure with her booted feet, the driver could jerk this strap tight up against her steed's crotch, pressing the shivering phallus even deeper and bringing a strategically situated extrusion hard against her clitoris, with predictable results. Even before the flag for the race proper, Fiona was gasping and drooling, biting hard into the rubber bit in an effort to fight back against her body's natural reaction.

And as the first inevitable orgasm began to build, she found herself hoping fervently that her opponent had even less will-power: for, if not, the prospect of spending the next week in this humiliating role was looming ever larger.

The two human ponies and their anonymous drivers did not seem to be racing in earnest yet, moving at a fairly leisurely pace: though, to Alex, as she lay beneath the screening bushes, clicking away with the small camera whenever the rigs came around to her side of the circuit, it seemed that even walking in those hideous boots would have been sheer torture.

Away on the far side of the track, the crowd had spread out, so that they now formed a thin line along most of the straight there. As yet, they did not sound too excited, but Alex clearly caught the sound of an occasional taunt or cry of encouragement. She heard two distinct names, Jasmine and Missy, though whether these referred to the pony-girls themselves, or to their drivers, she had no idea, and as to which was which, apart from the fact that one of the ponies wore white accessories and the other black, the only means of identification were the numbers on the drivers' rubber catsuits.

Alex peered down at the camera, trying in vain to see the little window that would tell her how many exposures remained. She had started with thirty-six and had now used at least ten, maybe twelve and she did not want to exhaust the entire film on this scene, no matter how bizarrely fascinating it was. Besides, she reminded herself, the photos she had taken so far would be of little use on their own in a court of law.

Pictures by themselves proved nothing, beyond the fact that these people shared some decidedly less than usual tastes in dress sense and sporting preferences. The drivers had whips in their hands, true, but that was not proof of coercion. She needed more and Alex knew that she was more likely to find what she wanted elsewhere on the tiny island. Tucking the camera safely inside her jacket again, she began to crawl backwards.

By the time Andrew had donned the tight leather trousers, boots and rubber shirt that Jonas had found for him and pulled on the leather mask helmet that he kept hanging on the rack inside Jessie's stable, the groom had finished getting the still sleepy-looking pony-girl into her tack and was harnessing her between the shafts of a standard buggy.

Seeing Andrew, when he had finally entered her stall for the mask, she had managed to smile around her bit and he had been rewarded by the sight of her large nipples beginning to swell instantly. He had smiled back and uttered a few words of encouragement, though he knew by now that Jessie would not even dream of questioning anything he told her to do. Dawn or dusk, noon or night, she accepted that Andrew was her master and now, as he lovingly fondled her heavy breasts while Jonas finished his task, they began to rise and fall with greater rapidity and Andrew did not need to explore between her thighs to know that she would already be wet there.

Jonas finished the last buckle, straightened up and stood back. He looked pointedly towards the nearest implement rack, but Andrew shook his head.

'No, she doesn't need anything,' he said. 'Not even a whip. She never does.' He stepped past Jonas and climbed up into his seat.

Nigel Hawkes checked the luminous dial of his wristwatch and muttered an oath under his breath. The two figures hunched in the bushes behind him stirred uneasily, sensing his growing impatience.

'What the hell are we waiting for, boss?' Kit Bates, a former corporal in the SAS, leaned forwards, hissing his question directly into Hawkes's right ear. 'We could have been in and out by now, surely?'

'The man's paying the wage bill,' Hawkes retorted, 'so we wait a bit longer. The target might not be down there, that's all, so he wants to make sure.'

'Bloody amateurs,' Bates sneered. 'This is a bloody fine time to be having doubts. I thought this was a quick smash-and-grab op.'

'It will be,' Hawkes said. 'It will be. Just keep down and keep quiet. We'll give him a bit longer.'

'And what if he doesn't show?'

'Then he's run into trouble and we go in and get him out of it.'

'Why don't we just leave him there? He's the one who changed the plan, after all.'

'You want to get paid for this job?' Hawkes grated.

'Yeah, of course.'

'Well, he's the guy with your wage packet, right?'

'Yeah. Right, boss.'

The two shadowy figures were moving so quietly that Alex very nearly didn't see them in time, and only the fact that they were intent on something in front of them saved her from being seen first. Heart pounding, she stumbled behind the nearest tree and peered around it, expecting to hear a challenge shouted out at any moment.

Except, she realised, as she watched their furtive progress, whoever they were, they were as anxious to remain undetected as she was. Her rapid breathing seemed unnaturally loud in the otherwise silent night air; with the wind – or what there was of it – in its current direction, even the sounds from the race spectators no longer reached her ears.

'So,' she muttered, under her breath, 'I wonder who you two jokers are?' All manner of possibilities tumbled through her mind, but nothing that seemed more or less likely than anything else. Alex pushed the myriad permutations on to 'hold' and concentrated on her more immediate problems.

Having finally extricated herself from the tangled undergrowth, she had back-tracked towards the path which the spectators had been using to get to the race course. They had all been coming from the one direction, so it was logical to assume that that was the way she should now go. If there was anything else to be uncovered, that was where she would be most likely to find it.

Alex had been moving cautiously enough, aware of the possibility of lookouts or guards, but they, she assumed, would not have needed to skulk in the shadows the way these two were doing – and that theory was proved a few moments later, when two more figures appeared, this time walking quite openly and carrying what looked horribly like short-barrelled rifles across their chests.

Ahead of her, the first two men dropped lower still and, for the first time, Alex saw that they, too, were armed, though with smaller hand guns. She ducked back behind the tree again and closed her eyes for a few seconds, thinking desperately. This was beginning to get far too heavy and although she hadn't tried the cellular phone for some time, she knew with a horrible certainty that the damned thing still wasn't going to get a connection to the outside world.

The flickering torches were like small shooting stars against a backdrop of dark silk, darting, swirling, growing and fading. Dimly, Missy was aware of the ground beneath her hooves, the tug of the reins pulling at her bit and driving the devilish invader in and out of her burning sex, her tail flicking against the backs of her legs, the faces, the voices, the clatter of wheels and the light sting of the whip across her shoulders.

The first climax had had her buckling at the knees and she had stumbled forwards for several metres before finally regaining something like equilibrium, but the respite had been short-lived. The second had followed as eagerly on the heels of the first as a puppy yapping in the wake of its mother and she had screamed into the bit, her head roaring and swirling.

Three, four, five times – Missy no longer knew, nor cared. All that mattered now was to run.

And run . . .

. . . and run . . .

* * *

At a silent signal from Boolik, the black garbed figures began to fan out. Already hardly visible in the darkness, they melted back into the trees and undergrowth, only the faintest rustle of leaves betraying their progress: but from all sides now night-vision scopes began to home in on the two unsuspecting targets.

'Walk on, Jess. Good girl.' Andrew Lachan shook out the reins and the dark-haired Jessica leaned forwards and began to move, pulling the small buggy behind her almost as if it were weightless. The groom, Jonas, stepped away, touching his forehead in a brief salute and Andrew permitted himself a wry smile as they entered the bottom of the wide tunnel that led up to the outside world.

Overhead, small fluorescent panels cast a ghostly glow and the sound of Jess's steel-shod hooves echoed against the rock walls, mingling with the creaking of her harness and the squeaking of springs, the rubber-tyred wheels passing soundlessly over the paved floor.

Andrew's smile grew wider as they approached the dark semi-circle that marked the end of the climb, and not for the first time he found himself entranced by the sight of Jess's magnificent buttock-muscles as she bent to her task. In his hands, the leather traces were becoming slippery and, transferring them from left to right, he wiped the sweat from his palms, making a dark patch on the thigh of his leather breeches.

Not long now. Just a few more strides and they would be out in the open, from where it would be but a steady few minutes' trot, collect Hawkes and his team, then unhitch, abandon the buggy and down the winding path to where the three inflatables lay waiting to take the raiding party back out to where the *Jessica* would be waiting to welcome them.

By this time tomorrow, Andrew told himself, Jessie would be safe and sound in her new stall. He shook the traces again and began humming softly to himself.

Kelly was running easily now, enjoying the warmth and the heightening of her perceptions, her every nerve alive and singing. Long ago now she had learned the art that every successful pony-girl ultimately had to master, that of rechannelling the energy created by the constant action of the dildo and the tail phallus, directing it down into her leg muscles and loping along in an almost trance-like state.

By now, she calculated, they had completed just over half the scheduled number of laps, although she knew better than to try to keep an accurate check. That was the job of the driver, who would use the whip, directing it between her shoulder-blades to indicate the moment when they began the penultimate circuit. There had been no verbal communication between Kelly and her anonymous driver but, presuming the girl was as experienced as she was supposed to be, the signal would surely come.

Meantime, Kelly was content to canter along behind her opponent, keeping just a few paces off the whirling wheels, using the other cart and driver as a windshield, letting the raw novice, Missy, make all the pace. Recalling her own racing début, Kelly grinned around her bit. By now, she knew, the arrogant bitch up front would be in a bad way, probably oblivious to her surroundings and, by the time it came to the final dash, unable to summon any reserves with which to make it a real contest.

It would be interesting, Kelly thought idly, as she eased past the start line and the gaggle of noisy spectators, to see how the former Fiona Charles reacted to a few days being kept harnessed and bitted and available to anyone who asked for her – and she made a mental note to ask permission to visit Fiona in the stables before her week's forfeit ended. If Kelly beat the bitch tonight, as she surely would do, she was confident Richard Major would accede to such a simple request.

Jessie had long since ceased to be surprised at anything that happened in her life, but the unexpected appearance of her master, Andrew, when she knew he was supposed to be away for at least the next two weeks, came close. She could hardly contain her eagerness as the groom, Jonas,

212

fitted her tack and had almost pulled the traces from his hands in her haste to get out to the cart area.

It had been a while since her master had driven her at night and a long time, too, since he had not personally bridled and bitted her and the novelty was not lost on her. She shivered with delight as she was handed over to him, already the complete pony, silent, obedient, eager to please, but a little saddened that he did not make his customary fuss of her before climbing up into the driver's seat.

No matter, she thought, as she began moving towards the exit tunnel, there would doubtless be plenty of time and he was probably eager to get her topsides to make the most of this unscheduled visit. The gentle kiss of the driving whip on her shoulder-blades made her tingle from head to toe and she shook her head, the long dark mane swirling in appreciation.

Out into the darkness they went, the clatter of hooves on stone replaced by the duller thud of steel on rough grass, the cool night air clutching playfully at nipples that hardened instantly to its caress. She blew air fiercely from her flaring nostrils, waited to pick up the pace at the next signal and then –

The dark figures came from both sides and she heard a yell from behind her, followed by a sudden dipping of the shafts as extra weight hit the cart. Another figure loomed in front of her, hands clutching at her bridle, jerking her head sideways.

A loud bang, followed by another. She staggered sideways, unbalanced by the drag on her harness, hearing the sharp scream from the rear. More figures. A curious violet flash, a skull-searing screech and a muffled groan.

A second screech, like fingernails scraping down a blackboard, another loud report and more shouting. Figures hurtled past her on all sides and she found herself being pulled around, the man almost hanging from her bridle, until a second black figure bore into him, carrying him away into the darkness.

With a frightened whinny, Jess started forwards again, trying desperately to turn her head in the stiff harness collar, praying to hear her master's voice and then suddenly her every fibre seemed to be tearing apart and she was falling, falling . . .

Nigel Hawkes threw himself flat, the Browning automatic unwavering in his two hands. Just behind him he heard a muffled oath, followed by the crash of something heavy falling into the brittle bushes, but only one compartment of his brain registered it as a man down.

Twenty metres ahead of him, two figures seemed to rise out of the ground, headed for the mêlée around the pony cart, and Hawkes hesitated only for the briefest of seconds before loosing off two shots, the unsilenced weapon sounding like a cannon as it bucked against his grip. He allowed himself just the smallest grunt of satisfaction as the two targets both crumpled, but by then he was already moving, rolling to his right, knowing only too well that the muzzle flashes from the pistol would have given away his position.

He was only just in time but, even so, the resounding echo inside his head was not what he had been expecting and there was no scrunch of a bullet ploughing into the earth nearby. He came back on to his stomach at the end of the second roll, squinting along the barrel, seeking the source of the shot.

He saw the silhouette, recognised that the weapon was some type of rifle, took swift aim and fired again. There was a loud yell and the figure staggered backwards as the hard rubber projectile took him square in the chest, but he did not go down. Hawkes lowered his aim, squeezed again and the second yell was accompanied by the satisfying sight of the would-be marksman finally buckling, his right kneecap at least dislocated, if not shattered, at that range.

This time, Hawkes did not bother to roll. Instead, he pulled himself up into a half-crouch, tensed and sprang, diving headlong back towards the bushes, and scrambling down into the small depression he had identified earlier, eyes already scanning in an attempt to separate friend from foe.

It was all going horribly wrong. Lachan had told them there were no weapons on the island, that there would be no resistance and probably not even any guard patrols – and yet there seemed to be men running everywhere now. Away to his left, he heard the staccato bark of an Uzi, registered the bright flashes and heard an agonised shout as at least one of the rounds found its mark, but the fire was answered almost immediately, tiny pin-prick flickers from three sources: yet no sound bar a yelp of surprise from the Uzi's owner and an awful, head-expanding squeal inside his own skull, that set green and purple lights dancing in front of his eyes.

Shaking his head to clear his vision, Hawkes was already reaching inside his combat jacket, fingers closing on the first of his spare magazines. With a muttered curse, he ejected the half-full clip of rubber-tipped projectiles and slid the replacement home in its stead. Except that it was not a direct replacement, for the fifteen bullets in this clip were coated with something a lot more deadly than vulcanised rubber.

The time for playing chicken was long past, Hawkes reflected, thumbing the pump mechanism; the first lead slug dropped into place. Whatever was going on here, these people were playing deadly serious and Nigel Hawkes, ex-Lieutenant, Military Medal and DSM, veteran of two war theatres on almost opposite sides of the globe, knew those rules better than most.

Alex switched off the mobile phone, shook it in frustration and only just resisted the urge to hurl it far into the bushes. Everything was lighting up that should light up, except that there was nothing showing where the signal strength reading should be, other than a curious blinking pattern on the first two bars. She wasn't any sort of telecommunications expert, but she was convinced now that it wasn't the phone's fault; something here on the island was blocking the signal and Alex doubted that it came from a natural source.

Meanwhile, something was going on here apart from the bizarre pony-girl race for, from her dark vantage point, she could see several figures creeping around among the trees and, from the manoeuvrings, she guessed that they weren't all on the same side. So far, there had been no direct encounters, but it appeared that at least one of the shadowy forces knew the existence and approximate whereabouts of the other, so it was surely only a matter of time.

Alone and unarmed, however, there was little she could do. She could see the dim semi-circle of light from what appeared to be a wide doorway leading into the side of a large hummock in the ground. It was possible that there would be some form of communications equipment in there, of course, but it would be madness to go that way. Even as she discounted it as too risky, she saw the figure of another trotting pony-girl emerge, pulling behind her a cart similar to the ones she had seen on the track, a black, featureless driver mounted on it.

Her only chance of summoning help remained with the damned phone. If there was some sort of blocking field in place, just maybe it wasn't kept switched on around the clock. Or maybe again, if she could get higher, perhaps it was possible to get above its range. At her back, the ground began to rise towards the hill that dominated the further end of Ailsa Ness. The photographs had shown plenty of cover on the slopes and, even if the phone still didn't work up there, at least she would be out of the way if any shooting started.

For a few seconds, she considered trying to retrieve her tent and the other things she had left at her temporary base camp but, the way things were beginning to look here, the sooner she put some distance behind her, the better. The way back to the tent would take her nearer the current action, not away from it. Besides, she reasoned, the stuff was well hidden and she could always come back for it later.

Stuffing the phone into a side pocket, she turned and began creeping quietly up the slope, just as the first shots began to sound behind her.

* * *

All thoughts of Andrew Lachan and his precious pony-girl were now abandoned and Nigel Hawkes's only remaining instinct was for self-preservation. The rest of his small task force could fend for themselves now, as their training dictated, but already Hawkes was certain that at least two of them were down and, to judge from the noise on all sides, they had not inflicted many casualties themselves in the process.

He pulled the pins on the first two smoke grenades, counted to three and rolled them out in opposite directions. A second or two later, twin dull plops heralded the billowing clouds rising up to either side of him, enveloping an already confused and impossible scene in a steadily expanding wall of complete visible impenetrability. Hawkes grunted, nodded to himself and tossed a third grenade straight ahead for good measure, ducked back into the bushes and adjusted the filter mask and goggles, all the while concentrating on keeping alive the mental map he had in his head.

The way back to the cove and the inflatables lay away to his right, but he had already discounted that – at least until he had had time to take stock – for it was likely, given the way in which they had been ambushed, that the enemy already knew about the place and attempting to retreat that way would be heading straight into a trap.

The underground entrance was to his left and slightly behind his current position, but that too was asking for more trouble. Ahead, across the immediate clearing, the trees offered the most likely sanctuary and behind that was the hill. Get the high ground, that was the invariable rule. Get above the enemy and let him come to you, if he could.

He checked the Browning again, felt in his pockets to make sure that the spare magazines were still there, drew out the first of the two stun grenades, flicked the safety pin clear with his thumb and took a deep breath. The smoke curled in around his hiding place as he closed his eyes, gauged the distance and lobbed it towards where he had last seen the fallen pony-girl and toppled cart and the dark figures who had been closing stealthily in on it.

* * *

Halfway up the hill, the going had become very much tougher, the steepening incline combined with thicker clumps of gorse and bushes that closed their ranks against her. Breathing heavily, Alex slumped to the ground, crawling behind the twisted stump of what had once been a tree and peered down at the scene she had left behind, a tableau slowly beginning to emerge in the first glimmer of the dawn light.

The shooting seemed to have stopped now, but the sounds of voices drifted up to her, even though the near-darkness and that drifting smoke still made it impossible for her to see properly what was happening, so there were obviously still plenty of people alive down there.

Suddenly, out of the edge of the smoke cloud, a black figure emerged, running low and zig-zagging as he crossed the narrow strip of clear ground separating himself from the trees at the bottom of the hill. As she watched, Alex saw him stop, jerk around and topple backwards, though there had been no sound of a shot.

He hit the ground hard but, even as the other two figures came out of the smoke, he was rolling, bringing up the weapon in his hand. Three flashes, followed by the sound of the shots themselves, but not before both pursuers had dropped amid cries of surprise and agony. And then the gunman was up again, only now he did not run so easily, his right leg dragging heavily.

Just before the trees, he turned again, aiming back towards any unseen pursuers, and loosed off four more rapid shots, before diving for cover just before the next three figures ran out into the open.

'Jesus H. Christ!' Alex exclaimed, in a fierce whisper. 'Cowboys and bloody Indians!' She tried the phone again, with predictable lack of results still, and then realised that she ought to start moving again herself. She didn't have a clue who was who in this mêlée, but one thing was certain beyond a doubt: none of them knew her, either, and as they appeared to be shooting on sight, if not earlier, the farther away she got from the action, the better her chances of remaining healthy.

* * *

She was going to lose, Fiona was certain of that now: for though she could not turn her head to see how close her opponent was, she knew the little rubber bitch maid could surely not be suffering as she was herself.

Even though her body seemed to have exhausted its ability to react to the still humming vibrator, the earlier stream of continuous climaxes had taken their toll and now only the tight pony boots kept her knees from buckling under her as she plodded remorselessly onwards, the regular flick of the whip between her shoulder-blades a constant reminder to keep going.

Tears stung her eyes as she ran, tears of frustration, humiliation and anger. Major had deliberately goaded her into this race, she could see that now, knowing that even one of his novice girls could almost certainly beat her. She groaned through the bit. This was going to cost her thousands to buy off the forfeit, even on top of the money she would have to pay Miko. The smug bastard was there now, though she could not make him out amid the hazy images of the crowd, probably already counting his winnings in his head and preparing a barbed little speech to greet her in defeat.

Damned great ape! She would find a way to get back at him sooner or later, Fiona knew, but for the moment he was the winner and he would milk the occasion for everything it was worth when she was finally paraded before her so-called friends in this degrading condition. She bit hard into the rubber, desperate to summon up any last remaining dregs of energy, for surely the finish could not be that far off now?

Maybe, just maybe she could lengthen her stride, perhaps open up some sort of lead that might dishearten the girl behind her? Maybe even the girl *was* as exhausted as she was? Fiona snorted in air through her flaring nostrils, trying to fill her lungs against the insistent pressure of the girth corset, willing her leg muscles to respond as she came off the bend and into the back straight again.

And then it happened and she screamed through the gagging rubber as the other cart eased slowly past her, the pony-girl, hair streaming, running easily and rhythmically, her diminutive driver sitting stock-still, the whip unmoving in her hand, already knowing that the race was won.

For the first time in many years, Alex Gregory was now seriously scared. Somewhere in the trees below her, the first figure she had seen was being hunted by the three who had come out of the smoke hard on his heels, while another lone figure, who had emerged into the open about a hundred metres to the right of the first, had begun running, only to be shot down by another two men who appeared from the furthest edge of the trees.

They had aimed at him with weapons that looked from a distance to be short-barrelled rifles, violet flashes from the muzzles indicating a discharge, although there was no accompanying crack of a shot to follow. Presumably, Alex thought, their guns were silenced, although she could make out no familiar bulge at the business ends, but their effectiveness was unquestionable.

Two shots, one from each rifleman, and the target flew into the air as though he had been hit by a car, landing several feet away, where he twitched spasmodically for a few seconds before becoming still. His two assailants did not even bother to approach him with the caution Alex had been trained to employ when approaching a downed target, simply strolling up to him and then walking on past without even stopping for a closer examination.

Their cold efficiency and total detachment sent a chill through Alex's spine. For all her years of experience, this was the first time she had watched a person die and it was not something she was in a hurry to repeat, especially as the next victim could well be herself.

From the trees below, she heard the sharp crack of two more pistol shots, followed by a louder, deeper explosion and leaves and birds flew into the air in all directions. Instinctively, she ducked, although she was still some way above the action.

'Let's keep it that way,' she whispered to herself, turned and began climbing again, heading for what appeared to be a little ridge about thirty feet above her. From her angle, it was possibly a path, leading up the side of the hill towards another clump of bushes that led around to the other side, away from the shooting, away from the danger. If she could make that, she knew from the photographs that she could get back down to the shore beyond, where there were rocks and, quite likely, small caves in which she could hide away until everything calmed down again.

What she could do then, she had no idea as yet, but at least she would still be in one piece and have time to consider her alternatives, few as they might be.

More shots echoed up from below, but Alex hardly heeded them now. Whoever was shooting at who down there, thankfully it was keeping them too busy for anything else, at least for the moment. She reached the ridge, pulled herself up and rolled over on to the path.

Except that there was no path there: just a sharp slope for about three feet and then a sheer drop into dark nothingness. With a scream of terror, Alex flung out a hand to grab the small outcrop of gorse, her boots scrabbling for a purchase that wasn't there. For maybe two seconds, she hung there, knuckles whitening from her desperate grip as she tried to reach up with her other hand for the small projecting edge of rock away to her left.

And then the roots gave, the lifeline of stems coming clear out of the shallow soil, the fingers of her left hand ploughing a furrow just short of the rock-hold and she slid slowly over the edge and down into the deep fissure and the darkness that rose up to grab her.

Fiona could barely stand as the two grooms unhitched her from the shafts, but they dragged her forwards, to where Richard Major, Miko and the rest of the crowd stood in an expectant semi-circle. Away to the left, other grooms were attending to Missy's victorious opponent, but all eyes were now on the beaten pony-girl.

As she was led towards them, she saw Miko lean close to Major and whisper something to him. Major smiled and nodded and Miko looked pleased, his lips curling beneath his mask.

'Not quite so easy, is it, my dear?' Major said, addressing Fiona. He nodded to the grooms, who quickly removed the bit from her mouth. 'You see, all our girls are very fit, but I thought you would have realised that, Miss Charles.' He grinned. 'But then you're not Miss Charles now, are you?' he sneered. 'At least, not for the next week.' Somewhere in the distance, Fiona heard a sharp explosion, but she barely registered it and none of the crowd seemed interested in anything but the immediate entertainment she was providing.

'OK,' she gasped, trying to stand upright, 'just name your price and I'll buy out the forfeit. You've all had your fun and I've made a fool of myself, which is what you wanted, wasn't it?'

'Well, precisely, *Missy*,' Major said, smoothly. '*You* made a fool of yourself, no one else, and *you* agreed to the terms of the wager. There can be no going back on that now and certainly no buying out, as you put it. You are now a pony-girl for the next seven days, as agreed.'

'But you can't!' Fiona exclaimed, horrified. 'Look, this is *me* we're talking about. I'm . . . well, I'm rich enough to pay your prices, and that should be enough.'

'Rich enough to pay my prices, you say?' Major mused. 'Well, of course, but now you must pay a different price. And, speaking of prices, I have already agreed one for your services for the next week.'

Fiona rounded on Miko, who was grinning smugly, his mask now off and in his hand. 'You better hadn't dare!' she screeched. 'I'll make you pay if you so much as touch me, you bastard!'

Miko waved a hand dismissively. 'But I've already paid,' he said, baring his teeth in a wicked leer, 'and largely with the money I've won off you, which makes it all the sweeter, don't you think? For the next week, pretty Missy, you're all mine – and aren't we going to have fun?' He laughed and looked around at the crowd, who were obviously enjoying her discomfort almost as much as he was.

'Well, *I'm* going to have fun, anyway,' he added, which brought a louder laugh from behind him.

'And you may as well start now,' Major suggested. 'I'm told there is a small situation over the other side,' he went on, just as two more sharp reports rang out from beyond the trees, 'but apparently things are now more or less under control, though it would be unwise for any of us to venture back that way until I receive the all-clear.' He held up the small walkie-talkie to indicate that he was still very much in the driving seat.

'Perhaps you'd like to mount your filly here?' he continued, addressing Miko. 'I'm sure the grooms will give you all the assistance you may need.'

Fiona searched the sea of faces, desperately seeking an ally, but all she saw were featureless masks and leering expressions, not the merest sign of sympathy anywhere.

'Please, Miko,' she said, 'let me pay you off. I'll make it worth your while. Listen, you know the score and even you wouldn't be that big a bastard, would you?'

'No? Well, I wonder what makes you think that, eh?' Miko retorted. 'Is it because I know you're a dyke bitch who'd go mad at the thought of a real cock invading her precious cunt, is that it? Well?' he roared, stepping forwards. 'You are a vicious dyke bitch, aren't you? You might as well admit it, if you think that's what's going to save you.'

'Yes,' Fiona muttered, lowering her eyes, 'I'm a dyke and you can call me a bitch if you must. I'm a dyke bitch and I hate the thought of having a man anywhere near me, as you well know.'

'Yes, indeed,' Miko chuckled. 'The rich and famous Fiona Charles, dyke bitch to the equally rich and famous. Except all I can see here now is a beaten pony-girl called Missy, with big tits and ringed nipples and even a shaved cunt, so she must be a real pony-girl.

'Of course, we must first decide what punishment this pony-girl deserves. I believe it's customary for a master to whip a beaten pony: is that so, Richard?'

Major nodded solemnly and Fiona stared at him with round eyes.

'No, please!' she howled, her stomach knotting painfully, the vibrating dildo still making its presence felt, despite her terror. 'Please, I'll give you anything.'

223

'That you will,' Miko said. 'Anything and everything.'
He nodded to the grooms at her sides. 'Put her bit back in
and get that thing out of her pussy,' he ordered. 'I've got
something much better for it, although I doubt our little
Missy will think so – at least for the moment!'

There was no pain, not since that first searing jolt, but
there was no other feeling either, just the slowly
brightening sky that seemed so far above – and the silence.
The shooting had long since stopped; either that or the
sounds could not penetrate down to the bottom of the
narrow fissure in which Alex now lay. She didn't much care
either way now. She was probably going to die here
anyway, whether they found her or not: and if they did,
there was nothing she could do about it.

Slowly, she turned her head, staring at her outstretched
right arm, willing the limp fingers to move, but although
her brain told her that they were flexing, her eyes told her
a different story.

'Shit!' she croaked, blinking away the tears. 'Shit! Shit!
Shit!'

And she knew, beyond any doubt, that her back – or
more probably her neck – was broken.

To Lulu's surprise, Higgy was not waiting to escort her
back to the stables after the race. Instead, she was told to
take her rig off to one side and wait, apparently until
whatever had been going on over at the far side of the
woods had been taken care of.

The thick latex hood muffled most sounds, apart from
when someone spoke directly to her, but even so she had
detected the short, sharp explosions in the distance and,
although she had no first-hand experience of it, Lulu had
seen enough television to realise that someone, somewhere,
was shooting at someone else.

Eventually, when the losing pony had been suitably
rewarded by her new master, one of the other grooms came
over and removed the heavy gloves from Lulu's hands,
tucking them and the whip behind the raised seat. He

patted her thigh and grinned at her as he opened the front of her mask and removed her spittle-soaked gag.

'Nice race,' he said. Lulu grinned back and nodded to where her pony stood patiently waiting for the signal to move off again.

'Nice pony,' she said. 'Supposed to be a complete novice, too.'

'Supposed to be, yeah,' the groom replied, and moved forward, running an appreciative hand down the silent girl's flank. 'Could do with getting her back soon, give her a decent rub-down.' He looked up at the sky, which had now finished turning from its dawn grey to a more promising pale blue. The clouds that had hidden both moon and stars such a short time ago were now far towards the horizon, heading, Lulu guessed, for Norway.

'Still,' he said, 'the sun'll be up any minute now, so she shouldn't get too cold.'

'She won't,' Lulu retorted. 'That I can promise you.' A little plan was already forming in her head – a plan that she knew would most certainly win Higgy's approval and if he didn't come back this morning, well, there was always Plan B. She climbed down from her position, tip-toed around to the front of the anonymous pony-girl and stood for a few seconds, admiring the proud breasts.

Not caring if anyone was paying her any attention, she stooped forwards, sucked one fat nipple into her mouth and began running the rough surface of her tongue over the engorged flesh. Above her head, she heard the appreciative snort from her mount's nostrils and, when she straightened up a few seconds later, even the bit could not disguise the fact that Jasmine, whoever she really was, was smiling broadly.

Richard Major stood in the window of his private sitting-room, watching the morning sun climbing steadily away from the flat blue horizon. Behind him, seated on opposite sides of the old stone fireplace, Amaarini and Dr Keith Lineker both looked pensive. In the centre of the room, standing almost at attention, Boolik Gothar looked grim. For several minutes, none of them spoke, Major deep in thought, the other three waiting for him to break the silence. At last, he turned back to them, his reptilian features impassive.

'You say the three wounded are stable, Ikothi?' He addressed the question to Lineker, who nodded. 'Then at least we have only lost two of our people,' he said. 'I suppose it could have been worse.'

'Much worse,' Amaarini agreed. 'Boolik acted with commendable speed and efficiency.'

'Yet it might have been better if he hadn't,' Lineker said. The security chief glared at him, but the doctor was unabashed. 'I don't mean that as a criticism, Boolik,' he said, 'and I *am* speaking with the benefit of hindsight. At the time, you did what you thought best – what any of us would have done, I guess.'

'And all because bloody Lachan wanted to keep his precious pony-girl all to himself,' Amaarini snapped. 'The man's an idiot, storming in here with gunmen shooting off like a crowd of wild west cowboys.'

'Apparently,' Boolik said, 'their guns were supposed to be loaded with rubber anti-riot bullets and they didn't use silencers as they wanted the noise to frighten off any of us who tried to interfere.'

'The two dead weren't killed by rubber bullets,' Lineker retorted. 'I saw my team pulling the slugs out of them.'

'That was the man Hawkes,' Boolik replied. 'All the other weapons we recovered did contain only rubber-tipped ammunition, but he apparently took the precaution of bringing along some insurance. The fellow aboard the cruiser was also armed with an automatic weapon.'

'I hear they are both dead,' Major said.

Boolik nodded. 'Yes, unfortunately Hawkes fell against a tree root when the stun charge hit him,' he said. 'He was dead before we could get him back to the doctor.'

'And the cruiser's captain?'

'Another unfortunate accident. He was trying to use his weapon and fell against the wheel-house. His trigger jammed and, sadly for him, he contrived to shoot himself through the head – three times.'

Major raised his eyebrows. 'You're sure about that, Boolik?' he said tersely.

Boolik shrugged. 'The boarding party all tell the same story and his was certainly the only projectile weapon aboard. It may be that one of them decided to take revenge for what happened back here, but I can't shake any of them.'

'You'll be able to remove traces of the wounds, Ikothi?' Major said.

Lineker nodded. 'It's already being taken care of,' he said. 'We'll have both bodies taken back aboard the *Jessica* as soon as I've finished with Lachan.'

'And my people will take her down south and stage a convincing maritime accident,' Boolik finished. 'A suitable explosion should cover any traces of the doctor's work.'

'And the other men?' Amaarini demanded. 'What's to be done with them?'

'They were only paid hirelings,' Lineker said. 'I suggest we keep them for a few days and then release them in various parts of the mainland, minus, of course, their memories of what took place here.'

'You're certain you can do that, Ikothi?' Amaarini said.

'For a period as brief as the one we are talking about, yes,' Lineker replied. 'Eventually, maybe we can handle long-term memory erasure, but that presents an altogether different set of problems. That is why we cannot afford to let Lachan go, too.'

'In the future, we shall have to be more on our guard,' Major said. 'We cannot afford another Andrew Lachan, I'm sure you all realise that. Even this incident could have serious consequences for us.'

'We'll be monitoring even more stringently than usual, sir,' Boolik assured him. 'I suggest that we call the police ourselves later today. They'll be wondering about the woman before too long, so I suggest we make it look as though she came down on Carigillie. Meantime, I can shut everything down tightly on Ailsa until after they've finished poking around.'

'Ah, yes, the woman who was also involved,' Major said, crossing to the small escritoire in the corner. 'From the local constabulary, I understand?'

'Yes, sir,' Boolik replied. 'She was nothing to do with Lachan's raiding party. Apparently she parachuted down from a friend's plane in the night. It would appear that certain recent deaths had aroused her suspicions, but her superiors did not consider she had enough evidence to continue her investigations by more normal means.

'Despite the events of this morning, there's still no reason to believe they'll change their viewpoint on that score. One renegade policewoman, trying to be a heroine. Just a loose cannon, that's how they'll see it, I'm sure.'

'I see,' Major said. 'Quite the little action woman, by the sound of it. You have been able to do something for her, Ikothi? She was badly injured, so I hear?'

'She slipped into a small ravine, or crevice,' Lineker replied. 'No one else was involved directly – it was an accident. She fractured her spine in two places when she landed on the rocks below and was paralysed completely when Boolik's men finally found her. She was lucky they did, I suppose.'

'But she will make a complete recovery?' Major persisted.

Lineker allowed himself the merest of smiles. 'She will,' he said softly, 'but then, don't they all?'

The stables, Missy rapidly discovered, were not a place where pride and arrogance survived intact for long. There was little, if any, actual cruelty from the grooms, but they treated her so much as though she were a real pony that any thoughts of rebellion were quickly crushed.

At first, after her public humiliation out at the track by Miko, who had instructed two of the grooms to hold her bridle and bend her forwards and then simply entered her already sopping tunnel, it had been a relief to be handed over to the grooms for the rest of the day, but even worse indignities lay in store for her. No sooner were they back inside, than it began.

Initially, the moment the first groom removed her bit, the old Fiona resurfaced, a stream of obscenities renting the confined air of the small stall. However, this was apparently not unexpected, for the second groom, coming up on her from behind, forced the nozzle attachment of a compact spray can into her mouth and squirted in a foul-tasting mixture. Immediately, Fiona felt her tongue beginning to grow, except that this was just an illusion, for in reality the spray was a powerful local anaesthetic and was actually numbing everything with which it had come into contact. Within seconds, any attempt at speech produced nothing more than comical glottal sounds – comic as far as the grooms were concerned, at least.

'Better,' said the first groom, grinning at his partner. 'Might be as well if we keep this one sprayed regular for a while, Jonas, even when she's bitted.'

'Good idea, Sol,' the second lad agreed. He grinned at Fiona. 'Ponies don't speak, you see,' he said. He touched her left nipple and she recoiled immediately, memories of Miko's massive hands kneading her defenceless breasts, as he pumped in and out of her, still too fresh in her mind.

'Have to do something about these,' Jonas smirked. 'Proper rings through 'em, I reckon.'

'No one's said,' Sol replied dubiously.

'And no one's said not,' Jonas retorted. 'So I reckon we do it. They won't say anything anyway. Bloke who's got her for the next week will probably thank us, if I'm any judge.'

'Well, you can take responsibility then,' the younger groom said. 'I always seem to be in the shit, whatever I do.'

'You worry too much,' Jonas said. 'Me, I just get on and do the job. Now, what say we change that mask, eh? Got something to make her look even more ponyfied in the end stall. I'll just nip and get it. You just stay here and play with her tits a bit; keep them nipples nice and hard.'

It took them an hour, maybe just under, to complete their work and by the time they had finished, Fiona was as completely Missy as she could have imagined, reduced to a pitifully subservient creature by their cool and expert handling, head now locked inside the new mask, with its equine-shaped rubber snout, even larger ears and flowing mane, formed in part by her own hair, drawn through strategically placed ports in the heavy latex.

A new bit was fitted, with a flanged plate that reached in and covered her thick and useless tongue and extra chains were clipped to the rings on each end of it, running down through the rings in her newly pierced nipples and passing beneath her pouched arms, coming up behind her to attach to the main driving reins, so that now any signal transmitted through them was received in two places simultaneously.

She peered out miserably, blinking through brown tinted lenses in the large horse eyes, her field of vision further restricted by the heavy blinkers attached to the new bridle, and did not offer even a token resistance when they finally led her back out, heavy tail swinging behind her, and harnessed her between the shafts of an elegant black sulky, taut straps from her collar forcing her to stand bent at the waist, buttocks projecting shamefully backwards. Her one consolation was that at least she had been spared the torturous vibrator, but that relief was short-lived.

She heard one of them stepping between the shafts behind her, felt strong hands grasping her buttocks and, as the bulbous head began to enter her, found herself trying to work out how many hours were still to go before she had finally fulfilled her forfeit. Too many, she thought, but then, as she found herself somehow responding to the steadily thrusting organ, she wondered if that was right after all.

D.I. George Gillespie drained the dregs from his pint mug and banged it back on to the worn bar counter. Beside him, Geordie Walker emptied his own glass and pushed it across the counter with slightly less emphasis. Sandra, the landlord's daughter, collected both empties in one swoop and removed them to the nearest tap for refills. As ever, mid-afternoon trade in the Mariner's Arms was slow and they were able to talk without any real fear of eavesdroppers.

'It's a fucking waste,' Gillespie snarled, when they had collected their drinks and retreated out of earshot of the few other customers in the pub. 'I can't imagine what possessed the girl, I really can't.'

'She was following her intuition, guv,' Geordie said. 'Mind you, I had no idea what she was planning, or I'd have tried to stop her. I'd like to charge that Dalgleish bloke with something, though. You'd think he'd have known better and to miss the island like that . . .'

'Except he's pretty damned certain he didn't miss,' Gillespie said. 'I've known Rory Dalgleish since he was a small boy and he's good at what he does, same as Alex Gregory was an experienced sky-diver and parachutist.

'If Rory says that Alex jumped over Ailsa, then Alex jumped over Ailsa, not Carigillie: and if there was virtually no wind that night, then she would have hit her target, fair and square.'

'So you think someone moved her body?' Geordie said, staring into his glass morosely.

Gillespie coughed, took a mouthful of beer and swallowed before answering. 'I don't know what I think,' he confessed. 'The post-mortem shows injuries totally consistent with a fall, but that doesn't mean there wasn't foul play. She could have come a cropper on Ailsa and someone moved her, or she could have somehow got across to Carigillie and someone did for her there.

'Trouble is, laddie, we've got nothing more to go on than the silly little cow had to begin with. You saw that Major fellow, smooth as you like, totally unworried, except for showing a decent amount of commiserative sympathy. If there was anything to find out there, it's gone now, or else it's so well hidden that the two of us aren't going to find it.

'The health place looks totally kosher; all those little chalet places were clean as a whistle and the guests looked a happy enough bunch. Some of 'em even looked healthy. There was nothing iffy out there at all and Ailsa was the same, only with less to see.'

'But why have that running track there and not on Carigillie?' Geordie demanded.

Gillespie shrugged. 'The man says it's for the ones who like to camp there and rough it a bit, so who am I to argue?'

'I don't quite buy it, all the same, this story about sponsoring the trust that runs the sanctuary side. I didn't see any unusual wildlife out there, did you?'

'Oh, and you're the expert, are you, mister city policeman?' Gillespie took another draught. 'Well,' he went on, 'as it happens, neither did I, but then these days they can slap a conservation order on something just because of a bloody rare weed growing there, so who's to say?'

'So we just forget the whole thing, eh?' Geordie said angrily. 'We just close the file, forget about poor Alex and the fact that she could have been murdered –'

'Murder is a strong word, Geordie, lad,' Gillespie cautioned. He looked around the bar to see if anyone had overheard, but no one seemed to be paying the two policemen any undue attention. 'You have to go careful before you start making accusations, even vague ones,' he said, in a fierce whisper.

'Word gets around fast up here. Apart from incest and shagging their bloody sheep, there's not much for this lot to do except drink and gossip, so keep your bloody thoughts to yourself. I didn't take much to that fellow Major, but he obviously has a lot of money to throw about.'

'But no locals among his staff,' Geordie reminded him.

'Maybe so, but nonetheless . . .'

'I still reckon he knows more than he's letting on,' Geordie persisted.

The older man laid a hand on his arm. 'So do I, lad,' he said. 'So do I, but unless we can get more than we have, we can't go storming in there with a search warrant to look any closer than we already have. At the moment, Sergeant Alex Gregory's death is officially down as a tragic accident, nothing more.

'But if I ever get any half-decent reason or excuse, I'll be back over those islands and turn them upside down and inside out – Major too, if I get even an inkling that he's involved in whatever happened to the poor girl.' He emptied his pint again and looked at Geordie.

'My round, I think,' he said, moving back towards the bar. 'Let's just get drunk tonight and tomorrow will be another day. Patience is what we need, old son, so patience is what we will have. And one of these days, tomorrow will bring us what we need, mark my words.'

Amaarini Savanujik stood in the open doorway of the little stall and her smile could not have been any wider. Before her, wide-eyed, bare-breasted and shaven in the usual manner of the pony-girl, one of the stable's two newest acquisitions stood quivering in her hooves and harness, bit drawn tightly back between full lips, head held erect by the stringent posture collar, nipples stiffened within their cruel ring clamps.

'My, my.' Amaarini laughed. 'And aren't you just the most beautiful creature now?' She stepped forward and the pony-girl tried to retreat, only to find her way blocked by the rear wall of the confined space. The huge eyes rolled in terror and confusion, but the only thing that came past the specially adapted bit was a thin stream of saliva. Amaarini laughed again, reached out a gloved finger and flicked the right-hand nipple-bell, which tinkled daintily. Its new owner cringed.

'Yes, very beautiful,' Amaarini said. She looked about the tiny stall area and nodded. 'Not what you've been used to,' she admitted, 'but then there's a lot you'll have to get used to now, isn't there? Like a new name,' she added. She raised her eyebrows and pouted a dry kiss at the frightened female.

'I thought maybe Bambi would be suitable,' she suggested. 'After all, you are quite a dear now, aren't you? I thought for a moment I was in Jessie's stable, you look so like her now. You'll make a fine racing pair, I think, once she's recovered from the bruising she got during the, er, fracas upstairs.' She reached forward, grasping the pony-girl's jaw in a powerful grip, dragging her face towards her own.

'And,' she whispered, 'seeing as you could be your dear Jessie's identical twin sister now, we can hardly call you Andrew any more, can we, Mr Lachan?'

At the sound of the heavy timber door being opened, Alex rose unsteadily to her feet, the metal links on her confining harness clinking in time to her every movement, seemingly adding their own mockery to an already awful situation. Between her teeth, the tasteless rubber bit prevented any speech and her arms were caught up in the tight pouches, preventing her from even trying to take it out, but the tall man who entered the little stall reached out and removed it with practised ease.

'Before you start screaming at me, Miss Gregory,' he said, holding up a warning finger, with such an air of complete calm and authority that the words died in her throat, unuttered, 'perhaps you should listen. It will be so much easier and save you a lot of questions. You may sit again, if you wish.'

Shuffling her feet in the hideous, hoof-shaped boots, Alex shook her head, hoping that the movement might even help to clear it.

'I'll stand, thank you,' she said, 'and I suggest you talk quickly. You're in big trouble, you know.' The threat sounded hollow, even to her own ears, and it certainly did not seem to have registered with him.

'Let me see now,' he said, smiling, 'what do we have here? Detective Sergeant Alexandra Gregory, aged twenty-eight, but then we don't, do we?' From the pocket of the curious tunic he wore, he pulled a folded sheet of paper, which he opened and held up for Alex to see. It was a copy of the local island newspaper and smiling out from it was a picture of herself.

'You will see,' the man said evenly, 'that this is an obituary – your obituary, complete with details of your funeral. They haven't gone into the details of how you met your death, but the death certificate gives the cause as a fractured spine and severe internal haemorrhage, both no doubt the result of your ill-judged parachuting attempt.

'Your body was discovered on Carigillie Craig, where you appear to have come down against a cliff and tumbled on to the rocks below.'

'But I didn't land on Carigillie –' Alex began, falling silent again as she realised that was hardly the point. Given an hour or two, they could have made it look like whatever they wanted, but there was one question that was still bothering her, though in the depths of her near subconscious she was already beginning to suspect the truth.

'Your body – your old body, that is – was identified by the police, when we called them in. They, of course, wanted to look around the island,' the man continued, still smiling. 'Both islands, in fact, but they found nothing, apart from our private running track where our more active members can train.

'Everything that might just interest your colleagues is, of course, hidden well underground and a lot of effort and money has gone into ensuring that it is very hard indeed to find.' He paused and indicated the low mattress. 'I do wish you would sit down, my dear Alex,' he said. 'You will still be very weak at this early stage and generally we do not move our girls to the stables until much later: but, given your situation, Amaarini thought this was the best place to keep you until you acclimatise.

'Perhaps I should explain,' he continued, 'and introduce myself, as well. I won't shake hands,' he added, grinning purposefully at her pouched arms.

'My name, in your language anyway, is Richard Major. My people here are the descendants of a very old race, much older than you could imagine and that really need not concern you.

'What is important is this. You discovered part of our little secret out here and I'm afraid that, even had circumstances been different, we could not possibly have allowed you to leave again. As things turned out, you fell in the darkness, into a rather nasty little ravine and did, in fact, break your back on some even nastier rocks.

'In the normal course of events, you would have spent the rest of your life in a wheelchair, paralysed from the waist down at least, probably even without any real use of your arms as well. However, luckily for you, my colleague, Dr Lineker, has developed certain processes far beyond anything known in the outside world and you have now been given a completely new body.

235

'In your case, it is not *that* different from your original one, though the breasts are slightly larger and the legs about four centimetres longer, I am told. The main difference is that it will not degenerate in the way your old body would have eventually, so you will remain fit, healthy and beautiful well into the next century and probably even the one after that.

'Of course, it will take you a little while to – oh, dear,' he said, pausing and shaking his head. 'I do wish you had taken my advice and sat down.'

But Alex, sprawled in an ungainly heap in the straw, wrapped in unyielding leather, her shaven sex gaping between sprawled thighs, was no longer listening to him. For the first time in her life, despite her new super-body, she had fainted.

The phone on Geordie's desk started ringing just as he reached the door of the office which he had, until so recently, shared with Alex Gregory. Dropping his small briefcase on the floor, he reached over and snatched up the receiver.

'Walker,' he snapped. The line was surprisingly clear.

'Geordie? Colin. How are you, you northern philistine?' Geordie would have recognised the cultured tones of Detective Constable Colin Turner even if he had been calling from the moon. Another university entrant and from a wealthy county family, he was nevertheless a damned efficient copper and Geordie had partnered him for several months during his stint with the Met.

'I hear they made you a sergeant,' Geordie said, easing himself into his chair. 'They must be getting bloody hard-up in London.'

'Probably are, old boy,' Colin said, 'but I'm not in London, as it happens. I'm down on the jolly old south coast, near Southampton. Place called Hamble, actually. Ever heard of it?'

'Vaguely. It's a river, isn't it?'

'A river and a village,' Colin confirmed. 'Forests of masts everywhere, all the snotty yachtie types and about a

236

squillion pounds worth of floating hardware. Attracts thieves and con men like bees to the old honey-pot. Of course, the River Police sort most things, but I'm here for something a bit different.'

'Oh, yes?' Geordie replied, stifling a yawn. 'Someone pinched the Royal Yacht?'

'Actually, old thing, we don't *have* a Royal Yacht any more, hadn't you heard?'

His laugh echoed in Geordie's ears and Geordie moved the ear-piece back an inch or so. 'Well, they don't tell us much up here, you know,' he replied, searching his pockets with his free hand for the ever-elusive cigarette packet.

'Still eat their children up there, I've heard,' Colin quipped, laughing again. 'But not to worry. At least you're out of the way for a while. Listen though, old chum,' he went on, his voice becoming more serious, 'there's something you just might be able to help me with.

'Don't want it common knowledge, but one of our billionaire types down this way appears to have gone out and blown his damned boat up, somewhere down off the coast of Cornwall. Actually, he's a Jock and not really local at all, but these rich bastards all seem to moor their expensive penis substitutes down here. This one was an impressive craft, as well, by all accounts – sixty feet plus, called the *Jessica*. All mod cons, including radar, ship-to-shore, satellite guidance. Just went bang, so it would seem.

'As far as we know, there were three people aboard her. The owner, his skipper and a guy who worked for him as some sort of security consultant, bloke by the name of Nigel Hawkes, ex-SAS type. Knew him at school, as it happens, but that's not my main reason for being interested.'

'Go on,' Geordie invited, 'what's the pitch?'

'Well, to be honest,' Colin continued, 'I'm not sure there is one. Boats do blow up fairly regularly, even ones like this *Jessica*, though usually there's a bit of warning.'

'And there wasn't in this case?'

'Ah, well, that's the point,' Colin said and Geordie could imagine him lying back, putting his feet up on some

237

polished desk, shirt open to the chest, trousers riding up around his calves. 'You see, there was a brief radio distress call, giving a position and saying they had a fire in the engine compartment. Then nothing.'

'So it blew before they could do anything more?' Geordie suggested.

'Maybe, but there's more. You see, our local coastguard chappies, here and along the coast, have recently acquired some rather tasty electronic gubbins. Helps in the hunt for smugglers and all that, much the same as your chaps up there.

'Well, the distress call was near enough triangulated – pin-pointed for position, in layman's terms – and, sure enough, a craft showed up on radar right on the noggin. However, among the few other craft in the area at the same time was another fix that suddenly went off the screen, just a few seconds after the call finished and at about the same time a fishing vessel reported seeing an explosion on the horizon.

'I've got a chart in front of me at the moment, with all the relevant positions marked, but I won't bore you with the foreplay details, just the vinegar strokes, as it were. Basically, the wreckage that's been washed ashore was from the *Jessica* all right and three bodies have been recovered – what's left of them, anyway, but enough to confirm IDs.

'However, if it *was* the *Jessica* that blew up – and we think it was – then that distress call came from another vessel about three miles from her at the time. A vessel which then headed away from the scene, not towards it, as you might expect, what with the jolly old maritime code and all that.'

'I see,' Geordie said, brain ticking now. 'So you think that the *Jessica* didn't so much blow up as she was *blown* up? Deliberately, I presume?'

'Spot on, my old Sherlock!' Colin exclaimed. 'That's what we think, though so far we can't fix a motive, other than that this guy was filthy, dirty, crawling rich, dripping with the stuff, in fact, so it could be that the old filthy lucre is at the bottom of it.

'However, the sole heir – heiress, in this case – is a younger sister living in Canada at the moment, well taken care of by big brother and half a world away from the action for at least the last six months. So, I'm detailed to dig a bit deeper, following up contacts, movements, that sort of thing.

'Fraud people are looking at company books and stuff, though so far it all looks clean enough and we've no reason to expect that to change any. However, there are a few personal details and contacts that might be worth following up.'

'So how can I help?' Geordie asked. He heard the sound of rustling paperwork from the other end of the line.

'Well,' Colin came back on, 'it's like this, old son. The dead guy – name of Andrew Lachan – was paying a lot of money to a lot of different places, not unusual, given he was made of the stuff, but there are a couple of quite interesting things.

'In his private safe was a banker's draft, made out to cash, for a lot of money. It was in an envelope, addressed and ready to go. The address was a sort of health farm place up somewhere near where you are, apparently on one of the islands.

'Of course, I realise there are over a hundred lumps of rock in that Godforsaken place, so you may not have heard of this one. Firm's called Healthglow and the island is apparently called Carigillie Craig. Ring any bells?'

'Ding-dong,' Geordie whispered and flicked his lighter into flame.